I0709055

Valentine's Warning

A Larry Macklin Mystery-Book 17

A. E. Howe

Books in the
Larry Macklin Mystery Series
(in order):

November's Past

December's Secrets

January's Betrayal

February's Regrets

March's Luck

April's Desires

May's Danger

June's Troubles

July's Trials

August's Heat

September's Fury

October's Fear

Spring's Promises

Summer's Rage

Autumn's Ghost

Winter's Chill

Valentine's Warning

St. Patrick's Cross

Memorial Day's Escape

Independence Day's Search

Copyright © 2021 A. E Howe

All rights reserved.

ISBN-13: 978-1-7346541-4-1

This book is a work of fiction. Names, characters, places and incidents are the product of the author's imagination or are used fictitiously. Any resemblance to actual events, locales, business establishments, persons or animals, living or dead, is entirely coincidental.

Except as permitted under the U.S. Copyright Act of 1976, no part of this publication may be reproduced, stored in a retrieval system or transmitted in any form or by any means, electronic or mechanical, including photocopying, recording or otherwise, without written permission from the author. Thank you for respecting the hard work of this author.

CHAPTER ONE

It was Friday and a perfect February morning in North Florida, with the sky as blue as a robin's egg. I took in a deep breath of fresh air as I walked out of the Adams County Sheriff's Office, feeling happy to have my second interview for the sergeant's position behind me.

"How'd it go?" asked Julio Ortiz. A recent addition to our criminal investigations department, he was walking toward the building as I headed for my car.

"They promised this would be the last interview, one way or the other."

"They're down to three of you?"

"Yep. Me, Pete and Phil. Pete's last interview is later this morning. Phil's already had his."

"Phil isn't even in CID."

"Phil has done a few stints as an investigator. Plus, when patrol's been shorthanded, he's served as acting sergeant. He probably has the best chance."

It was awkward interviewing for the same position as my best friend, Pete Henley, or Deputy Phil Eccles, both of whom had been with the department longer than I had. I wasn't sure which of them had the inside track. As for me, I was starting to have doubts about spending part of my day conducting reviews, handing out assignments and looking over other investigators' shoulders. Plus, a part of me was worried that I was only being considered for the position because I was the sheriff's son.

"If you or Pete are promoted, will they move someone else up to CID?"

"I—"

Julio's radio interrupted me. A trooper with the Florida Highway Patrol was requesting assistance from a violent crime investigator ASAP. Dispatch connected him to Julio, who was the investigator on call, and the trooper immediately requested to speak with him over the phone. There were still a lot of folks in the county with police scanners and there were some things best discussed out of public hearing.

"Maitland, what's going on?" Julio asked into his phone.

"It's bad. There's a woman with multiple stab wounds. She's been dead for at least a few hours."

Trooper Maitland gave Julio the location as he jogged to his car.

"You want to ride along?" he asked me.

"Sure, as long as you write all the reports." I got in on the passenger side, squeezing in around Julio's laptop. "I'll call Shantel and get her headed our way."

The body was located near the county's only exit to the interstate. It had been found behind an abandoned gas station that sat between a very active truck stop and the eastbound entrance ramp. The highway patrol frequently used the spot as a staging ground when they were working speed enforcement on that stretch of interstate. The empty parking lot also proved convenient for troopers who just wanted to take a break and write reports.

Trooper Maitland's distinctive black-and-tan Dodge Charger was parked in front of the old store and Julio pulled up next to it. As we were getting out of the car, a tall and lanky man in his forties who I recognized from a couple of accident scenes came around the corner of the building and walked up to us.

"I don't know why murder victims bother me more than accident victims," he said. "I've seen just about every horrible injury a person can suffer after going *mano a mano* with a hunk of metal that weighs a ton. Still, seeing what one human being can do to another… makes me lose a little faith each time." He pointed over his shoulder toward the back of the building. "She's back there."

"How'd you find her?" Julio asked as we donned protective gear and rubber gloves.

"I had to take a piss. Went around back and almost soaked my pants. Jesus!"

We walked toward the building and, as we came to the corner, the trooper stopped and motioned for us to go ahead.

"I don't need to see her again. She's out in the open. You can't miss her."

The woman's body was about fifty feet from the back of the building, lying at the edge of the cracked and litter-strewn asphalt. I was looking around for signs of tire marks or recent trash when I noticed that Julio had stopped in his tracks. I looked over and saw him stagger backward, his hand held to his mouth.

Julio let out an odd sound between a gasp and a huff. His legs gave out and he fell to his knees. With his hands wrapped up over his head, he began to sob heavily.

"What's wrong?" I asked, bending down next to him while giving the corpse a brief glance. I was confused and concerned for Julio. "Come on, talk to me."

"God help me!" he pleaded.

Looking into Julio's eyes, I saw pain and something more. Fear?

"What's going on?" I heard from behind us.

"Get me some water," I told the trooper, then turned back to Julio. "Listen to me. Focus." I tried to make eye contact with him. "Do you know her?"

I'd had a moment when I thought the victim might be his

wife, but while her dark hair was the right color, her apparent age and height weren't a match for the petite Dani Ortiz.

Julio moved his head ever so slightly up and down before he started pounding it with his fist.

I grabbed him by the shoulders and growled fiercely, "Get ahold of yourself! We have a job to do."

For the first time since he collapsed, Julio really looked at me.

"It's bad," he told me.

"The body?"

"I'm… in real trouble." Julio's eyes had a faraway look, like a person seeing a dark storm moving toward them.

I took out my phone and called the watch commander, telling him that Julio wasn't feeling well and that I would be taking over for him. After receiving his blessing, I used Julio's radio to tell dispatch that I was now in service and that Julio was off-duty.

"Let's get you back to your car," I said, pulling Julio to his feet.

Trooper Maitland had been watching us in stunned silence, a bottle of water held loosely in his hand. I waved him over to help me get Julio back to his car. By the time we came around the front of the building, Julio was walking on his own. He looked at the trooper, then back to me. I got the message.

"We've got this," I told Maitland. "Send me a copy of your report. I might need to talk to you later."

"Roger that," he said, looking a bit puzzled. "Is he going to be all right?"

"Just a blood sugar issue," I assured him.

"I know her," Julio said as soon as the trooper was out of earshot.

"The dead woman?"

"We had a thing. Only lasted a couple of months."

"When?"

"About four years ago."

I did some math and figured out that it was before Julio got married, which was a relief. "I can't imagine seeing an old girlfriend like that," I told him, my mind flashing back to images of my own father bleeding on the side of the road. That had been worse.

"There's more." Julio seemed to have more control over his emotions, but his breath still came out in a hitching wheeze. "Her name is Eva Calavera."

My eyes grew wide. "Ralph Calavera's *wife*?"

Ralph Calavera was one of the most famous and highest paid criminal defense lawyers in North Florida. His list of clients was a who's who of rich bad guys and the children of rich bad guys. My heart pounded a little faster when I remembered that the man who'd been responsible for my father's stabbing was being represented by Calavera. Neil Manning's father was just rich enough to be able to afford him.

"Yeah. You're getting the idea. More, man, there's more." Julio was hyperventilating.

"Calm down. You need to tell me everything about your affair with Mrs. Calavera."

He looked at me, hesitating. Or maybe he was just having a hard time formulating the narrative.

"Look, we only have a few minutes before the crime scene folks will be crawling all over this place," I pressured him.

"Okay, okay. I met her at the courthouse in Tallahassee when I was there giving testimony. Long story, but we ended up getting together for a couple of months when Calavera went up to Atlanta for a big case."

"When was the last time you saw her?"

"It's been a while. I swear."

"Okay, we can work with that," I said, relaxing a little. We'd have to distance Julio from the case because of his personal involvement, and his story would have to be investigated just like anyone else's. Still, the damage could be contained.

"The worst thing," he said, gasping, "is I got one of the emails."

"What?" I knew what he was talking about. I just didn't want it to be true.

"The anonymous emails. I got one. More than one. They laid out the whole affair and told me that bad things will happen if I don't tell Ralph Calavera and my wife about the affair. I don't know why the emailer insisted on me telling Dani. I barely knew her then." Julio was shaking and his voice turned panicky. "What if the person who's writing those emails killed Eva because I didn't confess about the affair? This murder could be my fault."

Now I was beginning to feel Julio's anxiety. A series of anonymous emails had been plaguing residents of Adams County for weeks. Almost fifty of them had been reported to the sheriff's office. The emails had uncovered secrets and spread lies across the entire county. We knew that most of them were completely wrong in their accusations, but many others were true or close to it. Some of the emails contained threats as well as the secrets they purported to reveal. They had been directly responsible for at least three physical altercations and several vandalisms. Two people had lost their jobs after their employers had received emails tattling on them for various offenses. Dad had finally gotten so fed up with the nasty missives that he'd given Pete the responsibility of tracking down the sender.

So far, Pete had come up empty-handed in the two weeks he'd been working on the case. What he *had* managed to do was to collect copies of all the emails for comparison—or at least what we *thought* was all the emails. He'd also enlisted the help of our forensic electronics expert, Lionel West, in an effort to track down the sender's internet service provider. Unfortunately, Lionel had found only frustration in the endless looping electronic trail.

"I know what this means," Julio said. "All of it's going to have to come out."

"It links the emailer to a murder," I said apologetically.

"My wife is going to be so hurt that I didn't tell her."

"You weren't even dating Dani at the time."

"But *Eva* was married. Her husband, what's he going to do? Now not only is his wife dead, but he'll find out she cheated on him."

I nodded. "We need to know his alibi, 'cause he'll be in hot seat number one."

"And me?" Julio asked, his eyes downcast.

"I'm not sure what your motive would be for killing Eva. Still, we'll have to investigate your affair. What you need to do now is go home and tell your wife what's happened. Better she hears it from you than through the grapevine. All the information won't come out immediately, but I think the sooner you tell her what's coming down the road, the better off you'll be."

"Yeah, you're right." He looked at his car. "I drove you here."

He sounded confused and I wasn't surprised. Experiencing such an intense shock could make even simple decisions and dilemmas seem insurmountable.

I grasped him by the arms. "You need to snap out of this. Do you have any food or water in the car?"

"My lunch."

"Sit in your car for a minute and eat and drink a little before you try to drive. Don't worry about me. I'll get someone to bring my car over. Concentrate on your driving. Last thing you need is an accident heading home."

Julio looked hurt at the suggestion that he couldn't drive. Even so, he nodded and got into his car.

"I'll tell anyone who shows up that you aren't feeling well and are going home."

I walked away and called Shantel Williams, the head of our crime scene and evidence division. She answered the call with: "We're only a mile away."

"Who's with you?"

"Clark," she said, referring to Clark Macon, one of our civilian crime scene techs.

"Marcus at the office?"

"He's going over a list of evidence that the State Attorney needs for that arson case last month."

"So he's busy. Okay, can you go back to the office, give Clark the keys to the van and you drive my car out here? You can get the extra key from the fleet locker." I explained that Julio was feeling sick and that I needed some equipment from my car. Plus, I thought that having them go back would give Julio time to leave without having to answer questions from anyone else.

"I guess." Shantel sounded a little perturbed.

"Bring my car and, when we get a break, I'll go to the taco truck and bring back lunch for all of us," I promised.

That did it. Ten minutes later I had sent Julio on his way and texted Pete to give me a call when he got done with his interview. Then I went back around the abandoned store to take another look at the body. I found a clear trail and walked a straight line, making sure that it was a path we could repeat to reduce contamination of the scene.

Eva Calavera had been wearing a red knee-length dress with a black belt around her waist. Now she lay on her back, her chest and abdomen a savage montage of stab wounds. I counted nine and guesstimated that the weapon probably had a two- or three-inch blade. From the lack of blood on the pavement, it didn't take a criminal investigator to deduce that the murder had occurred somewhere else. That was a mixed blessing. Without the blood pattern evidence from the murder scene, it would be harder to figure out how the attack took place. On the other hand, it also meant that the murderer might be driving around in a vehicle covered with evidence to tie him directly to the body and possibly the dump site.

I put in a call to Dr. Darzi's office. Adams County was too small to have its own morgue, so our coroner worked for us part time out of the hospital in Tallahassee. We took up our share of Darzi's time, but often other priorities came first. Today was one of those days.

"I'll send someone as soon as I can," said the assistant who answered the phone. "But it will be a couple of hours. There was a shootout near a laundromat this morning and a car wound up trunk-deep in the building. Four people dead of various causes."

"Understood." I was just glad that it was February and I wouldn't be spending hours waiting in the summer heat.

As soon as I disconnected that call, my phone rang.

"What's up?" Pete asked. "You want to hear how I bombed the interview?"

"We've got a situation," I said, ignoring the pleasantries.

"What's going on?" he asked, switching immediately to investigator mode.

"We need to keep a lid on it for a few hours at least, but I think your buddy with the poison-pen emails has upped his game to murder."

Pete let out a string of curses that would make a sailor blush. When I could finally get a word in, I told him where I was.

"I'll be there in fifteen minutes."

My next call was the one I dreaded the most.

"Hey, Carol, put me through to Dad."

Carol Braun was Dad's new assistant. She was still learning the ropes, but she was off to a promising start. She knew how to sort phone calls based on Dad's priorities and moods. Most importantly, she didn't scream whenever he showed up with Mauser, his one-hundred-and-ninety-pound moose of a Great Dane.

"What?" came Dad's usual greeting when he knew it was me. "I heard they found a body out by the interstate." From the way he said it I knew that he was assuming, as most of us normally would, that it was a homeless or transient person who had died or been dumped by the interstate.

"You aren't going to like this. It's a murder. Worse, the victim is high profile." As a department, we treated all victims with the same attention and respect. Unfortunately, the media and some families didn't always do the same. If our victim was indeed Eva Calavera, then we'd have the media and her husband breathing down our necks. And he might be our prime suspect. Fun times. "It's Eva Calavera. Not confirmed, but I'd put it at ninety-eight percent certain. Her husband is—"

"I'm well aware of who her husband is." Dad wasn't happy. "Have you talked with him?"

"No. I thought…"

"I'll do it. Fill me in on what you know right now."

It was the right decision, of course. Ralph Calavera was very sensitive to slights. If the sheriff called to deliver the news rather than a lowly investigator, Calavera would consider it a mark of respect and a sign that we were making the case a high priority.

I gave Dad all of the details, including the fact that Julio had once been involved with Eva. I couldn't let Dad get blindsided.

"Not good," he muttered. "Has Julio distanced himself from the scene?"

"I sent him home."

"*You* sent him home? I didn't know you'd already been promoted to sergeant."

"Cut it out. You know what I mean."

Dad sighed. "You did the right thing. I'll call Calavera and arrange to meet with him. If he finds out before we talk to him, he'll be headed your way."

It was not unusual for loved ones to want to rush to the scene of a crime and it seldom ended well.

CHAPTER TWO

As I was returning my phone to its holder on my belt, the crime scene van rolled into the parking lot, followed by my car with Shantel at the wheel.

"The body's around back," I said as she got out of the car.

"What's all this about? Is Julio okay?" Shantel asked as Clark started unloading equipment out of the back of the van.

"Long story," I said, hoping to avoid the conversation. But then I realized that Shantel would learn about it soon enough and she'd just be pissed off at me if she heard it from someone else. "Okay, here's the CliffsNotes version. Julio knows the victim and received a shock when he saw her. She's pretty messed up. And there's a darker side to all this."

"Darker than a stabbing?" She raised her eyebrows.

"Darker for Julio." I sighed, not wanting to add what I needed to. "Julio can't be involved in any way with this case. If he asks any questions, you need to refer him to me." Shantel frowned. "Also, let's try to keep his connection to the murder on the downlow for now."

Shantel suppressed her desire to ask more questions and gave me a curt nod.

"We'll start documenting the scene. We brought the drone and the laser mapping system."

Federal grant money had allowed the sheriff's office to purchase some of the latest techy crime scene gadgets, as well as pay for weeks of training for the techs.

"You won't need the mapping system. This is just the dump site."

"And I was hoping to test it out. Just take all my fun away," Shantel said, trying to make light of the situation.

"Aerial views with the drone would be great," I told her.

They unpacked the drone and got it ready for launch. While some recent tech innovations seemed more like toys for prosecutors to use to wow juries, others like drones could save a lot of time and provide new perspectives on crime scenes.

"I certainly appreciate not having to get up on a ladder to see if there's anything on the roof of the store," I said.

"We'll film the scene from the air first, then go around on the ground," Shantel said, flipping a switch and sending the drone buzzing into the air.

Pete pulled into the parking lot and I joined him as he got out of the car. The big man topped the scales at more than two hundred and fifty pounds, and normally his clothes accented his weight issues. But today was different.

"I see you got all spruced up for the interview."

He looked down at himself and brushed at the sleeve of his new suit.

"Sarah's idea. She's already spending the sergeant's pay that you're going to be making."

I shrugged off the suggestion that I was a shoe-in for the job.

"What have you got?" Pete asked, changing the subject.

"A middle-aged woman tentatively identified as Eva Calavera. The wife of lawyer Ralph Calavera."

The name elicited a whistle from Pete. "That kicks it up a

notch."

"There's more." I explained that Eva had had an affair with Julio several years earlier and that our emailer was onto it.

"Great." Pete spat out the word like a curse.

"Have you made any headway on discovering who the emailer is?"

"Ha! I'm closer to catching Jack the Ripper than I am to this guy. Lionel's already thrown his hands up. Say the jerk is using a bunch of repeaters or whatever to hide his location."

"Don't you need to provide some information to get an email address?"

"Apparently the emailer is using some crap he got off of the darknet." Pete saw the expression on my face. "No. I've already checked. The first emails were sent before Neil Manning was released on bail."

"I knew it couldn't be that easy. But how tech-savvy would the person have to be to hide his or her tracks?"

"I asked Lionel what level of skills are needed to hide location and identity. His judgment is that anybody with a little knowledge of how the internet works and the wiliness to get down in the muddy waters of the darknet could do it. Personally, I'd say we're working with a perp who's under the age of forty."

I heard the high, whizzing whine of the drone as it flew over our heads.

"How many of the poison-pen emails have you collected?"

"Fifty-nine as of yesterday. I guess I can add one or two for Julio. I've split them into three categories: accusations with threats, accusations without threats and simply threats."

"Sounds like the work of a charming person. How often have the accusations been true?"

"Less than half. I'm betting that there are more out there that aren't being reported because they *are* true."

"Like Julio."

Pete nodded. "It's blackmail. Most of the emails demand

that the person out themselves for the stated crimes. As a direct result, there's been an increase in the callouts for domestic violence and physical assaults. That's how I've found out about most of the emails—people fighting about their contents."

"I've read a few of the reports."

"I told Major Parks yesterday that I was afraid the emails were going to get someone killed. And here we are."

"Who would have that much knowledge about what's going on in the county?" I asked.

"If we can't track them down electronically, then answering that question is the only chance we have of finding them. Believe me, every person who receives one of these little love notes has a prime suspect. Unfortunately, all the suspects are different."

"Did Dad have a suspect for his emails?" Even the sheriff wasn't immune. Dad had received an email that accused him of misappropriating funds. Specifically, the federal money the department had received to help defray some of the costs of repairs from Hurricane Marcy.

"Several. He was almost too angry to name them."

I knew what Pete meant. When Dad had been stabbed shortly before Christmas, he'd also suffered a severe concussion that had left him with recurring headaches. In the last couple of months he'd had a very short fuse, and it hadn't been long to begin with. I knew that he was hypersensitive about the emails and I had avoided discussing them with him. No one likes to be accused of something they didn't do.

Shantel came over to us. "We're done with the aerial video. There's some junk up on the roof, but nothing that looks like it could be related to the murder. We also looked at the surrounding area. Nothing. We'll go ahead and start with pictures and video from the ground." She paused. "Does this have anything to do with those emails?"

"Why do you ask?" I was curious to know how she had figured it out.

"Just a hunch. Pete's the lead investigator on the emails. You called him… Doesn't take a mind reader."

"There does appear to be an email involved in this case," I confirmed.

"Do you know people who've gotten one?" Pete asked.

"I do." Shantel didn't look comfortable talking about it. "It's our minister's wife. She got one saying some pretty ugly things which she swears aren't true."

"How'd you find out?"

"Everyone knows I work for the sheriff's office. She came to me for advice."

"We need to see it," Pete told her.

"She deleted it."

"I bet it's not really gone. Could you arrange for Lionel to meet with her?"

"She's a sweet woman. They don't need this kind of trouble. There are already folks in our congregation who have knives out ready to stab—" As soon as the words were out of her mouth, Shantel shook her head. "I think I see how our victim might have ended up with a well ventilated chest."

"I promise that your friend's identity will be kept anonymous. The only person who has to see that email is Lionel. He can copy it with the names redacted," Pete assured her.

"I trust you. I'm just not sure she will." But she nodded. "I'll talk to her."

Clark and Shantel spent half an hour photographing and videotaping the area, then made a path for us to approach the body. Pete and I both donned gloves and paper booties, then walked slowly toward the body, looking for any evidence on our way.

Eva Calavera looked cold and lonely on the asphalt in her dress that had been meant for a night on the town. Her left shoe looked like it had been tossed at the body and rested about a foot from her shoulder.

"The killer dragged her out of a car," Pete said, pointing

to the leaves and dirt on her clothes. "Big knife. Those cuts are deep."

"It will be interesting to see what her back looks like." Had the stab wounds penetrated her body? That would give us some idea of how strong her attacker had been.

"I can't see any defensive wounds," Pete observed. "Though I can only see the palm of her right hand." Her left arm was half under her body. We couldn't touch her until after Darzi's people had arrived to take her temperature, bag her hands and take all the other notes that Darzi would use to make his proclamations on the time and cause of death.

"What do you think about the killer dumping the body here?" I gestured at the abandoned store, which backed up to an old field that looked like it was lucky to be mowed once a year. A quarter of a mile away, I could see cars and trucks zipping by on the interstate.

"It's an interesting choice. A little bit of privacy behind the building. But the killer could have easily found a place that's a whole lot more private. In fact, all he had to do was drag the body out into the weeds a few hundred yards and it probably wouldn't have been found until someone mowed the field."

"Just like the emails. This guy is making a statement."

"Is he targeting Julio? Calavera? What about all the other emails?" Pete wondered.

"Or did Calavera learn about the emails and decide to use them as a cover to kill his unfaithful wife?"

"Always look at the spouse first. What are you going to put out to the public?"

"What are *we* going to put out?" I said. "I think this is officially *our* case. We need as many of those emails as we can get our hands on, so I'd suggest a public appeal."

"I ran that by your dad when he gave me the job of catching the asshole. He said he didn't want to give the jerk more of the limelight. I agreed with him then. But now? This changes things. I think your dad will agree." Pete looked at Eva's body and shook his head sadly.

"We aren't going to find any useable car tracks on this asphalt." I looked around at the sand and litter that covered the cracked blacktop. The patches of sand were too dry to hold tracks. Every time the wind blew, the top layer shifted. "We might get lucky and find something that fell out of the vehicle when the killer pulled her body out."

"I'll get some markers from my car."

Pete headed back toward the front of the building, while Shantel and Clark put away the camera equipment and returned to their van to fetch evidence bags. Left with the body, I looked at her and around at my surroundings.

Both the victim and the location chosen by the killer could reveal a lot about the murderer and their motivations. This area implied that the person who did this was comfortable here, picking a spot so close to the interstate. And the body had probably been dumped late at night. The spot was too exposed during the day, which meant that it was someone who could be out at night without raising questions from their family. Most likely unmarried.

"Where did the murder take place? That's my first question," Pete said, coming back with the markers.

"Dad's going to notify her husband, which should give us a positive identification and some places to start checking."

Like magic, my phone rang with a call from Dad.

"I've decided to go to Calavera's office to deliver the news. Is Pete there?"

"Yep."

"Let him handle the scene. I'll pick you up in ten minutes. I've called Calavera and told him I'm coming to discuss an urgent matter. Get a picture of her or have Shantel text it to you when they have one so we can get a positive ID."

I took a few pictures of Eva and cropped one so that the more gruesome aspects weren't visible. By the time I was walking around to the front of the old store, Dad pulled into the lot. He was behind the wheel of his department SUV and wearing his dress greens.

"Is all of this for Calavera?" I asked, pointing at his tie.

"I have a Rotary talk at noon, which I might or might not make." He took a deep breath. "Let's get this done. Do you have the picture?"

I pulled it up and showed him.

"That'll do."

"Shantel is done documenting the scene if you want to take a look at the body."

"No," he answered and I wasn't surprised. One of his policies as sheriff was not to interfere in a case unless it was necessary. He wanted to be kept up to date so he couldn't be blindsided, but that was all. He knew that if he became involved, then the investigators might lean toward whatever opinion he formed rather than following their own path.

I climbed into the passenger seat and immediately felt like a twelve-year-old kid. Every time I was a passenger in a car with Dad, I became that scrawny boy headed to an afternoon ball game.

"Are you ready for the wedding?" I asked, trying to sound like an adult. He was marrying his girlfriend, Genie Anderson, in just over a week.

He looked at me. After a minute, he said, "I am. I wasn't sure for a while, especially after that knock on the head, but now I'm looking forward to having Genie move in and to settling down. Do you really want the sergeant's position?"

He almost gave me whiplash with the change of topic. This was the first time he'd brought it up since the selection process had started.

"I don't know," I said honestly.

Dad just grunted.

We drove the rest of the way in silence, looking out at the bare trees and brown grass of a North Florida winter. The glare of the sun added a crispness to the stark landscape.

Ralph Calavera's law office was in downtown Tallahassee near the capitol. More importantly for Calavera, it was near the Leon County courthouse. Though he lived in Adams County, there were only a few people there who could afford to hire him, so most of his business came out of the capital city.

We parked in the public parking garage and walked up a steep hill to his office. As we approached the impressive bronze door, I thought about Calavera representing Neil Manning and of Julio's involvement with Calavera's wife. Fate was weaving an odd web of connections.

Inside, the office was all gold, marble and French provincial furniture that seemed pretentious, even for a high-end criminal lawyer. To top it off, the man behind the front desk looked like a model from the pages of *GQ*.

"Sheriff Macklin and…" he said as we walked up to his desk.

"Deputy Macklin," Dad told him, causing a look of confusion until I took out my bifold and flipped it open to my ID.

"Have a seat and I'll let Mr. Calavera know you're here."

I could tell by the look on Dad's face that he wasn't going to sit down, which would have been an admission that he was willing to wait. He was not. Dad would give him five minutes before telling the coiffured assistant that he needed to see Calavera immediately.

After just a couple of minutes, Ralph Calavera came down the hallway and greeted us. The man was only five-foot-six, but he wore it well, his head up and a smile on his face. He was in his late fifties, but looked a decade younger. His right hand was already sticking out as he approached Dad.

"Sheriff Macklin, I appreciate you coming all the way over here. I assume this has to do with the Neil Manning case. I have to tell you, this is the first time I've been visited by the sheriff who arrested one of my clients."

"No, sir. It's not about the Manning case," Dad said in his most somber voice. "Could we go somewhere private?"

Calavera looked unsure for a moment before waving us

down the hallway. "We can go into my office."

Once we were enclosed in a room that looked more like a museum than an office, Calavera turned to us with an inquisitive expression.

"I'm afraid I'm here to give you some tragic news." Dad let that sink in for a five count before continuing. "We've found a murder victim in Adams County and we have reason to believe it's your wife."

Oddly, Calavera smiled. "That's preposterous. I'm sure my wife is fine." His eyes didn't look as sure as his words suggested.

"I hope that's true. Can you call her?" Dad asked.

"I… Yes, of course." Calavera stepped over to a desk the size of a dining room table and picked up one of the three smartphones that lay on what I assumed was a charging pad. He tapped the screen a couple of times before putting the phone to his ear. He repeated the process twice more before setting the phone down on the desk with slow deliberation. "She doesn't answer."

"When was the last time you saw or spoke with your wife?" Dad asked, sounding more like a concerned friend than a law enforcement officer.

"Yesterday, when I got home. I have to insist on seeing… some evidence or… something." His professional façade was crumbling. I was sure this was a side of Calavera the lawyer that few people ever saw.

"We have a picture of the woman we found." Dad looked at me and I took the cue to pull out my phone and bring up the image.

"What makes you think it's my wife?" Calavera asked, ignoring the phone in my hand.

"Someone identified her," Dad said.

"Who?"

"Please, just look at the picture and tell us if that is Eva Calavera."

Hesitantly, Calavera took my phone. For the second time that day, I saw a man's legs buckle. He grabbed the back of a chair to keep from going to the ground.

"This can't be real." He pushed himself back to his feet. "Tell me this is a sick joke." His eyes were pleading.

"I'm sorry," Dad told him.

"I don't understand. You said that she was murdered. Who did this?" With a shaky hand, he handed me back my phone.

"We don't know. Her body was found at an abandoned gas station by the interstate outside Calhoun."

"When was she killed?"

"I could let you ask questions, but most of the answers are going to be the same. Right now, we don't know much." Dad looked at me.

"The best we can say right now is that she was killed at least a few hours before she was found," I said.

"We came here as soon as we had a tentative ID," Dad said. "We wanted to save you finding out from someone else."

"I'd appreciate anything at all you can tell me."

"She was stabbed," Dad said bluntly. "Honestly, that's all we can tell you right now. If you can answer a few questions, we can begin to uncover more of the answers and track down the person who did this. I'm not going to treat you like some person on the street who doesn't know how this works, so we'll start out with a direct question. Where were you last night?"

Calavera nodded. "You're right. I know how this works, so I'll skip the indignation. I want you to go out and find this son of a bitch, and I'd like to be able to give you an alibi that would eliminate me and help you to focus on the real killer. Unfortunately, I don't have one. I got home last night at seven. Eva was getting ready to go out. We talked for a few minutes while she heated up some food for me. That's it. She went out. I ate dinner and spent the rest of the evening reading before going to bed around one in the morning."

"Where was your wife going?" Dad asked, and I leaned back against the wall to listen to the exchange.

"This is awkward. We've been living separate lives for several years. It's a satisfactory arrangement for both of us. The catchy name for it these days is a companionate marriage." He paused and I saw his hands clench and unclench. "I still love her. I think she has… had feelings for me. No. I know she loved me. The question was, could we live together? Were we still going in the same direction?" He balled his fists and pressed them against his head. "All sounds so stupid now."

"Are you saying you don't know where she was going when she left your house?"

"I asked her if she wanted to sit down and eat with me, but she said she was going out and would grab dinner in town."

"In town?"

"That meant Tallahassee."

"Did she leave in her car?"

"Yes. I noticed it was still gone this morning, but that's not unusual."

"We need the tag and description of the car."

Calavera had to call his insurance agent to get the tag number. Finding the car might go a long way toward finding the scene of the murder.

"It's a blue BMW five series," Calavera told us.

"Does it have GPS tracking?" Dad asked. Most newer, high-end models did.

Calavera hesitated, then said, "I'll call the dealership."

Ten minutes later we had a location for the car. As Dad continued to question Calavera, I stepped outside the office and called Pete to let him know that the car could be found in one of Calhoun's dodgier neighborhoods. He said he'd get in touch with Darlene Marks and ask her to send one of her officers to secure the site. Darlene was a former investigator with the sheriff's office and the current chief of police in Calhoun.

"You could also help us out by getting the phone company to release your wife's phone records to us," Dad was saying as I came back in the room.

Again Calavera hesitated. No doubt he was thinking of all the times that he'd advised a client to make the cops do their own footwork. Then he shook his head. "I'm thinking like a lawyer. Stupid. Yeah, I'll get that done. And kick the company's ass if they don't expedite it."

"We'd appreciate that." Dad gestured toward me. "This is my son, Larry. He's an investigator with our department."

Calavera looked directly at me for the first time since we'd arrived. Normally, this was the point where I'd stick my hand out for a shake, but the look on his face didn't suggest that we were going to be on a handshake basis.

"I know who he is. He arrested my client Neil Manning for a laundry list of crimes."

"Then you'll know that he's capable of getting his man." I thought I saw a little smile on Dad's face. "He'll be the primary on your wife's case."

Calavera was silent for a moment. "Your reports were well written," he finally said, his words flat without any inflection. It wasn't a compliment, but simply a statement of fact. Then he turned back to my father.

"I'd prefer another investigator." He looked at me. "Not because I doubt his skill, but it puts me in a strange ethical dilemma. As an attorney for my client, Neil Manning, I am duty-bound to oppose evidence presented by the prosecution, much of which will come from the work of your son. On the other hand, I'm going to want to work closely with the man investigating my wife's murder."

He had slipped into his courtroom persona and was presenting his argument as though speaking to a jury. I thought it odd that he was worried about his ethics when his wife was lying on her back with holes in her chest. Maybe this was his way of shielding his emotions.

"I see your issue," Dad said. "But that is *your* issue. Larry is the primary. You'll have to make whatever adjustments you need to satisfy your ethics."

Calavera looked confused at having his argument swept

away so casually. "I see," was all he could think to say.

"I'm sorry if this makes a horrible situation worse," Dad relented. "We're a small sheriff's office with limited resources. I'm doing what's best for this investigation."

"I'm sure. Yes. I..." Calavera looked like he had a bad headache coming on. "I'll get the phone company records as soon as I can. Is there anything else I can do to help?"

"We'd like to search your house." Dad was blunt.

"No. Not search. But I'll let you walk through the house."

"The sooner we can do that, the better."

"How about now? After you." Calavera indicated the door.

When we were in the foyer, Calavera told his assistant to cancel all of his appointments for the afternoon.

"I'll meet you at the house," Calavera said when we were on the street.

"We'll walk with you to your car," I said, getting a nod from Dad. I decided that I should start taking the lead.

"Of course you want to look at my car. Very well, follow me. I've got a reserved spot in the public garage." Calavera set a stiff pace back down the hill.

His car was just as impressive as his office, but not as tacky. It was a two-year-old silver Porsche that I was sure he'd bought new. Looking at the car, it was obvious that he hadn't crammed his dead wife into the trunk that would have been full with two small suitcases. The inside of the car was clean, but not too clean. However Eva's body had been transferred to the dump site, it hadn't been in this car.

"Thank you. We'll meet you at your house," I told him.

CHAPTER THREE

"Calavera seemed shocked when he saw the picture of his wife," I told Dad as we walked back to his SUV.

"A great criminal lawyer is a great actor. And Calavera is a great criminal lawyer."

"You think he was faking it?"

"I'm saying he could fake it if he wanted to," Dad said, clicking the fob to unlock the doors.

"Do you believe that part about the two of them living separately together?"

He shrugged. "Should be easy enough to find out the truth."

I watched Dad climb slowly into the SUV and thought that he was still showing some of the effects of the December attack. I tried not to think about Calavera representing the evil little spawn who had orchestrated the whole thing. I didn't want to be prejudiced against the man when I was evaluating evidence in his wife's murder. Maybe Calavera had a point about me working on the case.

Calavera lived just over the line in Adams County. The area was a cluster of expensive homes on ten- to twenty-acre tracts of land with a few old family farms mixed in to give the rich folks the full country experience.

The double wrought-iron gate opened as we followed Calavera up the cobbled driveway. Dad parked in the circular drive behind the Porsche.

"I couldn't even pay for the upkeep on this place," I mumbled as I got out and looked at the ten-thousand-square-foot faux Italian villa. There was even an acre of grape vines in a field beside the house.

"With homes like this in the county, you'd think we'd have more property tax revenue," Dad grumbled as we headed up the stone steps to the double doors. Calavera invited us in, looking small as he stood in the doorway of his cavernous house.

"You can go wherever you want," he said, waving toward the interior of the house.

"Why don't you show us your wife's bedroom first," I suggested.

He nodded with a grim expression. We followed him to an elevator that was ornate, but small. It would be a challenge to fit more than four people into the cramped interior.

"I put this elevator in with the thought that I wasn't getting any younger. I'm in good shape for my age, but even now there are days when the stairs to the third floor look like Mount Everest." Calavera closed the grate and pushed the button for the third floor.

Small but efficient, the elevator purred us up to the top floor of the house and opened up into a room larger than my whole doublewide.

"This is the master suite," Calavera announced as if he were an elevator operator taking guests up to their room.

The room had a California king bed hung with drapes and everything was done up in bright colors. Outsized windows looked out over the countryside for twenty miles in every direction. I had to admit that all the gaudiness could almost be overlooked for the view out those windows. For a moment I was captivated by the scenery.

"You two shared the room?" Dad asked and got a glare

from Calavera.

"No. I have a room downstairs. When we reached the point where our lives seemed to diverge, we did our best to give each other some space." He anticipated the next question and held up his hand. "It was my idea that she keep the master suite. I'm perfectly comfortable on the first floor. Like I said, the stairs are getting to be a challenge after a hard day. Besides, my office is there and I can work as late as I want without bothering Eva."

Dad and I walked slowly around the room. Everything was clean and tidy. The bed was neatly made. A pair of doors was open on the east side of the room that led into an enormous walk-through closet, which in turn opened into the master bath which would have been suitable for a Roman emperor. There were even murals on the walls and a sunken tub large enough to hold three people. I began to wonder how a criminal defense lawyer could earn so much money. Then I remembered his client list of drunken celebrities, politicians who'd hit their wives and over-the-hill sports stars who'd decided that murder would be their next game of choice. Neil Manning's father had a small fortune and I was sure he'd be willing to spend it on his murderous offspring.

Here and there throughout the suite were signs that a real person lived there. A pair of shoes laid out in the closet. A towel not folded but slung over a rack. A scattering of bath products and make-up on the counter. A tablet on a table by the bed. Yet there was nothing that spoke to who Eva Calavera was as a human being.

I picked up the tablet and flipped back the cover. The screen lit up and I heard movement behind me. Ralph Calavera had started toward me. I held up the device.

"Would you mind if we take this with us?"

He hesitated for a moment. "Of course not."

"I assume you have a maid?"

"We have a service that comes in twice a week."

"When are they due back?"

"Monday. They come Monday and Thursday."

"Would you ask them not to come this Monday? There's the possibility we might want to collect some forensic evidence."

His eye twitched as he forced himself to nod.

We toured the rest of the house. Some of the rooms, like his bedroom and office, appeared lived in, but most of the rest looked like an example for some decorating show on HGTV.

Calavera ended the tour in the foyer, an obvious ploy to push us out the door.

"When will you know more about what happened to Eva?"

He'd given me the perfect opportunity to bring up the emails.

"Your wife's murder is going to be a top priority for our department. Of course, we're also dealing with a number of other cases, including those annoying anonymous emails everyone in the county seems to be getting." I paused for a two-count, then asked, "Have you received one of them?"

"One of what?" he asked, appearing confused.

"The poison emails that have been going around. Have you gotten one?"

"No. I think Eva mentioned something about that."

"Did *she* get one?"

"I think she said a friend of hers did."

I watched his face carefully, looking for any of the tell-tale signs of deception. Though Dad was right—if anyone could lie with a straight face, it would be a criminal defense lawyer.

"Does your wife have any family?" Dad asked.

"I called her sister on the way home. Both of her parents are dead, but I'm sure that her sister will notify all of the distant relatives." There was a coldness to this statement which reminded me that he was on the list of suspects… A very short list that, so far, only included him and, as much as I hated to admit it, Julio.

"The autopsy will take place tomorrow or Monday," I said.

"The sooner, the better. I want to know who killed her," Calavera said firmly.

"Save some of that mojo for the labs when we send off evidence to be tested. I won't complain if you can put pressure on them. DNA samples can sometimes take a year," Dad told him.

"We *won't* be waiting a year."

"Do you have any idea who might have killed your wife?" I asked.

"I told you. We've been living separate lives. One of her new friends, maybe? I can't imagine any of our mutual acquaintances murdering her." He looked me in the eye. "There's something you might not know about me. I spent two years as a cop in New Jersey. I saw plenty. Then fifteen years as a criminal lawyer, the first five as a public defender. I've met my share of Dr. Jekylls, so I'm not going to tell you that none of our friends are Mr. Hydes when the sun goes down. It's *your* job to find them."

"What about clients? Are any of your past or present clients mad enough at you to…" I almost said "take a stab at your wife," but bit the comment back. "…go after Eva?"

"I'll think about that and make a list. Not everyone has been happy with the result of their case, even when it was better than they should have expected."

"Who is your wife's best friend?"

"Margaret Whittle. I'll text you her number." He took his phone out of the breast pocket of his coat. "What's yours?" he asked as he scrolled through the screen.

I hesitated for a moment. Should I give the prime suspect my cell number? *Wouldn't be the first time,* I decided. Though something about Calavera unnerved me. Maybe it was that stare, the same stare he used to intimidate juries. I knew it was part of what made him a great lawyer… or was it actor?

Finally I gave him the number and he quickly sent a group text explaining to Margaret Whittle who I was. In literally seconds, a reply came back. *Why are you sending this to me? Where is Eva?*

Calavera looked at the response before turning back to me. "You'll need to explain the situation to the woman. I detest her."

That's good to know, I thought. It meant that Margaret would be willing to dish about any trouble between Eva and her husband.

I dialed her number and she answered with a puzzled, "What's this all about?"

I explained about Eva. "I need to talk with you as soon as possible."

"What happened to her?" Margaret said through choking sobs.

"I'll be glad to tell you as much as I can if we can meet somewhere."

"I'm at work, but I don't think I'm going to… I don't know if I can stay."

"Do you have someone to drive you home?"

"I… no."

"Where are you?"

"I'm at Pineland Stables."

I'd heard the name, but wasn't sure where it was and asked her for directions. It turned out to be only a few miles away.

"I'll be there in ten minutes," I told her, and she said she'd be waiting at the barn.

We left Calavera looking a bit lost as he watched us drive away.

"He never cried," I said as much to myself as to Dad as we drove toward the horse farm.

"I'm going to drop you off at the farm," he told me. "You can get someone in patrol to pick you up and drop you back at your car."

"Gee, thanks, Dad."

"I've got to get to that Rotary meeting." He tapped his watch.

"Sure." There was no point in asking him for his opinion of Calavera. He'd just tell me it was my case.

"I think Cara is coming over tomorrow to work on the wedding with Genie. Why don't you come with her?" he said in an offhand way that belied the fact he never just invited me over to his house for no reason.

"What kind of work are you going to make me do? Just so I know how to dress." I didn't even pretend like I had a choice.

"No work. Just a… little project I could use your help with." He turned and looked at me. "Promise. No hard work."

"Okay," I said, highly dubious.

He dropped me off at a barn the size of Noah's Ark that sat on a hill overlooking acres of cross-fenced pastures that would be lush and green in spring. Near the barn, a rider was working a horse in a lunge ring. A tall, thin woman with long blonde hair, wearing riding breeches and boots, was standing by the fence. As I walked toward her, I could see that her eyes were wet and mascara was running down her cheeks.

"I'm Margaret," she told me, wiping at her eyes. "I'm sorry, I'm still in shock. I did a Google search while I was waiting for you. The *Tallahassee Democrat's* webpage mentioned that a body had been found in Adams County. Are they talking about Eva?"

"Yes, and I'm afraid that she was murdered." There was no way to soften the blow of those words, so I just said it.

"That son of a bitch!" she screamed.

Behind her, I saw the young lady on the chestnut horse pause trotting in circles and look over at us. The horse was almost as interested as its rider.

"Do you mean Mr. Calavera?"

"Of course that's who I'm talking about," Margaret growled. She saw me looking toward the ring and turned. "It's okay, Felicity. Reverse and do six more circles, then call it a day," she said and looked back at me.

"Ms. Whittle, what makes you think that her husband killed Eva?" I asked.

"Hell, you may as well call him her ex-husband, 'cause she was done with him. Look, I don't know what I think."

"Can we go somewhere and talk? I need to take notes."

"Let's go up to the lounge."

I followed her into the barn. The smell of alfalfa and Bermuda hay was pleasantly mixed with the scent of pine shavings and horse. Halfway through the barn the two rows of stalls ended. On one side of the aisle was a door with a sign that read TACK ROOM, while on the other side a sign announced LOUNGE. Pinned to the door of the lounge was a note reminding everyone that it was only open to boarders and students. I wondered who else hung out at the barn.

The lounge was large with tile floors and a couple of folding conference tables. Two couches were against the wall, and in the far corner were two refrigerators and a microwave oven.

We sat down at the nearest table and I took out my phone to take notes. It was a new skill that I'd been working on. Julio had pointed out that if I took notes on my phone instead of in my usual small notebook, I could cut and paste them into my reports and save a lot of time. There was also less risk of someone else reading the notes or me losing them. He'd been proven correct on all counts, but still I struggled with it.

"Do you mind if I record our conversation?" I asked and she nodded. *It allows me to focus more on the subject I'm interviewing anyway*, I thought, assuring myself that I wasn't just avoiding a task I wasn't comfortable with.

Freed of taking notes, I dove into the interview. "Tell me about your friendship with Eva."

"We met about five years ago when she started taking riding lessons. Eva was… I don't know how to say it. Maybe restless is the right word. She'd been married to Ralph for fifteen years by that time, and all Ralph thought about was his work and making money. She felt like one of his possessions and, from what I saw, that's how he treated her."

"Was there abuse?"

"Physical? No. He wasn't even controlling like some men. You know the kind, always calling and texting, following you around. Nothing like that. I guess I'd call it passive control. He just made it difficult for her to do anything he didn't want. He's a big man on campus and has lots of influence. Eva thought he had undermined her a couple of times when she was trying to get a job."

"What do you know of their current arrangement?"

"The living separately thing? More of his passive bullshit. With her on the top floor, he would know if she went out at night. She was sure that the maid service reported to him if they found any receipts or any other evidence of where she'd been."

"But she *could* go out on her own?"

"Yes. But the car he bought for her had GPS tracking."

I thought about Calavera's hesitation when I had asked him about the car's GPS locator. Had he really needed to call anyone to find out where the car was?

"You think he was monitoring her movements?" I asked.

"That's what Eva thought."

"Why didn't she divorce him?"

Margaret sighed. "I don't know. I asked her that regularly. Like all relationships, I think it was complicated. Her parents died when she was young. Maybe she just couldn't stand letting someone go from her life. Even if he was a pain in the ass. I also wondered sometimes, again because of her parents, if she actually *liked* the attention he paid to her. Even negative attention is attention."

"Do you really think he killed her?"

Margaret pursed her lips and squinted. "I know that was my knee-jerk reaction. I mean, that guy is constantly helping creeps get out of jail. That's his job. He must know a dozen murderers personally. Can that rub off on you?

"I say that, but he never struck me as a hands-on type of guy. You can tell the ones that will be physical. He was all mind games. Guess that goes with his job too. Could he have hired someone to do it?"

"We've just started to investigate. I can tell you that we'll consider every possibility." Murder-for-hire had already crossed my mind and, thinking about his client list, a cold chill ran up my spine.

The fact that Neil Manning was out on bail was already eating at me. One of the concessions that the State Attorney had received from the judge was that Manning was to be confined to his home, which was supposed to be devoid of all cell phones, laptops and desktops. Making sure that Manning was complying with the terms of his bail was moving its way higher up on my to-do list.

"What sort of motive would Ralph have for killing Eva?" I asked, focusing back on Margaret.

"He didn't like to lose. Anything. That's probably why he's such a good lawyer. I don't think he'd like Eva going off on her own."

"Were there any other significant relationships in her life?"

Her eyes narrowed as though she were suspicious of my motives. After a second she relaxed. "I guess I won't be doing her any favors by keeping her secrets." She took a deep breath. "I know for sure of one. It started about a year after we met. The man even came here to meet her once. Very handsome Latino."

I cringed, feeling sure she was talking about Julio.

"It was pretty short-lived. He was quite a bit younger than her. She told me later that it just happened and, while the relationship didn't mean too much, it kind of opened her heart. Let her see that she didn't have to live trapped in the world that Ralph had created for her."

"Anyone else?"

Margaret shrugged. "We really didn't talk about it. I'm sure she was seeing other people from time to time, but it didn't come up much when we were together. We spent most of our time here at the barn. She loved horses."

Margaret started to breathe heavily, then burst into tears again. She tried to get control of herself, but soon she was choking on her tears.

I walked over to the refrigerator and pulled out a bottle of water, then grabbed a few napkins from a pile on the counter by the coffee machine. I handed the napkins to Margaret and she wiped her cheeks.

"I'm sorry," she said.

"Nothing to be sorry for. Here, have some water."

I pushed the bottle toward her until she took it and drank some. After a cough or two, she regained a bit of her composure.

"I… I was just thinking how much I'll miss her. I remember a birthday party she threw for me one year. It was one of the best days of my life. She'd worked so hard to get all my friends and family to the barn, and she brought this beautiful cake with a horse on it.

"That's just the type of person she was. Very caring. She always wanted to help, whether it was volunteering at the animal shelter, or helping to organize various events in town. She just liked everyone to be happy."

Margaret stopped talking and clenched her fist, closing her eyes for a minute. "I want to help you. Whoever did this can't get away with it."

"When was the last time you saw or communicated with Eva?"

"I got a text from her around noon yesterday. She…" Margaret choked up again. "She invited me to go out to lunch with her, but I told her I was too busy."

"Would you mind showing me the text?"

She gave me an odd look. "You don't…"

"No. I don't think you had anything to do with her death. But I need to establish a timeline and the time stamp on that text will help."

Margaret had already pulled her phone out of the small

pocket of her breeches. A couple of clicks later, she handed it to me.

The text said: *lunch? On me. Somewhere good!* Margaret's answer was a frowny face emoji and: *Can't lesson at 12:30 then farrier.*

I used my phone to take a picture of the text message before handing Margaret's phone back to her.

"Do you own the stable?" I saw her look and raised my hand. "That's not part of the questioning, just curiosity. Sorry." I gave her a smile.

"Long story. My ex owns the farm, but I've got a lifetime lease. We've pretty much stayed friends. He doesn't have any use for the place, but couldn't quite bring himself to give it to me. He has a daughter from another marriage and thought he should keep it for her. I'm good with it. His daughter is sweet and comes out and takes lessons. Even her mother is okay with the arrangement. Modern life is pretty complicated these days."

"One more thing. Did Eva ever mention getting a threatening email?"

"Threatening?"

"It might have mentioned something she'd done in the past."

"No. I'd remember if Eva ever said anything like that."

I stood up and we walked out of the barn together. On the way out, I called dispatch and ask them to send any available patrol deputy to pick me up.

"I canceled my other lessons. I just want to spend the rest of the afternoon with the horses," Margaret said.

"I'll let you know if we need anything else from you."

"I'll do anything I can to help," she told me, her eyes still glistening with tears.

CHAPTER FOUR

"Larry!" The voice came from a truck that had just pulled up to the barn.

I turned to see Dr. Betty Horvath, the county's only large animal vet and my wife's part-time employer. Cara served as business manager for both Dr. Horvath and Dr. Barnhill, who ran the small animal clinic where Cara was also a senior vet tech.

The vet climbed out of her truck and walked over to me. "I was gonna ask Cara to have you call me."

"What's up?" I said, trying not to look at my watch. Even as we spoke, I could see one of our patrol cars pulling off the main road onto the long drive up to the barn.

"My cousin got a weird email the other day," she said, squinting at me. "Kinda threatening." Now my ears perked up.

"There's been a rash of poison-pen emails going around."

"That's what I'd heard. I told him to give your office a call, but he just brushed it off. I saw the email and it looked pretty creepy to me."

"I don't think I know your cousin."

"Doug Holloway, lives in town. Lost his wife a little over

two years ago. Nice guy. That's why I'm saying something. He's been depressed ever since his wife died, so when he mentioned the email… I just thought he might need some help. I told him I might say something to you and he just kind of shrugged. I took that as a yes."

"You say you saw the email. What did it say?"

"It implied that he was responsible for his wife's death."

"How did she die?"

"Hit by a car. The guy that hit her never denied it, so there's no way Doug was responsible. Besides, whenever I saw them together at the holidays, I got the feeling they really cared about each other. Like I said, he's still mourning her."

"The emails have run the gamut from true or semi-true all the way to basically false and completely ridiculous."

Dr. Horvath nodded. "This one is ridiculous. The thing is, at the end of the email it said he'd be in real trouble, or something like that, if he didn't confess and turn himself in."

"Glad you told me about it. We're trying to collect as many emails as we can so we can compare them. Pete has been assigned to find out who's sending them, but I'll get up with your cousin the first chance I get. Probably won't be until early next week. Not with the murder investigation."

Dr. Horvath narrowed her eyes. "Murder?"

"That's why I'm here," I said, glancing toward where Margaret stood at the entrance to the barn, waiting on Dr. Horvath. "Eva Calavera's body was found this morning out by the interstate."

"That's awful. I talked to her a couple of times when I was here on a call. Very nice woman. It's a crazy world."

"With a lot of crazy people," I agreed.

"That's why I work with horses."

I waved and trotted down to the waiting patrol car.

When I finally arrived back at the scene, Pete was talking to Shantel and Clark as they were loading the last of the equipment into the van.

"Here's Johnny-come-lately." Pete smiled. "One of Darlene's guys is watching Mrs. Calavera's car. We need to go check it out."

"We'll head on over there and start documenting it," Shantel said, climbing into the van and starting the engine.

"I'm thinking the killer dumped the car, which means he or she was inside," Pete said, holding up his phone to show me a photo of the car that the cop had sent over. It was banged up and the inside had been stripped. "Purposely left it in a neighborhood where it would get ransacked."

Pete and I made one last survey of the murder scene, but there was nothing to see. A few minutes later, we met back at our cars.

"Who came from Darzi's office?" I asked him.

"Linda and one of their interns."

"Nothing under the body?"

"No, nor in her hands. At least nothing I could see. Maybe we'll get lucky and Eva managed to dig her nails into the killer."

"And we can hope that the murderer used Eva's car to dump her body."

"Sanderson is meeting up with Darlene to see about pulling security camera footage," Pete said, referring to Matti Sanderson, one of our more dependable deputies.

Darlene kept an up-to-date map of all the businesses in Calhoun with security cameras, as well as a few in the county. Since Eva's car had been found inside the city limits, reviewing security footage was going to be our best way of maybe catching the killer behind the wheel.

I followed Pete over to the area of town known as the Ditch. Built on the east side of a creek that regularly flooded when we had a lot of rain, the area was populated by folks who were too poor to live anywhere else, or who found it convenient to live among other criminals, drug dealers and prostitutes. Mixed in with these were a few people who had bought starter homes in the '60s and still lived there, trying in vain to raise property values with a little landscaping and the occasional fresh paint job.

Eva's BMW was on one of the narrower side streets, backed into the driveway of an abandoned house. It looked like it had been there for months. Two of the windows were knocked out and the hubcaps were gone. I was surprised the wheels were still on it.

"Nice. These guys work fast," Pete said.

Shantel and Clark were parked about twenty feet from the car, next to a Calhoun city police car. I recognized the young officer, Jadyn Thomas, sitting in the driver's seat and working on his laptop.

"Great neighborhood," I said as I approached his car.

"Appreciate you letting me sit here for two hours watching your ragged-out car," he said with a grin.

"Didn't y'all just clean this area out?"

"We took out a meth operation and two sellers. The chief is working with the city to get a couple of the most dilapidated houses torn down. Until we can get that done, the crackheads just crawl back in every night. We'd have to spend every evening clearing them out. It's a big ol' game of whack-a-mole."

"I owe you lunch. We got it from here."

"Heard about the body by the interstate. Guess you have your hands full." He pushed his laptop out of the way and used the radio hanging over his shoulder to tell dispatch he was back in service.

I joined Pete and the others by Eva's car.

"I guess we should be glad they didn't burn it," Shantel said, then turned to Clark. "Go ahead and get the pictures."

I looked around. "The killer would have needed to park his car somewhere, but I'm betting it wasn't around here."

"No one in their right mind would park a functioning car around here," Shantel said.

"So he probably walked back to his car," I said.

"Closest place that is safe to park is about three blocks thataway," Pete said, pointing toward downtown.

"Yeah, just south of the courthouse. I'll check the security cameras in the area. At least we know that it definitely happened last night. We can figure sometime after nine and before six in the morning. The spot where they dumped the body would be too exposed after daylight."

"Makes sense," Pete agreed.

We spent more than an hour with the car, searching it and fingerprinting what the vandals had left intact. As evidenced by the partially ripped-out ignition, someone had even tried to steal what was left of the car.

"The same geniuses who tear the wiring out of houses did this," Shantel said, looking at the ham-handed destruction of the dash left in an effort to get some of the electronics out. "I bet they destroyed anything they managed to get."

We found traces of blood in the trunk.

"Now we definitely know how she got to the old store," I said.

"If he left any DNA, I'll find it," Shantel said. "Of course, I'm also going to find evidence from the swarm of tweakers that tore the car to pieces." She frowned at what was left of the car, then called for a tow-truck to have the hulk taken back to our impound lot for a more thorough examination.

"Let's go back to the office. I want to see what you have on the emails," I told Pete.

"Something to eat first. I did your job and got us all tacos for lunch, but that didn't exactly fill the void."

"Some of us have bigger voids than others," I joked.

"I'm telling you, it's my genes."

I looked at my watch. "Let's head to the Palmetto. They're between lunch and dinner, so they won't mind us taking up a table for a little while."

The Palmetto was the nearest thing to a nice restaurant that Adams County had. Luckily, the owner didn't hold it against us that we'd put her father in jail for a series of gruesome murders.

Seated at a booth near the back, we had a bit of privacy to talk about the emails and the murder. I filled Pete in on what I'd learned while he was working the crime scene.

"Do you want me to get with Horvath's cousin about the email?" Pete asked.

"No, I'll follow up on that one if you chase down the one from the wife of Shantel's preacher."

"Thanks a lot."

"We still don't have a clue where Eva was killed."

"Finding her phone would help. I've got Lionel working on getting the ping data for it."

"You think it's still on?"

"Doubt it. It goes straight to voicemail. But we can still see where it pinged last night."

"My question is: do you think all those emails have anything to do with the murder?" I very much hoped they didn't. The emails were a patch of quicksand that I wasn't looking forward to exploring. Plus, they linked Julio to the murder.

"I think until we learn otherwise, we have to assume that they do," Pete said, squashing my hopes.

I sighed. "I'm forced to agree. I'd better take a look at them," I said with less reluctance than I felt.

"Glad to have you on board, brother." Pete smiled and I gave him a subtle but distinct one-finger salute. "I'll put them in our shared folder when I get back to the station."

"You said you've got close to sixty. Plus the new ones from Julio, the preacher's wife and Horvath's cousin. How many more do you think there are that we don't know about?"

Pete sighed. "Could be hundreds. I don't know. Most of the ones I've gotten so far have been false. Maybe a fourth of them have contained truthful accusations. I'd say that most of those aren't being turned in."

"Any serious accusations?"

"A couple of them are pretty serious. The guy that runs the hardware store got one that accused him of a DUI with a fatality. That was true, but only sort of. Ten years ago, he was down in Tampa, stuck in a line of cars waiting for an accident to be cleared up where a woman *had* been killed. He'd been drinking and fell asleep at the wheel while he was waiting. A state trooper came along the line of cars and woke him up. When he smelled the booze, he gave him a sobriety test which he failed. The guy was arrested and charged. A reporter who was doing a story on the accident got his DUI conflated with the accident, resulting in him being reported as causing the wreck by some news accounts. It took a couple of weeks to get it straightened out; not that anyone had much sympathy for a guy who got a DUI."

"Interesting. So the email writer must have seen the incorrect newspaper articles and ran with it."

"Bingo. Thirty years ago, knowing the killer had access to old newspaper articles would be a lot more helpful. Today anyone can look at newspaper archives online. I did a search and found the articles in fifteen minutes. They were behind a paywall, but that doesn't do us a lot of good unless we can get the newspaper to reveal who's looked at those articles. I asked Lionel about it and his opinion was that they probably don't even have a way of digging that data out of their system. If he's right, then we'd have to get someone to write a program that could mine the archive's logs for the people who accessed the articles."

"You said Lionel couldn't trace where the emails came from, so whoever is sending them has enough tech skills to hide his tracks."

"Right." Pete leaned back as the waiter came over to deliver our food. I think I saw Pete drool as a burger covered in mushrooms and bleu cheese was placed in front of him.

"The New Year's resolutions are no more?" I asked, eyeing his burger and onion rings.

"Onions are a vegetable," he argued, glancing at his phone as a text came through. His wife and girls kept up a constant message barrage, but he never complained or failed to respond. Pete was good at his job and liked it, but he loved his family. Amazingly, he was one of those people who never seemed to be trying very hard, but always managed to accomplish what they set out to do. I, on the other hand, constantly felt the need to focus to avoid ending up crashed in a ditch.

"I've tried to find a pattern in the emails," Pete said through a mouthful of burger. "I thought I was onto something when I took all the place names mentioned in them and mapped them out. Halfway through and the place names were all on the southwest side of town. But then they started falling all over the county."

"Any connection between the people who've received them?" I asked as I dug into my own artery-clogging steak salad.

"There are relationships, but no more than you'd get in any small town if you pulled a couple dozen names out of a hat."

"How varied are the accusations?"

"You'll see. Several concern infidelity; a couple involve theft; one accuses the recipient of abusing his wife. All over the board. Oh, yeah, Sergeant Kirby got one accusing him of beating a confession out of a suspect eight years ago. I looked into that one. There was an internal investigation that exonerated him. I went further and talked to your dad about it. He remembered the incident. The bad guy and his lawyer were well known for filing unsubstantiated complaints."

"There are officers that I might question, but Sergeant Kirby isn't one of them."

Dill Kirby worked the front desk at our office from time to time. He'd passed the average retirement age years ago, but he'd found it hard to leave. Dad didn't mind having a man with so much institutional knowledge at the front gates, so he was allowed to stay as long as he could pass all the basic requirements.

"Even back in the day, he was known as a teddy-bear-type of guy," Pete agreed.

"Was the complaint in the paper?"

"Maybe."

"If so, our emailer might be getting most of his stuff from newspaper archives."

"Not the infidelity ones," Pete pointed out.

"Any of them true?" I thought about Julio. That one had certainly been on the money.

"One person admitted that the accusation was true. Her husband knew about it already, so she didn't mind showing me the email."

"So the emailer has some kind of insider information," I mused.

"Maybe if we get more emails we'll have better luck finding a pattern. I've asked Major Parks about doing a press release asking for folks to come forward with any they have. He's going to talk to your dad and get back to me."

"I assume you aren't going to mention the connection to the murder."

"If there is a connection."

"I'll talk with Mr. Griffin to see if he has any insight into the newspaper angle."

As the head of the local historical society, Albert Griffin was a font of local information. In addition, he'd done some work for the Calhoun paper before it had folded for good. Now the paper's entire morgue of articles resided in a number of file cabinets in his house.

"When they picked up the body, Linda said that the autopsy would probably be done on Monday."

"Did she hazard a guess on the time of death?"

"Sometime in the last twelve hours. Rigor mortis was just setting in when they got to the scene. Of course, she gave all the caveats about constant temperature, etc. She did a brief examination of the wounds and said that they appeared to be the cause of death based on the amount of bleeding. Which means that somewhere there are some big puddles of blood."

We ate in silence for a few minutes, simply enjoying the good food.

"I wish we had more people on the suspect list than the husband and Julio," I said glumly.

Pete's face looked concerned as he put down his fork and looked at me. "Is there any chance that Julio *was* involved?"

"I'd be a fool to think that isn't possible. Having said that, I know Julio and he's not a very good actor. What I witnessed this morning when he first saw Eva's body appeared sincere."

We finished our meal and Pete headed back to the office. After a moment's thought, I texted Julio and told him I was coming over to his place.

CHAPTER FIVE

Julio's face was grim when he answered the door and he looked like he was close to tears. I followed him into the small apartment, which was located in one of the only complexes in the county. Julio had told me that the landlord let him live there almost rent-free just so he could have a deputy on the property.

"Have you told Dani?" I asked once we were seated in the living room.

"She's gone to her parent's down in Tampa. She's not taking it well."

I didn't doubt it. Dani was Italian and could have a fiery temper. I knew that *I* never wanted to get on her bad side.

"You two weren't even dating at the time. I know that Eva was married…"

"You know that Dani's very serious about church. She's really upset that Eva was married. She's also mad that I didn't tell her about this earlier. I just hope she doesn't tell her father too much about what's happened. The man's never liked me."

"Who do you think sent the emails?"

"Ever since I got the first one, I've been trying to figure that out. I guess there are people who knew. Seems crazy now, but we weren't working too hard at hiding it. Eva told me her husband didn't care and I wasn't seeing anyone." Julio shrugged.

"When you two got together, where did you usually pick her up?"

"We met wherever. I mean, she did some volunteer work around here and in Tallahassee. I picked her up at the music theatre a couple of times, and out at the farm where she took riding lessons. At the animal shelter once too."

"Where would you go after you picked her up?"

"We'd have lunch or something. Maybe go to a park and... then... you know." Julio looked like he wanted to crawl under the couch.

"Where?"

"See, that was another thing that pissed Dani off. We'd come here. I've been in this apartment almost as long as I've been a deputy."

"Ouch!" I wondered if he'd gotten a different bed, but I wasn't going to ask. I could understand why Dani was so upset.

"I liked Eva. And even though she was older than me, there was a sweetness about her. You need to find out who did this to her," Julio said angrily.

"I wish you could help." I meant it. Pete and I had become reliant on Julio since he'd entered CID. Over the last year we'd had several people, including now-Chief Marks, go on to bigger and better things, leaving us short-handed. Julio had picked up his share of the slack and then some.

"I've let a lot of people down," Julio said morosely.

"One way you can help is to think about those emails. Do you know if Eva received one?"

"I haven't talked to her in ages. I thought about calling her when I got the email, but didn't know what I'd say. Besides, if it all came out, then I wanted her to be able to honestly tell her husband that we hadn't been in contact for a long time."

"One more thing," I said, hating to ask the next question, though I had to. "Where were you last night from midnight to… say, around five in the morning?"

"In bed. Dani was with me." His face was pained. "Do me a favor and wait a day or two before you ask her about it."

"It will take me a couple of days to get around to talking to her," I said and saw the relief on Julio's face. "Are there security cameras in this complex?"

"Yeah!" He started to pick up his phone and I put my hand on his to stop him.

"Don't call. Pull up the landlord's number and give it to me."

Julio and I talked for a few more minutes before I stood up. When I left, he was making a list of all the places he'd been with Eva and people who would have known that he was having an affair with her.

It was almost six o'clock by the time I headed home. The wind had turned and was blowing out of the north. I shivered and turned on the heater in the car. I was ready to get home and spend some time with Cara and our four-legged children.

"I heard about the murder," Cara said after giving me a welcoming kiss. "Dr. Horvath told me she'd seen you out at Pineland Stables."

Cara and I had texted back and forth a few times during the day as we usually did, but I always made it a point not to mention the cases that I was working on. It seldom mattered. Adams County had a very efficient gossip tree and Cara's position working for two veterinarians kept her in the middle of it.

"This is a tough one… and personal. Julio is technically on the suspect list until we can officially eliminate him," I told her.

"That's crazy. Julio?"

"Long story. I don't think it's a real concern." I reached down and petted Alvin the Pug, who was sniffing my pant leg.

"I picked up a pizza."

"Perfect. Pete and I had a late lunch."

Ghost, the latest addition to our small menagerie, was guarding the pizza box on the counter. The white cat looked up at me with his bright blue eyes, stretched out one of his long, lanky legs and yawned.

Meanwhile our tabby cat, Ivy, was participating in her favorite new pastime, which involved sitting five feet from Ghost and staring at him. I was pretty sure she was attempting to use her mental powers to make him disappear.

"You might as well give up. It's been four months. He's not going anywhere," I told Ivy as I gave her a treat before getting a plate out of the cabinet. Cara grabbed Ghost so that I could reach for a piece of pizza without having to share.

"Have you heard about any nasty emails going around?" I asked Cara later as we did the dishes. I was surprised when she shook her head.

"Nasty?"

"Threatening. Like telling someone's secrets."

"No. Does this have to do with the case today? The dead body?"

"Pete's looking into a bunch of complaints that have come in recently. People are getting emails that are borderline blackmail. They seem to be targeting folks who have secrets and threatening bad things if the people don't confess."

"Bad things?"

"The person will be outed, I guess," I said vaguely, not wanting to discuss the details of Eva's case with Cara. I'd done too much of that since we'd become a couple. It wasn't fair to Cara or the victims to be talking about the cases with her.

"Are you worried about *your* secrets?" she kidded me.

"Oh yeah, my closet is full of skeletons." I smiled.

We left the subject of the emails and got into a tickling contest that I lost. Things developed from there until we found ourselves relaxing in bed an hour later, naked and satisfied.

"Remember that I'm going over to your dad's to meet with Genie tomorrow," Cara said, getting up and heading for the bathroom.

"I won't forget because I'm going with you," I told her. She leaned out of the bathroom and gave me a quizzical look. "Dad wants my help with a project."

"What's that?"

"He was being coy about it. Which means it's something particularly unpleasant."

"Better wear old clothes," she said with a laugh.

"You're a big help."

I got up and threw on sweatpants and an old Henley. Outside the bedroom door, I found a trio of nosy animals that weren't happy at being shut out of the bedroom.

"Sorry guys, but we deserve a little private time," I told them. Then I poured a glass of iced tea and settled down at the table with my laptop to look through some of the emails Pete had collected.

I opened the folder that Pete had shared with me. Inside were several reports and dozens of emails that had been copied into Word documents. Pete had written everything up as a single case based on the first email complaint we'd received. All of the other people who'd received emails were considered witnesses to the case. This made sense from an organizational standpoint, though it could get tricky if we wanted to drop multiple charges on the bad guy.

All of the emails were roughly the same length and the threats were similar. The emailer usually wanted the person to tell their spouse, turn themselves in to the police or report themselves to their bosses.

I decided that the emails based on facts were most likely to lead to the sender, as they showed insider knowledge. The false ones were made up, or at least a guess. *Of course, they could all be guesses*, I thought. Without an electronic trail to follow, this was going to prove to be a difficult puzzle.

I made two new folders and put all the emails that, according to the recipient, were true into one folder and the rest into the other. Then I began to read through the true ones.

To Tamie Eckert: *You shouldn't sneak out on your husband. Confess now or suffer the consequences!*

Tamie was one of the deputies who worked at the county jail. She'd turned the email in to Pete, telling him that she and her husband had an open marriage and she didn't care who knew it. This was almost TMI for me. Tamie was a sweet, middle-aged woman who, in my narrow-mindedness, I'd never thought of as a particularly sexual person.

To Mickey Dennis: *You are a thief. Tell your boss or go to jail.*

After getting the email, Mickey had confessed to his boss that he'd taken a set of tools home and never brought it back. Mickey was thirty-three years old and had spent ten years working for a local, six-person repair shop for cars and small engines. His boss had asked him if he ever worked on projects at home. Mickey admitted that he did and the boss had told him to keep the tools. Then his boss had brought the email into the sheriff's office because he was worried about Mickey, who'd been freaked out by the message. Mickey was autistic and didn't handle some things very well. His boss wondered if someone was targeting Mickey for harassment and was a bit relieved when Pete told him that lots of people had been getting emails just like it.

To Chandel Baker: *You are a drug addict. Turn yourself in to the police or I will.*

Chandel had shown the email to her Narcotics Anonymous sponsor, who'd urged her to bring it to us. Chandel and the sponsor came in because they were concerned that someone at one of their meetings had sent it. Again, they felt better learning that other victims with no connection to NA had also received emails.

There were a dozen more emails where the accusations were purported by the victim to be true. After reading through them, I texted Pete to see if he was up for a phone call. I had some questions that I wanted to ask before trying to get a good night's sleep. My phone rang five minutes later.

"You saved me," he said. "My ladies are in full wedding mania and are trying to get me to wear a tux."

"Where are you?"

"Hiding in the garage."

"Did you tell them that Dad isn't even wearing a tux?"

"Makes no difference. They're going out tomorrow shopping for dresses and are determined that I dress in a manner to accent their couture or some such. Curses on your father for inviting us."

"Just hunker down in the garage. You'll be fine."

"You don't know what it's like living with three women."

"Enough about your torture chamber. I wanted to ask you some questions about these emails."

"Anything to take my mind off of that rental tux."

"I think you're right. There's probably a lot more of these out there."

"I spoke to your dad this afternoon and he did authorize a public plea for people to report any that they receive. There's already a post up on our webpage and social media. We even said that they can send them in anonymously with their email address obscured. We did ask them to indicate if the accusations are true or not."

"It will be interesting to see how many responses you get."

"How many responses *we* get, brother. You're in this with me."

"Then you're in with me on the murder investigation."

"Would I have it any other way?"

"You're right about there not being a clear pattern to the emails. The victims are all different ages, live in different parts of the county, different races, levels of education. You'd almost have to work to get a group of people this diverse."

"I know. One thing I did notice is that most of the allegations are based on things from at least two years ago. I guess that's something."

"It might just take a while for the gossip to get back to the sender of the emails."

"Gossip is a good word," Pete said. "That's what most of these feel like. Could we be looking at an older person? Or am I just stereotyping older women?"

"You're stereotyping. I don't think spending time at the garden club is going to get us anywhere. Little old granny ladies are seldom adept at diving into the dark web to pull up specialty software to hide their locations. Did Lionel say how hard it would be?"

"I got the impression that it would take someone with more skills than you or I have, but probably less than Lionel does."

"A talented amateur."

"Or maybe just a dedicated amateur."

"Great. We might have more success following the murder to the emailer than the emails to the murderer," I mused. "How many people have you interviewed so far?"

"I've talked to all of the ones where the emails are purported to be true, either in person or on the phone. I guess I've contacted a quarter of the ones that are false."

"Do you think any of the allegations that were reported as false might be true?"

"Absolutely. One of the accused cheaters sure sounded guilty to me. I think his wife had seen the email, so he had to act indignant and bring it to us. Different story when I talked to him. He was all *'Let's just forget about all this. I'm sure it's a misunderstanding.'* You know the routine."

"Another question. What was special about Eva? All of these emails, yet Eva is the one to get killed. We don't even know if she got an email. Why not kill Julio if his sin is so much worse than these others?"

"Maybe it points back to the husband. The emails were

just the catalyst to her murder. The emailer might even be shocked or upset to find out that his or her work led to someone being killed."

"Maybe. Reading them, they could be the work of a twelve-year-old."

"The emailer doesn't come across as very mature," Pete agreed.

"So why don't we just interrogate all the kids in the county middle school?" I joked.

"Who says the emailer is in the county?"

"Good point. We know the *killer* was in the county."

"Finding out where the victim went after leaving her house yesterday needs to be our number one priority."

"Agreed. Her husband won't be any help. Either because he doesn't know or because he's involved."

"He's the only witness to her even leaving the house," Pete reminded me.

"I'm not looking forward to picking a fight with one of the best defense lawyers in the country."

"If he's guilty then you'll need evidence, and a lot of it. You aren't going to break him down in an interrogation."

"Is it possible *he* sent the emails?" I asked.

"A lawyer hears a lot of gossip. He does a little local pro bono work, so he might be hooked into the Adams County grapevine."

"You're also a big grape on that vine. Did some of the email accusations sound familiar to you?" Pete was well known around the sheriff's office for keeping his ear close to the ground.

"I'd heard a couple of them. Most weren't of a criminal nature. Regardless of what everyone likes to think, I don't indulge in the more salacious gossip. Just the facts, ma'am."

We talked for a few more minutes before I heard the unmistakable sounds of Sarah entering the garage and dragging Pete back into the bosom of his family.

CHAPTER SIX

Cara and I were up bright and early Saturday morning. Dad had texted and asked me to be at his place by ten.

"Do you want to go see your big Uncle Mauser?" Cara asked Alvin. The little Pug had lived with Cara ever since being abandoned at the vet by someone who couldn't or wouldn't pay their bill. Wouldn't was probably the truth. Dr. Barnhill would never hold an animal hostage for nonpayment of a bill.

"Why you like that big lunk, I don't know," I told Alvin. Cara and I had taken care of Dad's Great Dane on occasion and Alvin always acted like the overgrown ox was his favorite thing in the whole world.

We loaded up the car with wedding paraphernalia and left the cats at home to enjoy a peaceful Saturday of napping.

When we turned into the driveway of Dad's small, twenty-acre farm, I saw one of the department's two K9 SUVs parked in the driveway. Printed across the back tailgate was "K9 Tornado." Tornado was Sergeant Mack Burrows's partner. I wondered what they were doing here.

I'd just gotten out of the car when I heard Dad yelling from the back of the house: "Come back here! Mauser, stop!"

I braced myself. "Here he comes," I told Cara as a one-hundred-and-ninety-pound, black-and-white locomotive came barreling around the side of the house straight for us.

Mauser's standard greeting routine involved running headlong at someone and then turning at the last minute, heading back the way he'd come before circling around for another pass. Usually he made the first turn before actually making physical contact. Usually.

This time, as the big guy charged toward us, he saw Alvin and slammed on the brakes, plowing into my legs and falling into an awkward-looking puppy bow in front of the dancing Alvin.

"Go on, play with him," Cara said, bending down and unsnapping Alvin's leash.

The front door of the house opened and Genie came out on the porch to greet us, tossing her long brown braid behind her head as she smiled. Dad trotted around from the back of the house to be met by Mauser and Alvin, who both proceeded to run a couple of circles around him before heading back to us.

"You aren't going to learn anything like that," Dad grumbled at Mauser.

"Has he *ever* learned anything?" I said in jest. Dad just glared at me.

"As soon as I get him under control, I want your help out back," he said to me in a sterner voice than he ever used with his four-legged son. "Cara, good to see you. Would you mind taking Alvin in with you when they're done playing?" Dad gave her a smile and a nod.

Where was my smile? I thought.

Mauser was soon lying on his back with Alvin running around him, playfully nipping at the larger dog as if he were a wolf who'd brought down a woolly mammoth.

"I think they're done," Cara said, looking at the two dogs. We'd just finished hauling boxes of wedding effluvium from our car into the house.

Sergeant Burrows came around the side of the house

with the large German Shepherd, Tornado, by his side. Burrows was the largest deputy employed by Adams County. He stood over six feet tall and weighed almost three hundred pounds, all of it muscle. With his rich black complexion, I'd heard people respectfully refer to him as the very shadow of a mountain. More than one suspect had tried to escape him at night, thinking he was part of the landscape.

"Hey, Larry!" he greeted me, holding out his hand. I took it and wondered if he could actually lift me off the ground as we shook. But he was careful and I got my hand back in one piece without ever feeling air beneath my feet.

I let Tornado smell my hand before reaching down to scratch his head. He tolerated it while watching his human partner to see if he needed to pin me to the ground. Burrows and I watched Dad try to stop Mauser from following the women and Alvin into the house.

"He asked me to come over and give Mauser some training as a scent dog," Burrows said in a half whisper so that there was no chance of Dad hearing him.

I raised my eyebrows. "Seriously?" I knew that Tornado was trained to apprehend suspects, but I didn't know much about the rest of his abilities. "Have you done much work with tracking dogs?"

"I've done a little training with trailing dogs."

"What's the difference?"

"With tracking, dogs mostly follow the scent left in footprints along soft ground. A trailing dog follows not just the scent along the ground, but also the scent in the air."

"Mauser isn't going to track or trail anyone," I said dismissively.

"Your dad thinks he can."

I shook my head as Dad came over with a panting Mauser on the end of his leash. The air was cool and crisp, so Mauser still had a little energy left after playing with Alvin.

"Let's go around back," Dad said.

"You're really trying to teach him how to follow a scent?" I asked, making an effort to keep some of my disbelief out of my voice.

"He's got a great nose."

Mauser was walking along between us and bumped me with his nose as if he knew what Dad had said.

"He has a *big* nose. I'm not sure that's the same thing." I got a glare from Dad that I remembered from the few times when I was a teenager and had come close to talking back to him. I'd learned early not to push him too far. "What do you want me to do?" I said, switching gears.

"Hide," Dad said as though that should have been obvious.

"So I'm the fox?"

"And you better do a good job or you can be the suspect instead and we'll work on Tornado's training," Dad said in a flat tone that left me wondering if he was serious or not. "Go out into... Wait, give my your overshirt."

"You know, it's still pretty chilly," I complained. While the sun was warm, the air temperature wasn't much above sixty degrees.

I got another look and shrugged out of my flannel overshirt, making up my mind to hide somewhere in the sun. "How far do you want me to go?"

"Over the ridge and out of sight that direction." Dad pointed to the rise on the back of his property.

I found a sunny spot on the other side of the rise near a couple of white oaks whose leaves had fallen off months ago. Lying there looking up at the clear blue winter sky and waiting for a dog that would never come, I thought about my life.

Dad was getting married to a nice woman who would do him good, but was he completely recovered from his concussion? This idea of Mauser as a scent dog caused me to question that. Then again, I could remember some of Dad's other crazy ideas. One of them had been running for sheriff after my mother died. When he'd first told me he was going to do it, I thought he was tilting at windmills. Now here we were years later and he'd won reelection twice.

Did I really want to be a sergeant? Was there any chance of me getting the promotion? What would it mean if I did? In CID, the sergeant had several duties. First was to cover his own cases, which he could pick and choose from the cases that came in. Second, he picked up any slack or assigned someone else to pick up the slack when an investigator couldn't cover their own cases. Finally, he was the supervisor over all the other investigators. This last duty was the one I was least interested in, and I didn't know if I could handle it. I had a hard time seeing myself sitting behind a desk and performing Pete's or Julio's annual evaluation. The image was comical.

The sun was warm on my face and I thought of Cara, wishing she was out there with me. I felt myself drifting off to sleep when a bear pounced on my chest, stepped on my groin and started licking my face.

"Get off me!" I yelled, trying to push Mauser back. His exuberance made it nearly impossible, then Dad came into view and told him he was a good boy, ramping up his excitement even more.

"Help me." I looked at Dad, who was laughing as I tried to ward off Mauser's lapping tongue and flapping flews. Seeing Dad really laugh for the first time in almost two months was worth the slobber and pain.

Dad pulled Mauser away while I got to my feet. Burrows was standing twenty feet away with a smile on his face.

"I told you he had a good nose," Dad said, ruffling Mauser's ears. Burrows cleared his throat with a loud, gruff sound and Dad nodded. "We did have to help him a little bit. I'll admit he'll never beat a bloodhound. Still, he can find something when he wants to."

We walked back to the house and sat on the patio in the sun with the two dogs, exchanging cop stories while Cara and Genie finished with their wedding prep. We offered to help at one point, but were told in no uncertain terms that the best way we could help was to stay out of the way. We could take a hint.

Around one o'clock, Burrows and Tornado headed home, leaving Dad and me alone.

"How are the headaches?" I asked after a while

"I still have them," he said with a shrug.

"It hasn't been that long."

"I know that." The words were clipped and sharp-edged, telling me to drop the subject.

"When do you think the committee will make a decision on the promotion?" I asked.

He gave me a small smile. "Are you hopeful?"

"I don't know. I have moments when I want the job and times when I think I'd hate having to manage other people." I heard the sound of a sawmill coming from around Dad's feet. Mauser had fallen over in a stupor and was now sawing some Redwood-size logs.

"You've come a long way. I remember when you didn't even want to be a deputy."

"I remember when you thought being sheriff would be the worst job in the world," I responded.

"I'll be honest. The last couple of years have been tough. Good news is, I can see the light at the end of the tunnel."

"You mean the money problems?"

Dad nodded. "Which have caused us to have staffing issues. Major Parks is on the edge of retiring, again, and I can't blame him. For months now he's had to oversee both CID and our forensic department while doing all his other duties."

"And since his main job has been to handle the budget, that hasn't been much fun," I said with sympathy.

"I don't think I could have gotten through the last two years without his help and advice with the budget. In fact, that's the reason for my current optimism. Parks has gotten us locked in with a federal block grant that's going to free up enough of our equipment budget that we'll be able to fill the lieutenant position that oversees CID and forensics."

A new lieutenant? I'd gotten used to just dealing with Major Parks since Lieutenant Johnson had left.

"A new sergeant *and* a new lieutenant?" I mused.

"This is good change," Dad assured me.

"Like your marriage?" I smiled.

"Exactly like my marriage. Speaking of which, we better check in with the women folk."

Dad stood up and Mauser lumbered to his feet expectantly. "You want a snack?" Dad asked, ruffling his ears.

The rest of the weekend flew by too fast. Cara and I cleaned up the yard and burned a pile of deadfall we'd collected. In the evenings, I re-read the emails and wrote out my initial report on the Calavera case. I worked hard not to color Julio's involvement in any way that would add suspicion beyond what the facts suggested. I debated when I should formally interview him. After the autopsy made the most sense. I'd know more at that point, and I wanted to avoid interviewing him more than once. A first interview would be natural considering his involvement, but if the reports showed we'd formally questioned him more than once, it could attract the attention of any defense lawyer looking for other people to blame.

CHAPTER SEVEN

By Monday the clear skies had given way to gloomy, overcast weather brought on by southerly winds blowing up off the Gulf. As soon as I arrived at the office, I received a text from Dr. Darzi's office informing me that Eva's autopsy was scheduled for ten, which just gave me time to check in at my desk before heading over to Tallahassee.

I found Pete and Julio at their own desks in CID.

"You want to go with me to the autopsy?" I asked Pete. Julio was sifting through reports, looking uncomfortable.

"No. I'm going to follow up on some of the emails," Pete said, and tilted his head toward Julio. He repeated the motion a couple of times before I figured out what he was trying to tell me.

"Julio, we need to schedule a formal interview with you."

He looked up at me with sad eyes. "Yeah, anytime."

"Let's give it a couple of days, let the shock wear off so you can give clear answers."

He just nodded.

I took pity on him. "Look, Julio, this isn't a big deal. You know the routine."

"I know. I've just never been... questioned about something like this. There's... different angles to it, you know? The relationship with an older woman… Besides, she was a really nice person." His mixed emotions and pain were clear.

"It's awkward for us too. Hopefully we can clear you and get past this."

"I was with my—" he started and I put my hand up to stop him.

"Save it for the formal interview. It's bad enough that we're all friends and colleagues. We don't want word to get around to some defense attorney that we were discussing the case and your interview informally."

"Right, right. Of course." Julio looked like a kid who'd been caught in a very embarrassing position and just wanted his parents to drop the subject.

I sat down and quickly checked my emails before I headed back out for the autopsy.

I got to the hospital's morgue with five minutes to spare and the receptionist waved me on into the main autopsy room. I slipped on gloves and a mask and entered the room to find Dr. Darzi and Linda at one of the tables with Eva already resting uneasily on the stainless steel. Or at least I assumed she was uneasy. I know I'd be, dead *or* alive.

"We got an opening and started without you, Larry," Darzi said after a quick glance up to see who'd barged into the room.

"That's okay. I don't need to see all the gory details," I told him.

"Never fear, the gory parts are still to come." He beckoned me to the side of the table.

"Great," I said with my sarcasm dial turned all the way up. I nodded to Linda who, as always, looked like she was having the time of her life.

Eva's body had been stripped and they had already taken samples of dirt, pollen and any other microscopic evidence off the body using a vacuum, a high-tech version of sticky tape and a few other methods for getting at all the places on a body that gathered lint and other debris. Now they were using their eyes to examine the body from toes to head.

During the examination they talked almost constantly, so that the microphone over the table could pick up the details of inspection and analysis. I didn't know if they used transcription software or if some poor sod did it manually at a computer.

"I have one observation for you." Darzi interrupted his own dictation to point at the various holes left by the knife. "She was unconscious when the stabbing took place. See here."

He pointed to one of the wounds. "The blade cut cleanly into the body and came out without opening up the wound in any way." He waved his hand across her torso. "They're all the same. If any of them had been done while she was conscious, they would have shown signs of her struggles. Nothing."

"Could she have already been dead?" I asked.

"From the appearance of the body, she lost large amounts of blood, so her heart was still pumping."

"Unconscious, then, but not dead. Drugged?"

"And they say you aren't a quick study." Linda smiled.

"I will give very detailed instructions for the blood and tissue analysis, with an emphasis on the more easily accessible drugs and widening out to the less probable," Darzi assured me.

The rest of the autopsy was routine and uninformative except for what they didn't find. No recent sexual activity, no signs of physical abuse, no other wounds and no unknown medical conditions.

When I got out to the car, I called the number that Dr. Horvath had given me for Doug Holloway and made a mental note to run a records check for information on his wife's accident.

"Mr. Holloway, this is Larry Macklin, a friend of Dr. Horvath," I said when he answered. "I'm an investigator with the sheriff's office and we're looking into the rash of threatening emails that have been sent out in the last couple of months."

"Betty said she might tell you about the emails I've gotten. I don't know whether to be angry, sad or puzzled by them."

"I'd like to come by and talk to you if I can."

"I'm on a job right now, but I can meet you at my house in about an hour."

I told him that would be perfect. To kill time, I drove to a Publix and got a sandwich and drink from the deli. As I ate my lunch in the car, I used my laptop to search the department's archives for information on Mrs. Holloway.

Even with just a last name, it didn't take me long to find the accident report. Kristy Holloway had been killed while crossing the road during the Fall Family Festival that was hosted every year by a couple of churches in downtown Calhoun. Phil Eccles had been the responding officer. His report was detailed and well supported by graphs and an understanding of physics.

The accident had happened at eight fifty-six in the morning. Visibility was poor due to early-morning fog that was just starting to lift. Eccles also noted that the road had been damp due to a storm the night before. Kristy had been a successful romance author and had been planning to sign some of her books during the festival. She had been unpacking books from the trunk of her car and had stepped out into the road when another car, driven by Daniel Zywicki, had struck her and sent her flying headfirst back against her own vehicle.

The investigation had determined that Zywicki, then thirty-one, had been going slightly below the speed limit when he'd struck Kristy. Zywicki said that he'd seen her at the back of her car and had expected her to see him and wait for him to pass. Instead, she had simply turned and walked right in front of his car as if she'd never seen him at all.

Zywicki had slammed on the brakes when he'd realized

what was about to happen and there were long skid marks in the road to prove it. The final assessment was that he was not at fault in the accident. It was just one of those tragic incidents that ends a life and changes so many others. I didn't see any way that Doug Holloway could be responsible for what had happened. The report even made it clear that he had been home at the time of the accident.

I finished my lunch and headed back to Adams County to meet with him.

Holloway lived in a modest yet upscale house in one of the nicer subdivisions that had been developed fifteen years earlier, before the housing market collapsed. The house and yard were well kept. A white panel van was parked in front of the garage. I pulled in behind it and read the small sign on the back that said: Holloway Electric Repair & Supply.

By the time I got out of my car, Doug was standing on the porch.

"We can sit out here if you want. I printed out copies of the emails," he said, gripping a few sheets of paper in his hand.

"Thanks," I said, climbing the stone steps to the covered porch.

Holloway was an inch or two under six feet with dark hair showing touches of grey around the temples. I would have guessed his weight to be a little over two hundred without any fat. I wondered if he spent much time in the gym.

"Have a seat," he said, shifting a couple of rocking chairs so that we could sit facing each other.

"Nice place you've got here."

"I thought about moving after Kristy was killed, but this was her dream house. Maybe because of that I just couldn't sell it. Staying here helped me stay close to her and gave me a chance to think about the future."

I looked down at the emails he'd handed to me. There

were three of them and all followed the same theme: *You killed your wife. Turn yourself in to the police or suffer the consequences.*

"Why would someone accuse you of killing your wife?"

"Because I did."

I stared at him. He had turned his head and was looking off into the distance as his hands gripped the arms of his chair.

"How do you mean you killed her? I've read the accident report. It's pretty clear what happened."

"By letting her go by herself to that damned festival. She was so excited when the festival committee asked her to do a book-signing. I should have gone with her, but I didn't want to sit in the park all day. I thought I had better things to do." His knuckles were turning white as he gripped the chair.

"I understand how you feel—"

"No, no, you don't." Holloway shook his head.

"You'd be surprised," I said quietly. "A friend of mine was killed awhile back. A bomb went off. I can't help but feel like I could have saved him."

"The one that went off by the courthouse? I remember that."

"You can't blame yourself for what happened," I said, repeating advice that I'd received myself.

"Apparently *someone* blames me for her death." He pointed to the emails.

"Do you have any idea who could have sent these?"

"Her parents were certainly angry with me. Froze me out of their lives." Holloway managed a small smile. "If the email came from their ISP, I wouldn't be surprised."

"Have you talked to them since you got the email?" I asked.

"We haven't spoken since the funeral. I did go back and look at some old emails from them. The address is different."

"If it's like other emails we've looked into, then the address isn't real and the sender went to a good deal of effort to hide their ISP."

"That wouldn't be Bill or Kendra then. They needed Kristy's help to set up a new TV. But I really can't think of anyone other than them." He looked aside for a second before turning back to me. "Look, I'm being too harsh on them. They lost their only daughter, who meant the world to them. They have a right to be angry, and I guess I'm the only one left for them to blame."

"What about the driver of the car?"

He gave me a funny look. "I would have thought you knew. Daniel Zywicki died of a drug overdose six months ago."

"Where?"

"I don't know exactly. Some place in Tallahassee. They found him in a park, I think."

That explained it. Since Zywicki's death had occurred in another jurisdiction after the accident report had been closed, there hadn't been any reason to go back and make a note of his death in the original file.

"Did you have any contact with him or his family after the accident?"

"I heard he got into drugs after it happened. I know it tore him up. His mother called me up before the funeral and asked if he could see Kristy. She said he didn't want to disrupt the funeral by attending. He just wanted to have a moment with her to tell her how sorry he was. At the time I was still angry. Even so, a part of me was touched by the request. I told her to call the funeral home and tell them that he had my okay to see Kristy an hour before the viewing."

"Is it possible that *his* family blames you for his addiction and death?"

"I hadn't thought about that. I guess anything's possible. The only time I've spoken with any of them was when his mother called me."

We talked for a few more minutes before I left, figuring I'd gotten all the useful information that Holloway was able to give me. The list of emails was getting longer, but I didn't feel like we were getting any closer to finding the sender.

Back in the car, I saw a text from Cara asking if I would pick up cat food and something for dinner on my way home. I texted her a thumbs-up and started the car. Then I called Lionel to find out if he'd had any luck getting the tracking data from Eva Calavera's phone or car, but I had to leave a message.

A mile from the office, my phone rang. Figuring it was Lionel, I was surprised to see Ralph Calavera's number. I hoped he was calling to schedule a full, sit-down interview. But as I answered the call, I could almost feel an Arctic blast of hatred coming through my phone.

"I want to let you know that I've already begun the process of filing a lawsuit against you, your father and the sheriff's department, as well as a civil rights violation complaint against all of you."

I was stunned, having no clue what had set him off. "Excuse me?"

"You son of a bitch, if you think you can get away with this type of intimidation, you're in for a surprise. I'll take you all down!" Calavera's voice sounded just like a classic supervillain.

"I swear I don't know what you're talking about," I assured him.

"The email, you asshole!"

I'd seen Calavera in court half a dozen times and he'd never lost his cool. It was gone now.

"If you received an email, it wasn't from me."

"Don't think a phony email address is going to fool me," he growled. I think my phone actually quivered in its holder on the dash.

"Meet me at my office and I think I can explain everything," I said.

There was a long pause on the other end of the call.

"I can be there by four o'clock. I also want information on my wife's autopsy and when her body will be released for burial." The words were sharp and clipped.

"I'll see you there." He wasn't going to get too many

details from the autopsy, but he did deserve to know when he could bury Eva.

Calavera disconnected the call, probably missing the days when you could slam a receiver down. I had a few memories from my childhood of Dad slamming the phone down so hard that I'd sneak over and inspect it later, just to see if he'd actually busted it or not.

When I got to the office, I headed straight for Lionel's desk in the evidence department. He hadn't called me back, but that didn't mean he wasn't in. He had a reputation for burying his nose so deep into his work that sometimes he had to be tapped on the shoulder and encouraged to go home.

"Do you want to look at the items we picked up at the dump site?" Shantel looked up from her monitor when I entered her kingdom.

"Did you see anything that stood out?"

"There was a water bottle that looked fresh. I went ahead and processed it for prints and got four good ones."

"Have you run them?"

"Our network's been down. Lionel's promised to get it up and running before we close up shop today."

"If you get the chance, see if the prints come back to anyone. I'll look through the rest of the stuff later. Is Lionel in his office?" I asked, nodding at his closed door.

"He's been hiding in there half the day trying to fix the network."

I debated bothering him in the midst of his crisis. *There's always a crisis*, I thought and went over to the door and knocked.

"The network should be up shortly!" Lionel shouted.

I opened the door.

"If I'm interrupting, I'll come back," I said, not really meaning it. If he told me to come back later, I was still going to tell him what I wanted before I left.

"You can come in. I'm waiting for some software to finish updating so I can get everyone off my back," Lionel told me with a grin on his ebony face.

"Have you had any luck with Eva Calavera's phone or car?"

"I've got the request in for the full data spread on both. The warrants made the difference."

To hopefully speed up the process, I'd asked our county judge to issue warrants for the information. It was just a formality, but sometimes necessary. The companies in question wanted to help, but they also didn't want to be seen by their customers to be handing out personal information whenever law enforcement asked for it. In a case like this, it was easy. Dead people have no right to privacy.

"Let me know when you hear back."

"Could be five minutes, or it could be two weeks. I gave them some of the gruesome details, trying to play on their civic duty. Nice woman stabbed multiple times. Both the people I talked to sounded interested in helping. Now whether that will translate all the way down the chain of command to the person who actually has to get off their butts and do the work..." Lionel shrugged his shoulders. "Who knows?"

"Appreciate your effort. If you don't hear back soon, let me know. Calavera offered to push them." I paused to change subjects. "I did wonder something. How do you think our emailer got everyone's addresses?"

"You mean their *email* addresses?"

"Exactly. It's not like he's sending out spam. He's targeting specific people with specific messages. How did he get those emails?"

"Good point." Lionel looked thoughtful. "The addresses could have come from the same list. I'll check around on the tech boards and see if anyone around here has been hacked."

I thanked him and left him to work out his network issues. Having a little time before the meeting with Calavera, I helped Shantel prioritize the items we'd picked up at the dump site.

The best of the bunch was the water bottle. Everything else looked like it had been out there for a day or more. But who knew? If Eva had been transported there in the back of a pickup truck, then some of the junk could have been dragged out when the killer took her body out of the bed of the truck. If that was the case, then even the stuff that looked old and faded might be relevant to the case. This part of forensic work was all about the numbers. In a perfect world, we'd be able to test everything. As it was, we had to play the odds.

"I'll let you know about the prints from the bottle as soon as I can put them in the system," Shantel told me.

"They won't come back to anyone. We never get that lucky," I said as I left.

I was halfway down the hall when the rookie holding down the front desk called me. "There's a man here who says he has an appointment with you."

"Short, well dressed, angry-looking?"

"That's him."

"I'll be there in a minute."

CHAPTER EIGHT

Ralph Calavera was pacing around the reception area.

"We can use the small conference room," I told him. I hadn't bothered to shake hands. He wasn't in the mood.

"Go on down. I'll be right there," I said, seeing the look on his face. "Don't worry, I'm not going to keep you waiting."

With a glare, he walked on ahead. He'd been to our office often enough with clients to know where our two conference rooms were.

We also had a couple of rooms we used for interrogations, but they were small and intimidating. Just what you wanted for an intense interview, but not when questioning a witness or wanting to put a suspect at ease. I wasn't sure which I would be doing in this interview.

I jogged back to CID and was glad to see Pete sitting at his desk. "Good, you're here. Would you mind coming down to the conference room and helping me explain the crazy situation with the emails to Ralph Calavera?"

"I need to be there anyway to make sure you don't go off on him," Pete said, standing.

"You make me sound like a hothead. I know he's just doing his job with Neil Manning. I'm just pissed that

Manning can afford a lawyer as good as Calavera."

"I hear you. Are you going to ask him about Neil now?"

"I'll leave that up to you. If he really was in jail when some of the emails were sent, then I don't see how he could have done it."

"Snuck a phone in?" Pete suggested. "Wouldn't be the first time."

"You've got a point. The emails are your case, so I'll leave that up to you to ask. But I don't see why Manning would kill his lawyer's wife."

"Payment," Pete said.

We'd almost reached the conference room. I turned to look at him to see if he was serious.

"That's not the dumbest thing you've ever suggested," I said, considering it. "Sounds crazy, but…"

"I shouldn't have mentioned it right before we talk to him."

"You're right. Now is not the time to antagonize Calavera. We don't want him to stop cooperating with the murder investigation." I opened the conference room door.

Calavera was standing on the other side of the table. As we entered the room, his eyes were locked on us like he was assessing the members of a jury.

"This better be convincing or I'll report you to FDLE and the State Attorney for further action."

"Remember the threatening emails going around the county that I mentioned to you on Friday?" I said. "More than one of them mentioned your wife."

I watched both Calavera and Pete for their reactions. Calavera's aggressive stance wavered and he reached out for the back of one of the conference room chairs. Pete looked at me sharply as if to ask: *Do you really want to do this now?* I gave him a reassuring smile that, truth be told, was hiding my own uncertainty. With a man like Calavera, our only chance of catching him off guard was a quick, sharp sucker-punch.

Calavera straightened, recovering quickly from the first blow. "What did the email pertain to?" he shot back at me.

"An affair that she had," I responded and saw him take the second punch with less aplomb. Then a sneer crossed his face.

"Now you really are angling to be thrown in your own jail." The words were heavy with menace. "I've already told you that we were living separate lives. I didn't know about her… affairs, but I wouldn't be surprised if she saw other men."

Calavera was treading lightly. He knew that we were talking about motive. A motive that any jury would recognize, while most would have a much harder time understanding the Calaveras' separate living arrangement.

"Maybe it was something you were comfortable with, but I'm thinking a public display of your cuckoldry would be a different situation," I said.

"If you sent that email then I'll have you strung up in court."

Pete placed a folder filled with copies of the poison emails on the table. Calavera reached out for the folder like it was a bag full of rattlesnakes, then he flipped it open and started going through the emails.

"This doesn't prove that you didn't send the email to me," he said, sounding less sure of himself.

"And me telling you that I didn't for the fifth time won't convince you either. Let's deal with what we can agree on. You have a motive for the murder of your wife."

Calavera's face turned red and his jaw clenched as he glared at me. Here was a man who had spent his entire career making people mad on the stand so they would say something stupid. He was familiar with the trap I was laying. I watched him take a deep breath and relax all of his muscles.

"I can see how someone might think that."

"Would you also agree that you don't have an alibi for the time of the murder?"

"I don't know when the murder was committed."

"Let's do broad strokes. Say between midnight Thursday

and six Friday morning. During which time you were at home… alone," I said, trying not to smile as I watched his left eye twitch.

"Yes. That's true. I accessed my emails and used my phone to send several texts during that time."

"But no one was with you?"

I could see that he wanted to make some kind of snide remark, but he settled for, "No." He was obviously frustrated. "Look, I'll grant you access to the ping data for my phone. I can't give you access to everything since my phone contains privileged communications between myself and my clients." He paused again. "We can probably work out a way to let you see the time stamps and have a neutral third party verify the purpose of the texts that I sent that night. Same goes for my laptop." He folded his arms as though to say: *This far and no further.*

If I'd been interviewing anyone else, I might have asked him what he'd say if I told him that I had a witness who claimed to have seen him leave his house that night. But a cheap trick question like that would only earn me more scorn from Calavera. I'd already forced him to make a concession, so it was time to move on to another possible suspect.

"I want to check Neil Manning's ankle monitor and ask him some questions."

"Why?" Calavera blurted in the same voice I'd heard him use to shout *Objection!* in a courtroom. "You don't have to ask me for permission to check his ankle monitor. As for asking him questions, I've advised him not to speak to anyone but me."

"He might not take your advice."

"I think his father can persuade him otherwise."

"You do know that he kidnapped a woman and tortured her?" I asked.

"A court of law will decide his guilt or innocence." Calavera was clearly losing patience with me.

"No. They'll decide his fate under our legal system. His

guilt is a fact."

"And your tunnel vision is likely to be a focus of his defense. There is no point in us discussing his case, because I'm not going to." He leaned back against the wall. "If you continue to pursue asinine lines of inquiry, I'll talk to the State Attorney. The person who killed my wife is out *there*," he said, pointing dramatically at the door. "And I will hold you and the sheriff's office accountable if you fail to track them down."

"At last we find ourselves on the same page. I promise you…" I pointed at him in an equally dramatic fashion. "…that I *will* hunt down and imprison the murderer of your wife… no matter who he is."

Calavera stared back at me. It was a classic standoff. He didn't want to start a knockdown, drag-out fight with me at this point. I was the lead investigator on his wife's murder. If he was the murderer, then it wouldn't serve his purpose to raise my ire further. And if he was innocent, then it wouldn't help to have me focused on him. For my part, I didn't want to cut off all ties with a man who could provide me with information in the death of Eva Calavera. So far, he'd been helpful in obtaining data from her car and her cell phone, and he'd offered to provide some information from his phone and laptop.

"Are we finished?" His eyes were hard and cold.

"Truce," I said, raising my hand. "Let's agree to work together on your wife's murder." I dropped my hand and stuck it out toward him.

"I'm not shaking your hand," he grumbled. "I have been cooperative and will continue to be. Your antics during this interview don't scare me or surprise me. Do what you have to do to satisfy yourself that I didn't harm my wife, then get on with the business at hand. There is a killer on the loose. Do your job." He headed toward the door of the conference room.

I dropped my hand. "One more question. When I find the person who stabbed your wife to death and dumped her behind an abandoned gas station, are you going to be their lawyer?" I couldn't resist a jab at a man who had represented some of Florida's most heinous citizens.

"No. It would be a conflict of interest. Though I would hope that he'd get a highly qualified attorney." Calavera looked thoughtful for a moment, then added, "Of course, if the person you charge with the murder *is* guilty, then I will be glad to see the State of Florida exercise the full weight of its authority and inject him or her with a lethal dose of chemicals until their life is extinguished."

I thought he was done, but he gave me a twisted smile and said, "You know, Old Sparky is still authorized for use in executions." With that, he turned and left Pete and me in the interview room, staring at each other.

"You were quiet," I said to Pete. I was used to him cutting in with a couple of penetrating questions during interviews.

"I thought you were doing a fine job of digging your hole deeper on your own." He smiled.

"Calavera and I came in disliking each other already and that's where we were when he left. I don't think I did myself, or the case, any harm."

"Probably not. No offense, but he's above your weight class when it comes to verbal sparring. Mine too, for that matter."

I wanted to argue, but Pete was right. As much as I disliked Calavera, I knew he was too smart to be caught in any mental trap I could set. If he was guilty, only hard evidence was going to put him in jail.

"I've got to go." Pete looked at his phone.

"Dentist appointment?"

"What?"

"Your face. You look like you're going to your own execution. That's the way I feel going to the dentist."

"Same idea." He sighed. "Doctor."

"Ouch! Good luck."

"I'll need it." Pete rubbed his well-padded middle. "I

wish I could find some overweight, cigar-smoking, whiskey-swilling doctor who wouldn't nag me about my own bad habits."

I looked at my watch. It was almost four o'clock. "Isn't it kind of late for an appointment?"

"I always get the last one of the day. I figure they won't fool around since they want to get out of there and go home."

"Does that work?"

"Only about half the time. The other half of the time, they're backed up from emergencies and I don't get out of there until after six."

I saw him out the door, then went back to my desk and worked on some of my other cases, trying to keep an eye out for any that might be related to our mysterious emailer. The way he was blanketing the county with his poison-pen messages, we could have any number of domestic disputes or assaults popping up that had been caused by them.

Cara gave me a call at five-thirty.

"I'm going to stop off at Sarah's house. I want to talk to her about something," she told me.

"What?" I asked, a little suspicious about what she might have to discuss with Pete's wife.

"Just an idea," she said vaguely.

"That's okay. I'm going to make a stop myself at Albert Griffin's."

"The cats are going to be mad that their dinner is late."

"They'll live. I'll make it a point not to beat you home so I don't get all the angry meows," I kidded her.

"Coward," she told me before we said our goodbyes.

I packed up and headed for Mr. Griffin's. I wanted to ask him about the emails. If anything like this had surfaced in the past, he'd know about it.

CHAPTER NINE

The winter sun had dropped below the trees as I pulled into the driveway, and I could see lights on in the back of the house. I also noticed that the garage apartment where Eddie Thompson lived was dark. Eddie had been my confidential informant during his days as a drug addict. He had a pretty good excuse for his poor start at adulting. A large chunk of his close family had been involved in the drug trade.

I knocked on the kitchen door. "Mr. Griffin, it's Larry," I called out, not wanting to make him get up from the table if he was eating.

"Come in!" he shouted back.

Inside I found him eating a bowl of New England clam chowder while trying to persuade his stubborn black cat, Brutus, not to take a few licks from the bowl. As I neared the table, the cat gave me a soul-sucking glare before turning and jumping down to the floor.

"Have a seat. Can I get you some soup?" Mr. Griffin started to get up and I waved him back down.

"No, I'm fine. I just wanted to see how you're doing."

"And ask me some questions about the emails going around town?" There was a glint in his eye that said he knew why I'd come by.

"I think you're getting smarter in your old age." I smiled.

"I know you pretty well by now, Larry. Though I'm a little surprised that you're worried about emails when the wife of one of Florida's most prominent defense lawyers was found dead last week." He looked thoughtful for a moment, then snapped his fingers. "Ah ha! There must be a connection between the two."

"Elementary, my dear Poirot," I said, mixing my references. "But I am neither confirming nor denying your assumption."

"I've still got a little of the journalist in me, but never fear, I—unlike most of the world—don't need an audience these days. What is said inside these walls stays inside these walls."

I sat down across from him. "Don't let me interrupt your dinner."

With a wink, he picked up the bowl and drained the last of the soup before setting the dish on the floor for Brutus, who was slinking back around his ankles. The cat licked the last dregs from the bowl while keeping one eye on me.

"So what have you heard about the emails?" I asked.

"Heard and seen. I got one of my own. Well, actually two." He smiled at the surprised look on my face.

"Why didn't you report them?"

"You obviously have no idea how many threatening letters newspapermen get. When I freelanced for the paper, I'd sometimes get two or three hate-filled letters a week. Some were nasty, some vindictive, while others were taunting. Occasionally they were deadly serious. I've been physically attacked three times."

"I didn't know about the attacks." I was surprised. "I hope you don't take this wrong, but I can't imagine anyone being that mad at you."

"I was just a focal point for their anger, which was usually more about their own perceived impotence than anything else."

"I'd think being attacked would have made you more

inclined to report the email threats now."

"Hundreds of threats over the years and only three attacks. Most people got it out of their system by writing it down. I'm not a fan of zero tolerance policies. I think we need to cut each other a little slack. Sometimes people just need to vent. Every word we utter or write down shouldn't be set in stone for all eternity. One of the problems I have with our digital age."

"Can I see the emails?" I asked.

"Sure. Come on back to my computer. I guess if I was more tech savvy, or had better eyes, I'd just pull them up on my phone." He tapped the smartphone lying on the table as he stood up.

"A full-size monitor doesn't break my heart," I said, following him back to his office. The old Victorian house smelled of yellowed newspapers, aged wood and leatherbound books.

He sat down at his desk while I stood behind him and looked over his shoulder. His email was open and, with a couple of clicks, he pulled up the first email which read: *You embezzled the newspaper's funds and forced it to go out of business. You should pay for your crimes.*

"Pretty silly since I never actually owned the paper and I was the one who volunteered to house all the archives. And, honestly, *should pay* is not much of a threat," Mr. Griffin said, pointing to the words on the screen. "Pretty weak tea. Why not *you will pay* or *shall pay*? Or maybe *I'll make you pay.*"

"You've got a point."

"And the idea that there were any funds to embezzle." He chuckled softly. "Why do they think the paper folded in the first place?"

I looked at the email address of the sender. Like all the others, it was a mishmash of letters and symbols. I pointed to it. "Lionel tells me a program can generate bogus email addresses."

"I assumed that wasn't the actual address of the sender. Anyway, that was the first email, and I wasn't even sure that it wasn't some type of spam, randomly generated and sent out. The newspaper bit might have been a lucky hit. But the second email hit a little closer to home."

He clicked a couple of times and pulled up a second email. This one read: *Your ambition and self-righteous attitude killed Betty Armitage. Justice would be served if you were found hanging from a tree branch.*

"Who's Betty Armitage?"

"The wife of Harold Armitage. She killed herself after one of my articles exposed her husband as, ironically, an embezzler."

"Harold Armitage… That name rings a bell. He worked for the county, right?"

"He was the assistant to the clerk of the court. The county manager found out that he had stolen close to two hundred thousand dollars. This was in 1999. It was going to be a huge embarrassment to everyone in the hierarchy of county government, so a deal was worked out where Armitage would quit and pay back the money. And he probably could have just about scraped together enough after selling his house and some land that his father had left him."

"So what happened?"

"I did. I got tipped off by a friend who worked for one of the commissioners. He thought Armitage should go to jail and, of course, I thought the people had a right to know what was going on. The plan was ill-conceived anyway and, sooner or later, it all would have been exposed. When I interviewed Mrs. Armitage, she pleaded with me not to publish the story. Their daughter was going to get married in a few months and she didn't want the scandal to come out before the wedding. But I rode my high horse all the way to the printing press. The morning after the story was published, Mrs. Armitage was found hanging from an oak tree in their backyard. The wedding never happened and Harold's health collapsed until he finally died three years later. I took a year off from writing articles for the paper."

An unusual sadness clouded Mr. Griffin's eyes.

"You weren't responsible for her husband's actions," I said, but he shook his head.

"I took my time and thought long and hard about my motivations. I don't think this email is far off." He tapped the monitor. "Which might be another reason I didn't bring it to your attention before now. Dredging up the worst moment in my varied career wasn't something I wanted to do."

"So who do you think sent these emails?"

He looked thoughtful. "Clearly someone who knows my past. Having said that, there is nothing in the emails that wasn't or isn't public knowledge. I was open about my feelings when I took a year off from writing. Is it someone with deep roots in the community? Probably. But the first email went wide of the mark."

"So we have a swing and a miss followed by a home run." I looked at the time and date on the two emails. "Two days apart. Did you tell anyone about the first one? Maybe make fun of the fact that it was a laughable accusation?"

"I see where you're going. Did the email writer hear that he'd missed the bullseye and decide to take a second shot? Unfortunately, I just ignored it. Like I said, I half thought it might be spam."

"What other threatening emails have you heard about?"

"Several folks mentioned getting one. I advised them to report them."

"Did you tell any of them that you'd gotten a couple?"

"I just said that I'd received a lot of crazy letters and emails over the years without mentioning these." He tapped the monitor again.

"Who were these other recipients?"

"Let me talk to them again. I don't want to break a confidence."

"Did they sound like they wanted you to keep quiet about them?" I asked.

"One said so specifically. The other two... I'd say they

implied it."

"Did they tell you what was in their emails?"

Mr. Griffin held up his hand to stop me. "Let me talk to them, then I'll get back with you."

"Fair enough."

"This reminds me a little of the Circleville, Ohio letter writer."

"Who?"

"It was in 1976. I don't remember the exact details, but let me think. A married woman was supposedly having an affair with the mayor or a school principal. I can't remember, but she started getting letters telling her to end the affair. Eventually her husband got a letter, followed by at least one phone call, which caused the husband to drive off into the night, thinking he knew who had called and planning to get revenge. The husband was found dead in a single-car accident that night. Anyway, the letters went on and, at one point, there was some kind of bomb or something that almost killed the woman. That's all I remember. You can Google it."

I made a note to research the case.

"From the emails I've seen, the writer knows a lot about our county," I said.

"But the emails aren't always right. You're looking for a watcher. Someone who observes from the outside. They see things, but aren't really intimate with the details."

"Good point."

"What about the murder? Do you think the emails are connected or just red herrings?"

I shrugged. "They seem random. They could be from the killer or from someone else. All bets are off."

Mr. Griffin looked thoughtful. "I wish I could be of more help. I tried to think who could be sending the emails to me and didn't come up with anyone. Or maybe I should say, I came up with a bunch of folks, but none of them were a perfect fit. I mean, why me after all these years? I can't remember the last time I got into a phone argument with anyone other than some unhelpful rep from a corporation. And I don't think that someone from Verizon or Comcast is going to take the time to stalk me 'cause I complained about an increase in rates or their poor customer service."

"Unlikely. I'd appreciate you encouraging anyone else who has gotten one of these emails to contact us. I keep thinking that if we have enough of them, we might be able to see a pattern."

"I can think of half a dozen cases of people who have received anonymous letters and harassment over the course of years. But it's usually directed at an individual, a family or a company."

I remembered my interview with Ralph Calavera. Curious, I asked, "Did you ever see Old Sparky in action?"

Mr. Griffin gave me a sad smile. "Worst day of my life. I was a witness for the execution of John Spenkelink in 1979. He was convicted of killing his roommate in Tallahassee. He got two shots of whiskey before the sentence was carried out. There were about thirty people there to watch. Ten of them were newspapermen."

"The electric chair can still be used, right?"

"Old Sparky has survived every challenge," Mr. Griffin said, nodding. "The state is holding it in reserve in case lethal injection can't be used for some reason. Just thinking about that night gives me nightmares." He gave a little laugh and his eyes looked away.

"Sorry."

"I'm not opposed to the death penalty in principle."

"I'm surprised. I would have thought you were more… forgiving… or maybe reform-minded."

"No. There are some people who can't be redeemed. They've committed hideous crimes. No question they did it either. In those cases, I think execution is the most humane option. I've seen the cell on Q ward in Raiford. We are fortunate that true monsters like Ted Bundy and Danny Rolling are rare. Living in a four-by-eight concrete box for twenty-three hours a day for the rest of their lives is not compassionate. In my opinion, neither option—execution or life as a trapped animal—is good. I just think that execution is more humane. Though not necessarily at the hands of Old Sparky."

"How's Eddie doing?" I asked after a while, wanting to break the silence and stop the uncomfortable thoughts we were both having.

"Okay. He misses Jessie. She's concentrating on her classes at the academy. I'm impressed that he's being good and giving her some space."

Eddie had met Jessie Gilmore while working at the library. They had become good friends, despite Eddie's past and Jessie's penchant for stumbling into my investigations. Eddie had mixed feelings about her decision to enter the law enforcement academy.

"He's not home yet?" I said, looking out the window at the space where he usually parked.

"They've been letting him close up the library."

"Wow. Eddie… a man of responsibility," I joked. I stood up, figuring I should get home before Ivy and Ghost starved to death.

"You saved him," Mr. Griffin said solemnly.

"No. I gave him a little room so he could save himself. When we met, he was hungry for a chance to escape his family and the life he'd drifted into."

Mr. Griffin followed me out to my car.

"There's a front coming," he said, looking up at the clouds sliding across the moon.

"It's going to bring rain and temps in the twenties by tomorrow night. Stay warm," I said, getting into my car. February in North Florida could be anything from mild to frigid. Sometimes both in the same day.

I made a quick stop for cat food and dinner, then I spent the ride home thinking about the arbitrary nature of the emails. I still couldn't make up my mind if they were connected to the murder of Eva Calavera or not. If not, I was wasting time obsessing about someone who just got their jollies by stirring up the muck.

I managed to beat Cara home. When I opened the door to our house and turned on a light, Ghost rushed over to me. Ivy, on the other hand, gave me her most judgmental glare from the back of the couch.

"I'm home. What do you want?" I asked her.

Ghost reached his claws halfway up my leg and Ivy gave me another glare before jumping down and heading for the kitchen. "I'm coming," I told her. "You two aren't going to starve to death."

Once I'd fed them and changed clothes, I warmed up the fried chicken I'd bought at the store. I pulled up the radar on my phone while I listened to the microwave whirr. A dark red line of storms was only about twenty miles away.

Before I could decide whether I should text Cara and warn her about the weather, I heard her car come up the driveway to the house. I relaxed and finished loading my plate.

"It's going to storm," Cara said as she came through the door. I kissed her, then we talked weather for a few minutes before she went to change.

"What did you want to talk to Sarah about?" I asked once Cara had joined me at the table. I considered being nosy an asset to my job and practiced whenever I could.

"Genie won't let us have a bridal shower for her," Cara said, picking a piece of skin off her fried chicken and popping it into her mouth, "but I still want to do something for her."

"If she said she doesn't want one, then she doesn't want one. Genie isn't one to play games."

"I know. And we aren't going to give her a shower, but Sarah had a great idea. We're going to have a small get-together with some of the wives and husbands of deputies after the wedding. You know how Sarah made me feel welcome and talked me through the whole what-it's-like-to-be-married-to-a-deputy thing. We want to do the same thing for Genie... maybe as an informal support group for law enforcement spouses."

"We're so bad you need to have a support network?" I asked with a smile.

"You know what I mean," Cara said, kicking me under the table. "But I don't think you can be married to a law enforcement officer and not think about... the consequences." She paused and gave me a smile. "Besides, y'all are a pain in the ass to live with."

"I get it. High rates of divorce, drinking, moodiness, suicide, etc., etc. But Genie doesn't—" I almost said that Genie didn't have to worry about Dad, but then I remembered seeing him lying on the ground bleeding and all the headaches and moodiness that had followed. "I see your point."

"We just thought Genie might like to meet a few more of the spouses."

"It's a good idea. Part of being the sheriff's wife is being the *sheriff's* wife. It's an elected position and she'll have to play politics too. Even if it's just in the form of going to some public functions."

"Exactly. I think she'll go for it. Her main objection to a bridal shower was that she didn't want anyone giving her presents."

"Did you see Pete?" I asked, just to make conversation as Cara finished her dinner.

She surprised me by putting her chicken leg back on her plate and looking over at me.

"He didn't seem himself." She let the sentence hang in the air.

"What do you mean?"

"He was quiet."

"Did he look okay?" I remembered the doctor's appointment that he'd had scheduled for that afternoon.

"I guess. Just not his regular, crazy self."

"He had a doctor's appointment today."

"That could explain it. Getting poked and prodded is enough to make anyone a little quieter than normal," she said, then saw my expression. "You don't think there's anything wrong with him?"

"It's probably what you said. Who enjoys a trip to the doctor? He seemed fine at work. There was just something about the way he was acting. Normally he'd be making jokes about the prostate exam."

"Maybe I'm just so used to him being… funny that it's a surprise when he's just acting normal." Then she deftly changed the subject. "Why did you stop by Mr. Griffin's on your way home?"

"To ask about the emails. He had a few ideas." I reminded myself to look up the Circleville letter writer later.

"How's Eddie doing?"

I told her that I hadn't seen him and filled her in on what Mr. Griffin had told me. Then we cleaned up the dishes and settled down in different corners of the house as the rain pounded on the roof. Cara relaxed with a paperback that had well-armed badgers and armor-plated cats on the cover, while I did some work at my laptop.

I read about the Circleville incident. The story was even stranger and more convoluted than Mr. Griffin had made it out to be. Mary Gillispie and her husband, Ron, had received a number of letters before he received the phone call that had sent him running out into the night. Ron's death in the single-car crash was ruled an accident, but there were a number of inconsistencies about his death. For one thing, he had taken a gun with him when he went to confront the person he thought was on the phone. When his wrecked truck was found, the gun had been fired. More letters were sent to residents of Circleville after the accident, claiming that the sheriff was covering up the truth in Ron's death.

Mary received additional letters and accusatory signs began showing up around town tacked to trees. When Mary finally got fed up and attempted to tear down one of the signs, she was almost killed by a boobytrap.

The sheriff became fixated on Paul Freshour, Ron's brother-in-law, after the gun used in the boobytrap was found to be registered to him. Against the flow of evidence, the sheriff and district attorney managed to get Paul convicted of setting the trap. But even with Paul in jail, the letters continued. In spite of the prison warden swearing that there was no way that Paul could be sending the letters, the sheriff still insisted he was guilty.

After reading a couple of accounts online and watching the episode of *Unexplained Mysteries* about the case, I pondered the similarities and differences between the Circleville letter writer and our anonymous emailer. Our emailer was accusing a broad spectrum of people of all manner of malfeasance, while the Circleville letter writer had concentrated on Mary and Ron and the events surrounding them. Most people believed that the Circleville case was never really solved. I hoped that we could do better with our malicious emailer.

CHAPTER TEN

When I got out of the shower the next morning, I noticed a text from Pete on my phone.

Sorry, I'm taking the day off, it read. He followed this with a list of chores he wanted me to take care off.

I texted back and asked if he was okay.

I just need a day. I owe you.

"What's wrong?" Cara asked when she saw me standing by the kitchen table, staring at my phone.

"Pete's not coming in today." I was still frowning at the phone, trying to figure out how to make it give me more information. I wanted to know what was going on. Did it have anything to do with his doctor's appointment? Or maybe he really did just need a day off.

"You're worried about him."

"Yeah, I am. This is weird. I can't remember the last time he just up and decided to take a day off. He schedules plenty of time off, but he doesn't do it on a whim."

"He's probably fine," Cara said, rubbing my back in a reassuring manner. "Maybe he got stressed out over the promotion selection process."

"Maybe. I think he does kind of want the promotion, but we're both pretty sure that Phil Eccles is going to get it."

Outside, the skies were clearing after the previous night's storm, and the north wind buffeted the pine trees. I pulled my coat tight as I rushed to the car and its warm heater.

Once I was at the office, I pushed concerns for Pete out of my mind as I tried to come up with a plan for the day. The first thing on my list was easy. Before I even woke up my computer, I called Sergeant Moses Hudson, who oversaw the county's home confinement program.

"I checked on Neil Manning three days ago," he told me.

I explained the situation to him.

"I'll be at his house in an hour. You can meet me there."

I'd worked with Moses on a couple of cases where suspects had jumped bail. He put new meaning to the phrase "no nonsense." When he narrowed his eyes at someone on probation, it meant they had better come up with the right answers.

"I'll be there," I promised.

I opened my email and scanned the two new cases that had been assigned to me, then did a quick interview with both victims. One of them had been beaten up in the laundromat because of an argument over a dryer. The other was a schoolteacher who had been attacked with a golf club by a teenager. The boy had done a number on the woman, striking her a dozen times around the torso. The responding deputy had included pictures of the bruises that were taken at the hospital. The boy had already been arrested and charged, but I'd been asked to investigate a little deeper to see if additional charges were warranted. These were the types of cases that left me shaking my head about the state of the world.

I had to hurry to get to Neil Manning's on time to meet Moses.

Manning had a nice place in a new development on the edge of town. I parked across the street until I saw Sergeant Hudson pull into the driveway. I knew his routine. He didn't call ahead. The person out on bail was supposed to be home when he showed up, so he gave them every opportunity to prove that they were trustworthy.

He unfolded himself from the older model marked car. The sergeants who worked out of the jail got the older cars since they were used primarily for routine trips around the county. At six feet, Moses was as tall as I was and had a dark black complexion. Though over fifty, he looked like he could go toe to toe with anyone on the WWE circuit. I'd never heard of a prisoner who hadn't been high on drugs giving him a hard time. And if he didn't feel like wrestling someone to the ground, he also carried a Wilson Combat .45. Pete told me that Moses was one of the quickest draws in the department, with double-taps anywhere he wanted them on the target.

"Macklin, I don't want to have to remind you that this isn't an interrogation, only an inspection," he said with the smallest hint of a smile.

"Scout's honor," I said, holding up two fingers. "Unless he *wants* to talk to me."

"Not likely. I had to argue with Calavera just to get the house cleared of possible internet access." Moses reached into his car and pulled out a briefcase.

"That was the court order," I said, surprised that Calavera would even argue the point.

"He was fine with the internet, but Manning complained to him when I ordered the cable removed. Calavera made me go before the judge and explain that, in these enlightened times, a person can communicate with others over all types of systems, including games accessed through the TV."

"Good point."

"The judge gave Calavera a talking-to. Even threatened to raise bail for dragging us into a meeting for something that should have been obvious."

We had walked up to the front door. I watched as Moses shifted his focus to the job at hand. He rapped on the door three times. After waiting for ten seconds he knocked again, this time hard enough to rattle the windows. I saw him tense up as though expecting Manning to have flown the coop, but he relaxed as soon as we heard the sound of heavy footsteps approaching the front door.

"What?" Manning called from the other side of the door. The voice wasn't aggressive, just matter-of-fact.

"It's Sergeant Hudson. I'm here to examine your ankle monitor and to inspect the premises to be sure that you are in compliance with your—" Before he could finish his sentence, the door opened.

Manning started to smile and then caught sight of me. With a grimace, he tried to push the door closed, but Moses's boot was in the way.

"Deputy Macklin is simply here to monitor the process," Moses informed him.

"I don't want him in my house." Manning was still wearing a back brace, had a cast on his arm and had a number of raw scars on his face from the accident caused by his reckless attempt to avoid capture.

"You're refusing the inspection?" Moses said as though it didn't matter to him one way or the other.

"And if I am?" Manning's voice was high-pitched and his eyes danced around.

"You aren't stupid." Moses sounded like a disappointed teacher.

"I know you can take me to jail."

"Your choice," Moses said, and this time I caught a little smile. "If you're in jail, it saves me the trouble of driving out here. I can just look at the monitor and see that you're locked up in your cell."

Manning backed away from the door. Moses followed him to the dining room, where he dropped down in a chair and stuck out his right foot.

"I'd like to have it moved to the other ankle." Manning was acting like a petulant child, which was exactly what he was. A violent, psychopathic, petulant adult child.

"No problem." Moses unlocked the ankle monitor and inspected it, then opened his briefcase and switched the monitor with one of the three he'd brought with him. After making sure it was charged and working, he placed it on Manning's left ankle.

"Have you ever met Mrs. Eva Calavera?" I asked without any expectation that he'd answer the question.

"No," Manning said and gave me a smirk. He turned to Moses. "He tried to kill me. We're going to file a civil suit against him and the sheriff's department."

"I'm going to look through your house for any violations of the terms of your bail." Moses ignored his comment.

"Do whatever you want." This time Manning went with a sneer instead of a smirk. Moses didn't point out that it had been a statement, not a request.

Manning leaned back in his chair and had a hard time hiding the pain he was in. I probably should have been ashamed at the pleasure I got from watching him wince and cringe, but I couldn't help but feel that he deserved to suffer after what he'd done to Terri Miller and his culpability in my father's injuries.

"Have you ever sent an email using a fake address?" I asked as though it was normal small talk.

Manning gave me an odd look. I couldn't tell if it was because he didn't know why I was asking the question or because he was concerned that I'd asked it.

"Why would I answer any of your questions?" he said, awkwardly trying to adjust his back brace.

"Because you're bored," I answered with a dry smile.

"You're damn right about that. This all sucks." He pouted. "I loved her."

After the accident, when we'd tried to question him about Terri Miller while he was still in the hospital, his father and Ralph Calavera had stepped in and prevented us from doing anything beyond what we were allowed by law. Manning had been on enough medications that Calavera could have gotten anything he'd said blocked from use in the trial, but it hadn't mattered and we still had a lot of holes to fill in the investigation. But I wasn't going to take the bait now. Manning had kidnapped and brainwashed Terri Miller.

Love had nothing to do with what he'd done

"You're good at hiding your tracks. We have a guy who's sending anonymous emails. I'm assuming you can do that?"

"It doesn't take a genius. Get me a computer and I'll show you."

"We know how it's done. I just wondered if *you* could do it."

"I don't know about you, but most guys under thirty could do it. Hunt up the right program. On the dark web, people will sell you all kinds of shit."

"What have you heard about the death of Calavera's wife?" I switched subjects.

"What the hell is that man doing?" It took me a minute to realize that he was talking about Moses. "Is he going through my underwear?"

"He's going through everything you own," I told him. Of course, that wasn't even close to true. We'd had to work overtime finding all the toys this rich brat had scattered on properties all over the county. His father's house still had a room filled with his junk.

"Whatever. You know I'm going to be acquitted of all those charges." He went back to baiting me.

"Funny how there is another violent death among your acquaintances."

"I never even met that woman," Manning said with some irritation.

"Calavera becomes your lawyer and a couple months later, his wife is murdered. I'm just sayin'."

"Hell with you. Why would I kill a woman I've never even met?"

I shrugged. "Maybe as payment?"

"You're crazy. I'm going to tell Calavera what you said." The more he talked, the more I realized that he had the maturity of a twelve-year-old.

"Do what you want," I said, then decided to rub a little salt in the wounds. "Except leave the house or communicate with anyone online or access the internet in any way."

He made some rude finger gestures as Sergeant Hudson came back into the room.

"House appears to be clean." He picked up his briefcase.

"I'm done," I told him and we started for the door, ignoring the dangerous and pathetic man-child struggling to get up out of his chair.

"Come back anytime," Manning said sarcastically as he followed us to the door.

"We will," Moses said over his shoulder.

We stopped at his car.

"I'll take a look at his monitor, but I don't think it's been tampered with," Moses told me. "I looked at the data that we've gotten and there's nothing out of the ordinary."

I nodded my head before I became aware of something confusing.

"I don't understand. If there isn't any wi-fi in the house, how do you get the information from the monitor?"

Moses grinned. "Lionel figured that out. Your buddy in there isn't the only creep we've got on house arrest who can't have access to the internet. Of course, the ones who aren't allowed to surf the web are usually the ones who can hack a router. What Lionel came up with is a router that we put on the outside of the house with a well-encrypted password." He pointed to the corner of Manning's house where the power box was located. Another metal box was screwed to the wall. "That's it. The bad guys can't even get to the box because if they try it, the alarm on their monitor goes off and a signal is sent to us before they can reach the router."

"And if the power goes off?"

"Lionel wired a battery backup."

I saw Manning watching us from the window. "It's nice to think that he's boxed up in there. I wish I could believe that he's really neutralized."

"He is until the trial."

I thanked Moses and moved my car out of his way. After he left, I parked on the side of the road and watched the house for a few more minutes, thinking about the situation with Manning. If Calavera wanted to use him to kill his wife, then he'd bring him whatever he needed. We weren't able to watch Manning twenty-four hours a day. It wouldn't be impossible for Calavera to bring him a phone, laptop or both. Manning could set up a personal hotspot and then do whatever he wanted on a laptop.

Should we do a more thorough search of the house? I wondered, but decided that the time wasn't right. I had no hard evidence pointing to Calavera. From what I knew of the man, jealousy seemed like a pretty feeble motive. I left Manning's house feeling decidedly unsatisfied.

CHAPTER ELEVEN

I was working at my desk when Julio came into the office.

"You look like last week's leftovers," I told him as he dropped down in the chair at his desk.

"You don't want to know," he said without a trace of humor.

I rolled my chair over to his desk. "Tell Uncle Larry all about it."

"I'm screwed. Dani is still at her parents'. When I call her, her dad or mom answers the phone. Her cell phone!"

"Wow!" I said, not knowing what else to say.

Julio entered his computer's password. "Pete's out?"

"Yeah. I don't know what that's about. Have you noticed anything going on with him?"

Julio looked down at his desk for a minute. "No. Maybe been a little less… Pete."

"Yeah, that's what Cara said." I looked at the sad frustration in his eyes and added, "It goes without saying, if you need anything, let me know."

I got a grim-faced nod from him before I wheeled back to my desk.

Finished with a laundry list of chores that included Pete's list, phone calls about my other active cases and writing up notes in the Calavera case, I glanced at my watch. Lunchtime. I looked at the two lists on my desk—names of people I needed to interview about Eva Calavera and a to-do list I'd come up with in hopes of opening up new leads on the anonymous emails. My stomach growled. I needed food.

I could double task, I thought and picked up my phone.

Want to go to lunch? I texted Chief Darlene Marks.

Her: *Your treat?*

Me: *Tacos?*

Her: *Sure.*

"Do you remember the dark days before the taco truck?" I asked Darlene a little later as we stood in line behind a couple of guys from the electric co-op. The air was cold and brisk. Only the warm sunlight made the wait tolerable.

"You're depressing me just by bringing it up," she said while scrolling through her text messages. She sent a couple of people thumbs-up emojis before clipping the phone back on her belt. "Be the chief of police, they said. It will be fun, they said."

"You know you love it."

"Sometimes it's good to be chief… other times, not so much. Which reminds me, any word on your big promotion?"

"Nothing yet. Pete's out today. I figure they'll wait until we're all available and then let us know who's the winner and which of us are the losers. Though I'm not sure what I mean by loser. I have days when I can't imagine supervising other officers."

"You just need to tamp down all that compassion and understanding," Darlene said with a grin.

We stepped up to the counter and ordered. I got two Mediterranean tacos and barbecue fries.

As we took our places at one of the picnic tables, Darlene asked, "Is Pete out at the range today?" As the department's firearms instructor, Pete regularly spent time at our shooting range helping officers to get qualified.

"No, he took a mental health day," I said before taking a

bite of the best tacos east of the Mississippi.

Darlene looked at me over her shrimp taco. "A mental health day? *Pete?*"

"Exactly. I can remember him missing a day or two a couple of years ago when he had the flu, but other than that… The time he was suspended during the whole Ed Landon incident is the only other time I remember him not coming in when he was scheduled."

"Maybe the women in his life needed him," Darlene said.

Knowing Pete, that made sense. Still, the doctor's appointment nagged at me.

"Did you and Sanderson pull video camera footage for the night that Eva Calavera was killed?"

"I gave her the locations. She said she could handle it."

"We're still trying to find a link between the anonymous emails and the murder," I said as a lead-in to picking her brain. When she was my partner, I'd always felt like she was a little smarter than me.

"That brings up a point that's been sticking in my craw," Darlene said, and I thought she was taking my bait. She set her taco down and leaned across the picnic table. "Why haven't I gotten one of these emails? Does this asshole think I'm too good to have skeletons in my closet? I'm kind of offended." She gave me just a hint of a smile before going back to her lunch.

"Don't feel bad. I haven't gotten one either."

"Everybody knows you're a goody two-shoes." She dismissed me with a wave of her hand. "My corporal got one. It threatened to expose his affair." She paused. "Which is kind of interesting since the affair happened three years ago and, since then, he's dumped his wife and become engaged to the… other woman."

"And that's interesting?"

"It's like the information is old news," Darlene pointed out.

"We've been thinking that too. Still, a lot of the emails have been altogether wrong."

"The email he got was *very* precise. Even named the woman in question."

I considered this from several angles. "You have a point. Why would this person be using information that is several years old? Where are they getting it from?"

"Maybe they lived here in the past and moved away."

"That's possible. Which raises the question of why they're sending the emails, and does that eliminate them as a suspect in the Calavera murder?"

"People can hold grudges for a long time. Maybe they didn't feel safe sending the emails until after they'd moved. As to your second question, maybe yes, maybe no. A lot would depend on how far away they moved. If they only moved as far as Tallahassee, they might be out of the gossip loop but still able to commute to Adams County to kill Eva Calavera."

"There has to be a clue in the emails. I don't care whether they're connected or not. I just need to know one way or the other so I can move the murder investigation forward."

"You could call in some experts."

"I will, even though I don't have much faith in syntax analysis to find a suspect. Maybe it can help to exclude or confirm suspects, but what am I going to do—take writing samples from everyone in the country?" I threw up my hands dramatically. "We don't even know that they *are* in the country."

"They're certainly fluent in English. Believe me, I've read enough emails from Nigeria, India and China from people trying to get into my bank accounts to know how bad some foreigners' English sentence structure can be."

"That's one point for us. It wouldn't hurt my feelings if you'd take some time to look over all the emails we've gotten and give me any thoughts you have."

"Cool, gossip. I like it." Darlene gathered up her trash and put it on the tray. I did the same with mine and stood up.

"Back to work," she said. Her phone had buzzed constantly during lunch, but dispatch had left her alone. She keyed her mic and told the 911 operator that she was done with lunch.

The sheriff's office and the Calhoun Police Department used the same dispatch system, and the operators would send whoever was available to calls within the city limits. Unlike a lot of chiefs, Darlene had told them that, if she was out in her car, she was willing to respond to calls. Another point that had earned her the respect of her officers.

I headed back to the office and had just pulled into the parking lot when Sergeant Dill Kirby at the front desk called me.

"I've got a woman with one of those emails."

"I'm right out front. I'll be there in a minute," I told him.

I saw her pacing back and forth through the glass door as I walked up to the entrance.

"That's him." Dill pointed at me as soon as I opened the door.

The woman was in her forties, with poorly cut brown hair that she kept pushing behind her ears. She wore stretchy blue pants and a red sweater that, even to my colorblind male eyes, didn't go together. In her hand, which shook slightly, she held a sheet of paper.

"Are you the detective that's hunting this bastard?" she blurted before I'd had a chance to introduce myself.

"I'm Larry Macklin. Yes, I'm one of the investigators looking into a series of anonymous emails. Let's go to our conference room where we can sit down."

"I want to make a report. This guy needs to be caught. There's an email address on it, but my neighbor said it's bogus…" She kept talking as she followed me through the inner door and back to the smaller of our two conference rooms.

"Have a seat." I pulled out a chair for her and moved to the other side of the table. "First, may I have your name?"

"Oh yeah, I'm Rhonda Padilla."

"If I could see the email you received." I held out my hand.

She looked uncertain. "I don't want… I… I guess I have to let you see it." She handed the piece of paper over to me.

There was the usual email stuff at the top, along with the sender's fake email address. The subject line was: *Die*. The body of the email read: *You killed your mother and father. Your type disgust me!! Do the right thing and kill yourself.*

I read it twice.

"Are your parents dead?" I asked, putting the email down on the table between us.

"Yes," she said in a small voice as she looked down at the table.

"May I ask what happened to them?"

"They were killed in a car crash."

"I'm sorry. When did this happen?"

"I was fourteen." Her voice trembled. "The emailer is right. It was my fault."

"How exactly was it your fault?" I'd done the math as well as I could without knowing the woman's exact age. The best I could tell, the accident would have happened sometime in the 1990s.

"I'd gone over to a friend's house. A bunch of us girls were having a pajama party. I… I got in… to…" She was having a hard time getting the words out and she was almost hyperventilating. "The girls wanted to watch *The Sandlot*. I'd seen it like a dozen times. So… so… I got mad and wanted to go home. I threw a real fit. I guess I was… a spoiled brat."

Somehow she'd gotten ahold of her breath, but her voice was now small and childlike. "I called Mom and Dad. I didn't know what they were doing. I just wanted to go home."

She paused so long that I didn't know if she was done or if her sniffling was going to turn into crying. Instead she cleared her throat and continued. "I guess they'd been doing some drinking with me out of the house. The autopsy said

Dad's blood alcohol level was .14. They didn't test Mom 'cause she wasn't driving."

The woman put her forehead down on the table for a moment before taking a deep breath and sitting back up.

"I know this is hard for you," I said kindly.

"Everybody blamed me. My brother… he was older than me. He still doesn't talk to me unless he has to."

"I'm sorry. I've investigated a few accidents and… I'm sorry, but if your dad was drinking, then getting behind the wheel was his poor decision. Like you said, you didn't know he'd been drinking. You couldn't know what the consequences of your phone call were going to be. Have you talked to someone about this?"

"I'm not as messed up as you're thinking. I mean, I've talked to a whole bunch of counselors since the accident. Most of the time I hold it together pretty well." She tapped the email on the table. "This just caught me by surprise." She shook her head. "Not that I didn't know about the emails going around. I did. That's why I came straight here when I got this. I knew y'all are looking into the creepo who sent it."

"Where did you learn about the emails?"

"Eddie at the library. He put up a sign on the door that said anyone who got one of these…" She tapped at the email again. "…they should bring it to the sheriff's office."

"I appreciate you bringing this to our attention. We've had a lot of reports and we're working hard to track down the… person who did this."

"Why does he hate me?"

Her question made me want to grab the asshole responsible for these emails by the neck and throttle him or her.

"I don't think they're targeting you. They're just trying to upset as many people as possible." Even as I said it, I noticed something different about the email she'd received. Most of the emails had been bland statements of fact. Only a couple had made threats. This email was one of the most direct in expressing the author's contempt for the recipient.

"Do you know of anyone who might hate you enough to send you this email?"

"My brother? Maybe. I haven't talked to him in years. I just don't know. No one else." Her eyes looked like those of a child lost in the wilderness.

"Where do you work?"

"I'm a graphic artist. I work from home. People commission me to design webpages, logos, that sort of thing. People like my work." Rhonda sounded surprised at the idea that anyone could dislike her enough to send a poison-pen email. And working from home eliminated an office environment as a source of possible enemies.

"Any other significant issues?" I asked as delicately as I could.

Rhonda shook her head without further comment.

"Where were you all living when the accident occurred?"

"Thomasville. I grew up in South Georgia. At least until the accident when I moved in with my aunt. She treated me like a daughter."

"Who around here would know you felt guilty about the accident?"

"I don't know. Lots of people, I guess. I kind of talk about it when I'm sad. That's what my therapists always tell me to do. Talk about it."

"You've been a big help bringing me this email," I told her, seeing no point in prolonging the interview. "Hopefully we'll be able to shine a light on this jerk."

I escorted her to the front desk and gave her one of my cards.

"We'll let you know as soon as we have someone in custody," I assured her.

"Sure," she said, looking at my card. Then she turned away and walked off to her car.

Nothing made me feel more useless than sending a wounded soul back out into the world without being able to answer their questions. With a sigh, I turned and headed for Lionel's office.

CHAPTER TWELVE

"Hey, Sandy," I said when I found Deputy Matti Sanderson. She was sitting at a desk that Lionel had set up for anyone in the office who was drafted into reviewing video footage. He had a couple of programs on a desktop that could zoom in, improve contrast, bookmark and enhance images and sections of footage.

"I'm already bored," she grumbled. "I don't mind when I know what I'm looking for, but without a car or a description of the individual…" She tossed up her hands.

"You're looking for Eva Calavera's car."

"I *know* that part," she said with a look that shut me up. "That's where I've started, looking at footage from cameras that might have captured her car heading to the crack den where it was abandoned. But what about after that? I figure the perp wouldn't have hung around for very long after ditching her car, so I'm also looking for anyone leaving the area within half an hour of her car going in."

"Good plan."

"Trouble is: I haven't even been able to catch a glimpse of *her* car. That area is a few blocks from any of the business cameras." She put up a finger to stop me. "Don't even go there. I've already done my door-knocking without finding anyone who would admit to having a camera facing the street. You can't expect drug dealers to have doorbell cams."

"You sound like you have all the bases covered," I said, thinking it was time to consider retreat.

"Where's that intern, Jessie? She was great at reviewing footage."

"She's at the academy."

"Why are we ruining a great unpaid intern? All we're going to get is another patrol deputy who grouses about every little job." She pointed a finger at herself in recognition of the irony of her complaint.

"How many hours of footage do you have?"

"Since we don't know exactly when the body was dumped, I got a bunch. A whole bunch. Hours and hours. This isn't going to be done in a day, or probably even a week. If you see anyone who wants to help, I'd appreciate it. Did I mention this was my day off?"

"You're a trooper," I told her. "I'll take some of it home with me. Just label a box and tell me what I'm looking at."

"You're a peach," she muttered.

"Where's Lionel?"

Sanderson shrugged. "Wasn't here when I got here."

"I'll be back in a few hours. If he comes in, find out if he's gotten anywhere with the car's or her phone's GPS."

She nodded. "I'm hoping to be able to pair that data up with this video footage."

As I walked back to my desk, I had to restrain myself from texting Pete. What good is a mental health day if someone from work chases you down? *He'll tell you what's going on when he wants to*, I told myself.

Ralph Calavera called as soon as I sat down.

"You've been asking my client questions," he said as soon as I answered my phone.

"Good afternoon to you too. I can ask your client questions. What I can't do is make him answer."

"Cut the crap. You know as well as I do that he's not... stable. I'll make sure that anything he says won't be able to be used in court, and any evidence you get as a result of the answers he gives you will be tainted."

"Keep your shorts on. He didn't tell me anything. Now don't you want to know how the investigation into your wife's murder is going?"

"Of course I do."

"It's an ongoing investigation. That's about all I can give you. Have you spoken to her sister?"

"She's coming in from North Carolina tomorrow. I wouldn't be surprised if she wants to meet with you."

"I'll look forward to talking to her. Unless you object," I said in my most sarcastic tone.

"I've spoken to the State Attorney about you."

"My ears are burning."

"You better get your feet set on the right path soon, or I'll have you removed from the investigation."

"That sounds more like a treat than a trick."

"Your distaste for me doesn't do you credit. You know it's ignorant for police to hate on defense attorneys. If you want to blame anyone for criminals getting back out on the streets, you should look in the mirror. Every case I've won is because some cop stepped on their own dick."

"Yeah, don't forget to place some of the blame on crappy judges. If you're done, I'm going to get back to work."

Calavera seemed to think about this for a moment before giving me an abrupt goodbye and ending the call.

I looked at the phone, thinking about the conversation. It seemed oddly out of character for the slick defense lawyer. In court, I'd never known him to do something that didn't advance his cause, but I couldn't understand for the life of me how calling me up had done anything for him. Was he just taking the temperature of the investigation? Maybe. And if so, why? Was it because he was interested in seeing the criminal who'd killed his wife brought to justice, or was it because he was the killer and the call was equivalent to someone being chased looking over his shoulder? Maybe.

I spent the rest of the afternoon working on my other

cases. At five, with my eyes blurry from screen fatigue and my arm sore from holding the phone to my ear, I shut down my computer and cleaned some of the junk off of my desk in preparation for going home. Cara had texted earlier to let me know that she was going to be late because she had a bunch of supplies to deliver to Dr. Horvath. On a whim, I decided to stop at the Supersave to pick up a sandwich and chips for dinner.

The Supersave was an institution in Calhoun. When I was in high school, half the senior class had worked there at one time or another, and every family in the county got their Saturday afternoon grilling meat of choice from the Supersave butcher. Nowadays there was a Walmart just over the county line where many people shopped, and there were rumors from time to time that they were going to build a Publix in town. Still, the Supersave had its loyal followers, of which I counted myself a member. It had the musty smell of a dowager, but there were no self-checkout lanes, the clerks were people I knew by name and there was always the murmur of gossip just out of hearing.

I hate to admit that my situational awareness was down as I walked through the automatic glass door. My mind was on the Calavera case, so as I grabbed a shopping basket I was startled to hear a man shout at the top of his lungs.

"Get out of here, you son of a bitch!" screamed Archie Something-or-other. He was one of the managers at the Supersave, a smiley, round-bellied young man who was always asking everyone if he could help them. Now he appeared to have come completely unhinged. He stood behind a counter near the store office, pointing his finger at a raggedy old man who looked stunned.

Archie literally rolled across the counter, sending a credit card machine clattering to the floor. As I started toward them, Archie grabbed a metal display rack and swung it back and forth, chewing gum flying in all directions as he advanced on the older man, who was holding up his hands and backing away.

"You ruined my father's life, you bastard!"

"I don't know who you are!" The old man was bald and looked like his life had been one of hard work and rough living. The look on his face was an equal mix of confusion and dread.

"Archie!" I shouted, trying to draw his attention.

I was only partially successful. He made a feint at me with the display rack before going full berserker at the old man. He got in a couple of good swings, but fortunately the old man was nimble enough to dodge the first one and lucky enough to fall out of the way of the second pass.

I was behind him as Archie set up for another swing. I moved forward and did a leg sweep that he didn't see coming. The bigger they are, the harder they fall, and Archie was no exception, slamming to the tile floor. He was stunned, so I took the opportunity to throw myself on top of him and get his hands cuffed behind him before he could recover his senses. By measure of my extensive handcuffing experience, this one was pretty easy. No drugs were involved, and all of Archie's aggression was focused away from me. Even as I was pulling his arms back, he was sputtering obscenities at the old man and trying to crawl over to him.

"Settle down," I growled in Archie's ear. I put a little backward pressure on his arms to get his attention.

"Owww!" he yelped.

"You can end this here and we'll go out to my car and talk about it, or you can continue yelling and fighting until I have backup that will haul your ass down to the jail," I said in a harsh whisper. I was hungry and ready to go home. This had not been on my evening's agenda.

"Arrest *him*! Arrest him and I don't care what you do to me!" Archie spat into the tile floor.

I looked over at the old man, who was being tended to by a couple of customers and employees. He looked less confused and more horrified.

"Why do you want me to arrest him?" I asked.

"He attacked my father. Blinded him in one eye. Made him have seizures. He did." Archie's frustration had him close to tears.

"Did your father report the attack?" I looked at the old man, who couldn't have weighed more than a hundred and twenty pounds soaking wet, and found it hard to believe he could do that much damage to anyone.

"Yes, yes." Archie was crying now.

"Okay." I pulled out my phone and called for backup. I couldn't take both of them in my car. Leaving Archie on the floor, I walked over to the old man.

"Are you okay?" I asked him.

"Yeah, maybe. My hip hurts." He was being helped to his feet by one of the employees, but he seemed unsteady. Everyone else in the store was beginning to return to their normal business.

"You'll need to stay here until we can get this all sorted out," I said, and the old man nodded.

"Mr. Bauman?" A middle-aged woman in a Supersave apron was looking down at Archie. "Should I call Miss Trent to come in?"

"Yes," Archie said from his position on the floor, with his face still flush against the tiles.

Five minutes later, I had talked to the old man long enough to find out that his name was Rob Hartman and that he was fifty-eight years old. I had also gotten Archie up off the floor and put him into a chair. He was explaining his seeming over-reaction when Darlene walked through the door in full uniform and headed straight for me.

"Macklin, what are you doing? People are trying to shop and get home for dinner," she said when she was close enough not to be overheard by the half dozen spectators still hanging around.

"Thanks for your concern," I said.

"I heard you needed backup, and I needed a quart of milk, so I thought I'd come help," she told me cheerily.

"Thanks. All our guys are dealing with accidents and

afterwork crime reports, so I guess I should be grateful for any help I can get."

"Thanks, cowboy. I know that was from the heart." She looked at Archie. "Seriously, what's going on here?"

"I was just getting to that. Mr. Bauman was explaining that Mr. Hartman over there attacked his father. Which might or might not be true." I gave Archie Bauman a hard look. "The attack took place thirty years ago. I haven't seen the report, but according to Archie it occurred on Tennessee Street in Tallahassee outside the Beer Barn."

"Thirty years ago?" Darlene raised her eyebrows.

"1990," Archie said.

"Almost thirty years ago," I corrected myself. "The rub is that the man who attacked Bauman's father was never identified."

"I did it," the older man mumbled. I turned to see him staring down at the floor. The store employees had found a wheelchair for him to sit in until his hip could be looked at. An ambulance was en route, but like our patrolmen, it would take them awhile to get there.

"Mr. Hartman, I need to inform you of your rights." I turned to Darlene. "If you'll watch Mr. Bauman, I'll take Mr. Hartman somewhere so we can talk."

"My pleasure," Darlene said. "I'm dying to hear the whole story." Then her face lit up. "The anonymous emails!"

"Exactly. I've already read Mr. Bauman his Miranda rights, so feel free to question him. He'll tell you the whole sordid story." Ever since I'd gotten the handcuffs on him, Archie had turned into a sad heap of self-pity. Just before Darlene walked in, he'd told me about the email he'd received and the answer that it had contained. An answer that he'd been looking for ever since his father had been beaten.

Rob Hartman was slumped in the wheelchair looking like the very image of the Ancient Mariner.

"I'm going to push you over there so we can talk in private," I said, pointing to a corner near the store's office.

He nodded.

"Do you want to tell me your side of the story?" I asked him once we were settled. In truth, it didn't matter whether he'd beaten Archie's father or not. The only way that the statute of limitations wouldn't have passed would be if the State Attorney could charge him with attempted murder, which seemed very unlikely in this case.

"I was drunk. He was drunk. We'd been playing pool when we got in an argument over football. Drunk, stupid drunk. He shoved me. I swear to God he laid hands on me first." Hartman looked up at me. "Now, I was kind of crazy back then. I told him if he wanted to fight, then let's go to the vacant lot a street over and do it right. I knew I'd beat the snot out of him. I was small even back then, but it didn't matter 'cause I was scrappy. Learned to fight down at the docks in Mobile. Long story short, I was getting in a bunch of good hits and he was stumbling. I gave him one to the kidney and figured I'd made my point. I turned to walk off and he threw a rock at me. Hit me in the shoulder."

Hartman grew quiet and looked over to where Archie Bauman and Darlene were talking.

"What'd you do then?" I prompted.

He looked me in the eye and, for the first time, I saw the thirty-year-old guy who'd been tough enough to pick a fight and duke it out in a vacant lot.

"Didn't matter that I was drunk. I'd have done the same thing if I'd been sober. The guy pitched a rock at me when my back was turned. There are rules. Pissed me off bad. I went back and dropped the hammer on him. You can bet my hands were sore for a week after the pounding I put on him. I wasn't gonna kill him. Stopped short of that. Had a lot of friends back then that wouldn't have. I left him breathing. All the next week, I waited and waited for the cops to come knocking on my door.

"At the time I thought the guy had been smart enough to keep his mouth shut, but I learned later that he'd been beat so bad he didn't remember what had happened. Of course, he'd been drunk too, so that might have had something to do with him not remembering nothin'. Five years ago when I'd been sober for two years, I saw him. He'd lost his eye and his jaw didn't look quite right; still, I knew it was him. I'd heard about the eye way back. Kind of felt bad when I found out, but hell, I wasn't sober so… things kind of don't sink in. That's the point of staying drunk."

"I guess you thought of trying to make amends when you got sober?" I knew it was a stupid thing to say the minute the words were out of my mouth. How could you make it up to a guy when he'd lost an eye?

Hartman nodded. "I did. I really did think about going to him and apologizing. Part of the twelve step program. Step eight, being willing to make amends. But I used the escape clause in step nine and convinced myself that it would do more harm than good for me to approach the family. Then two years ago he died."

"Who else knew about the fight?"

"Lots of folks. I've told the story in AA meetings a hundred times. It wasn't my low point, but it was the worst physical damage I ever caused. I believe I died a little inside that night. I'd been in fights, got the snot beat out of me dozens of times. Never in all those fights did I ever come close to killing anyone. I was one punch away that night. If I'd hit him one more time, he would have been dead. The sick part, the thing that haunted me, was how much I'd wanted to hit him one more time." His voice trailed off.

I sighed. Leaving Hartman slumped in the wheelchair, I went back to where Darlene and Archie were talking. Archie, shoulders sagging, looked pathetic in handcuffs.

"I'm going to have to arrest you for assault," I told him. "Unless you want to do it?" I asked Darlene.

She shook her head. "You were the first officer on scene."

"I knew you were going to say that."

"What about him?" Archie nodded toward Hartman.

"We'll look into possible charges," I said.

"He ruined my father."

"Mr. Bauman, think about it. With the statute of limitations having expired for every other crime he could be charged with except attempted murder, what do you think the odds are of getting a conviction? Even at the time, there were no witnesses. He's confessed, but not to attempted murder. When he told me what happened, he was quite clear that he knew where the boundary was between a beating and a murder, which he said he purposefully stopped short of."

"So you're just going to sweep this under the rug?" Archie was looking less pathetic and more defiant.

"What I'm telling you is that the State Attorney is unlikely to do anything with it."

"That's insane!" He was getting agitated again. "I've wanted to find the man who did that to my father for decades. Now here he is and you're telling me that no one cares?"

"Everyone cares. But the extenuating circumstances make it unlikely that the courts are going to punish him." For a moment I hesitated to give my opinion, then decided to just speak from the heart, even knowing that it could get me into trouble. "Look at him. He's sober now. Used the story about what he did as a reason to become a better person. Shared the story at AA meetings as encouragement to others to get sober and stay sober. I believe he's truly sorry for what he did to your father."

"And my family! I swear I'll kill him!" Archie was shifting his weight from leg to leg as though preparing to run over to Hartman and attack him.

"Stop!" Darlene barked, causing both of us to turn and look at her. "You talk like that and you'll be the one who's locked away in prison. We won't let you take the law into your own hands. I'll admit that this is a pile of crap. Who knows what would have happened if he could have been found and arrested when your father was attacked? I can tell you that it wouldn't have repaired your father's eye or taken away his scars. Would your dad have wanted to see you arrested?" She leaned in and stared hard into Archie's eyes, pushing him to answer.

"No," he said in a small voice.

"Just like your father's attack, what happened tonight is history. No matter how bitter, you'll have to take your medicine. Give us your pledge that you'll leave Mr. Hartman alone and Deputy Macklin and I will write up our reports so that they put you in the best possible light."

Archie nodded. "Yeah, okay. I don't like it but... I see your point."

Darlene's chastisement had reduced Archie to a petulant but obedient child. Unfortunately, I doubted that the effect was permanent.

After getting Hartman's information and making sure that the EMTs gave him a thumbs-up, I took Archie to the jail and booked him. I charged him with simple assault, which was only a second degree misdemeanor, so he wouldn't have too hard of a time with bail. I warned him that I'd make sure the fires of hell came down on him if he interfered in Mr. Hartman's life. In return, I promised to look into the records of his father's case with the Tallahassee police.

All the way home I thought about getting my hands on the person writing those emails. My mind ruminated on the case of the Circleville letter writer. They hadn't even been sure if the letters were all written by the same person. Could we end up with multiple emailers? I still wasn't sure how easy it would be for an average Joe to send emails from a fake email address. I decided to talk to Lionel the next day and have him walk me through the process.

CHAPTER THIRTEEN

I rolled up at the house around nine o'clock. The temperature was plummeting now that the sun had gone down.

"Do we need to wrap the well?" Cara asked as I came through the front door.

"First I need something to eat. I never did get what I went to the store for," I grumbled before giving her a kiss.

"Sorry. I think we've got some canned chili, though it's probably not anything to write home about."

"At this point I'll take anything."

"Go get a hot shower and I'll heat something up."

After a shower, some food and a few minutes spent covering the pipes to the well so that they wouldn't freeze, I was feeling more human and could finally relax.

"You need to get a good night's sleep," Cara told me as we leaned against each other on the couch, listening to classic folk music. Alvin and the cats had already turned into faceless bundles of fur, curled up in their various favorite spots in the room.

"Sleep sounds good. What I really need is just to be able to turn off my brain. These emails are driving me crazy, and

I need to be concentrating on Calavera's murder, which may not even be connected to the emails. On top of that, I can't help but feel that something is up with Pete."

"You've got to let that one go. He'll be at work tomorrow and you can ask him then. What about the promotion?"

"What about it?"

"Aren't you a little curious about that?"

"It'd be different if I knew I wanted it."

"I think you do," Cara said softly.

"Why do you say that?"

"I know you. You wouldn't have gone through the interview process if there wasn't a part of you that wanted it. Like becoming a deputy. You weren't sure about that for a few years, but it turned out to really suit you."

"True."

"I think deep down there's some gut feeling that knows what you want. Even when you aren't sure, you're already moving forward."

"You been reading psychology books lately?" I joked, nudging her. Then I wrapped my arms around her. "What I want doesn't matter. It's in the hands of the committee now. My guess is that Eccles will walk away with it." I thought about Pete. "Maybe that's what Pete's mental health day was all about. He might have a backup plan somewhere else if he doesn't get the promotion."

"He wouldn't leave Adams County." Cara dismissed the idea.

"He has mouths to feed and college tuition to pay. He might have gone to a job interview today."

"Where would he go?"

"Another agency. State or federal. Maybe even private security. They can pay big bucks for the right man."

"You'll find out tomorrow. Don't let him weasel out of telling you what he's been up to. But for now you need to push all that to one side." She leaned in and kissed me.

Before long we found ourselves wrapped around each

other in bed. Afterward, I settled down and pulled the thick quilt up to my neck. We had the thermostat turned low so the heat wouldn't run any harder than necessary. Florida homes are not made for cold temperatures. I drifted off contentedly, thinking how nice it was to have a friend, a wife and a bed warmer all rolled up into one.

Much too soon, I heard my phone go off and opened my eyes to find that it was still dark. Flailing my arm around, I managed to knock the phone off of the nightstand. Groggy and irritated, I had to hang off the bed to retrieve it.

"What?" I answered gruffly.

"I've got a car accident that's turned into a gunfight," reported Deputy Roland Ericson.

"I'm not on call," I grumbled. I felt Cara roll over to listen to the conversation.

"I called Ortiz. He's… sick." Ericson was a good deputy. He'd been in the Army for eight years before getting married and joining the sheriff's office. I knew that he wouldn't have called if he didn't really need me.

"Okay."

I got dressed and moaned when I realized that it was three o'clock. The worst. By the time I got done dealing with whatever stupidity had gone down, it would be too late to come back home and get any more sleep.

I found the location Ericson had given me, a rural crossroad now flashing with red and blue lights. A truck was in the ditch and an old SUV sat half on and half off the road. There were a number of spectators and hangers-on standing around and watching.

"It's freezing," I complained as I walked up to Deputy Ericson.

"Yes, sir." He used ma'am and sir to a disconcerting amount. "We have one man in the ambulance and the other is in the back of my patrol car. There's one witness who was in the truck with the man who got shot. She's over there." He pointed to the ambulance, where a woman was talking on her cell phone.

"We'll get to all that in a minute. You said Julio is sick?" I was still trying to figure out why I was standing there with my hands and feet going numb in the middle of the night.

He pursed his lips and shook his head. "I believe he was drunk."

"Really?" Anger started to burn in my stomach. "Forget it," I said, then I saw Ericson's look of suspicion and held up my hand. "I don't mean that you should cover it up. I just mean for now, let me deal with it."

Ericson's father was a preacher at one of the largest African Baptist churches in town. I'd gone there with Dad a couple of times when he spoke to the congregation. Ericson's father could hurl fire and brimstone with the best of them, and I'd gotten the idea that the acorn hadn't fallen far from the tree.

I was thrilled to learn that the accident and shooting were over a normal bit of jealousy caused by wandering eyes at a party. No mysterious emails were involved.

I spent the next couple of hours conducting interviews, making notes and taking measurements, all done while my hands and cheeks were numb from the cold. At least once every fifteen minutes, I muttered a curse in Julio's direction.

The sun was coming up and the ground was white with frost as I came out of the jail after booking the shooter. Cold and tired, my choice was to go home and get a hot shower and clean clothes, knowing that I'd have to walk by my bed half a dozen times without being able to lie down for even a short nap... or I could go straight to the office and get in an hour or two of work before anyone came in. With a deep sigh I headed across the street to the office, hoping that someone who knew how to make decent coffee had left a pot on in the breakroom.

I hit the jackpot. A kind soul had left half a box of Krispy Kreme donuts on the counter next to the coffee pot. I grabbed two and a cup of coffee that might not have been good, but was certainly hot, and headed to my desk.

Then I remembered that I had some unfinished business.

Just thinking about it made me feel warmer, but not in a good way. I left the donuts and coffee on my desk and ducked into a conference room where there wasn't a chance of being overheard. Then I hit Julio's name on my phone.

The phone rang and rang. When it went to voicemail, I disconnected and called again. I did this four times, getting more pissed off each time, until he answered.

"Wha'?"

"You had better throw a glass of water in your face and sober the fuck up," I growled.

"Larry?"

"Yes, it's the man who had to get up out of his warm bed to do your job this morning. The man who'd like to throw your ass under the bus."

"Hey, man, Larry, listen… I…"

"I don't want to listen to your drunken babble. You need to get your ass in gear and get in to work this morning with a convincing story for Major Parks and last night's watch commander. You're also indebted to Deputy Ericson, who could have called the watch commander instead of me when you answered his call drunk and unable to do your job."

"I'm hearing you." Julio was still half slurring his words. "Hey, good news! My wife came home. Oh, wait, bad news. She made me move out. I'm at the Roads Best Motel."

I sighed. "Okay, forget coming in. Call in sick. Make it damn convincing. We'll talk about this tomorrow," I said and disconnected the call.

As I headed for my desk, I noticed that I was still clenching my fist. I took a couple of deep breaths and tried to relax my muscles and clear my mind.

With my reports on both the supermarket fiasco and the run-them-down-and-shoot-them party from that morning mostly done, I looked up to see Pete striding into the office. He gave me a big smile, which I returned with squinted eyes.

"The grapevine tells me that you had to cover for Julio last night," he said, sounding sympathetic.

"Oh, yeah."

"Is he okay?"

I took a deep breath. Now wasn't the time to go into it. "He's not doing well. I'm pretty sure he's taking the day off."

"Probably best."

"Speaking of taking the day off, what were you doing yesterday?"

Pete shook his head. "You'll hear all about it shortly. I just needed to think a few things through."

"Shortly as in ten minutes, or as in days? 'Cause I'm not in the mood for suspense."

"Like nine o'clock. We have a meeting with your dad." As if from his mouth to Dad's ears, I got a text message from Dad's assistant, Carol, telling me that I had a meeting with him at nine.

"No donuts?" I noticed that Pete wasn't carrying his usual bag of breakfast goodies.

I swear I saw his left eye twitch. "No. I'm going to be cutting back on the donuts." There was not an ounce of his usual good humor in the statement. I could see something hard and a little distant in his eyes.

"Does the nine o'clock meeting have to do with the promotion?"

"That's part of it. I'd rather let your dad go over it. Honestly, I don't know everything."

"Sounds like *you* got the promotion."

"Just wait," he assured me.

"Nine then," I said, letting it go. When Pete made up his mind, it wasn't worth the effort to try and change it.

At eight-fifty, I got up and met Pete in the reception area of Dad's office. Phil Eccles, wearing his uniform and looking like everyone's image of the ideal deputy, came down the hall toward us.

"Gentlemen, I guess this is about the promotion?"

I shrugged and Pete kind of nodded.

"May the best man win," Phil said with a smile.

I thought about what it would mean working under Phil. He was all cop all the time, which had its upsides and its downsides. With Dad being a deputy, I had grown up with an understanding of the culture, and some of them lived and breathed law enforcement. They couldn't imagine another life. Phil fell into that category.

"Y'all can go in," Carol told us. "Major Parks is already here."

We filed in like schoolchildren visiting the principal's office. I looked around to see if Mauser the monster dog was around, which was completely unnecessary. If he'd been there, he would have been greeting everyone as they came in. Apparently Dad had left him at home to be waited on by Jamie, Dad's critter sitter.

Major Sam Parks was seated next to Dad's desk, facing the three chairs set up for us. Behind his desk, Dad was typing something into his phone and only looked up after we'd all been seated.

"Big day," he said with a wicked smile as he looked at each of us in turn. "I want to start off by thanking you all for stepping up. Being willing to take on a leadership role in law enforcement is commendable. Now I'm going to turn it over to Major Parks so he can tell you what the promotions committee is recommending."

Parks was past retirement age and had only stayed on as a favor to Dad. His experience and skill with matters of budget and management were the cornerstones of the department. Many of the deputies made fun of his pedantic nature while admitting that the man was almost always right.

"I'm sorry that the other two members of the committee couldn't be here today. I'm sure you understand that they have other commitments. Like the sheriff said, we appreciate your willingness to put yourselves through the selection process. Thanks to some grant money and the sheriff's determination to fully staff all of our departments for the first time since before the hurricane, we have been able to make recommendations that will meet each of your career goals, as well as our plans for the future of the Adams County Sheriff's Office."

I wondered where this was going and stole a brief glance at Phil and Pete. They looked like they knew what was coming. What did *that* mean?

"Yesterday Deputy Henley…" Parks nodded toward Pete. "…came to us with a request. As you all know, Sergeant Martin oversees the tactical squad. In August he is going to be moving to Arizona where his wife has gotten her dream job."

I was trying to figure out what this all had to do with us, and was beginning to blame my inability to track the conversation on sleep deprivation.

"Pete is a member of the tactical squad and would like to take Martin's place."

I glanced at Pete again. Now I knew that my lack of sleep was causing me to hallucinate. Pete was a great deputy and would make a terrific sergeant, but our SWAT team was required to meet higher standards of physical fitness than the average deputy. The only reason Pete was allowed on the team was because he was the undisputed best shot in the department. If someone was going to be on a rooftop with a rifle, we all knew it should be Pete.

"Deputy Henley admitted to us that he would need to work on his physical fitness in order to take over from Martin," Parks continued. "He also explained to us that this lines up with some personal health goals. The committee is recommending—if Pete can meet the SWAT team's fitness standards—he be elevated to the rank of sergeant upon the departure of Sergeant Martin."

Now I simply stared at Pete, who looked back and gave me a smile and shrug. At least this helped to explain his lack of donuts that morning.

"Now, on to CID. As you all know, CID is down not just a sergeant, but also a lieutenant. When Lieutenant Johnson left, I took over his duties. I did that because of the budget crisis we were in as we waited for the federal government to fulfill its obligations to reimburse us for monies that were spent during and after Hurricane Marcy. We have those funds now, as well as a budget plan that allows us to move forward with filling all of the current vacant positions."

This was what drove deputies crazy about Major Parks. Anytime he was given the opportunity, he would slip into professor mode. When that happened, you may as well settle in for an hour-long lecture.

"All of this is to say that we are recommending that Deputy Eccles be promoted to lieutenant."

I almost fell off my chair. I looked around the room and appeared to be the only person surprised by this development.

Dad held out his hand to stop Parks and said, "I understand that there is going to be some consternation over this decision. I would like to point out, and expect you all to remind everyone else, that Phil has been an acting sergeant on several occasions. I've thought long and hard about this. None of our current sergeants have experience in CID, but Phil does. He was in CID for three years before returning to patrol. The only sergeant who I would feel comfortable promoting to lieutenant and placing over CID would be Sergeant Toomey. The problem there is that he has a very special skillset when it comes to investigating auto accidents. I'm not going to move someone who is a perfect match for their job when I don't have anyone to take their place. That being said, if I don't promote Phil to the position, then I'd be looking outside the department. I don't think anyone would be happy about that." Having explained his rationale, Dad motioned for Parks to continue.

"That leaves us with the sergeant's position, which was our original undertaking." Parks gave me a small smile, like one you'd give to the kid who comes in last but has put in a good effort. "We ended up with one candidate for one position. Fortunately, we all agreed that you are qualified."

I was stunned at the amount of change that was being proposed. Pete gone—at least I had several months to prepare for that. A new lieutenant—Phil was a good guy, qualified and a known quantity, so that should be okay. But now I was going to have to step up and take on more responsibility, including responsibility for other people. With Pete and Phil in line for the job, I had never really imagined that I'd end up with it. It may have been by default, but that didn't change the end result. Now I was going to have to figure out if I could do the job.

"I've approved the committee's recommendations and will announce it immediately. We'll have the pinning ceremony next week. Congratulations!" Dad stood up.

Everyone else followed suit, with me lagging behind. In a daze, I shook hands with Dad and Major Parks, wondering what I'd gotten myself into.

CHAPTER FOURTEEN

"What just happened?" I asked Phil and Pete as we walked down the hall toward the breakroom.

"You just got a promotion." Pete clapped me on the back.

"I can't believe you're going to get in shape so you can be a sergeant on the SWAT team," I said in all seriousness.

"No choice." Pete looked at Phil as though he wasn't sure if he wanted to share the next bit, but he must have decided it didn't matter. "My doctor's appointment didn't go so well. I was told in no uncertain terms that diabetes and heart disease are lurking in my future if I don't make some drastic lifestyle changes."

"Yikes," I replied.

"So I took yesterday off and Sarah and I talked about it. I needed a real goal, something I wanted to do that would get me off my ass and moving. Martin told us he was following his wife to Arizona, so bing, bang, boom. I get to be the SWAT team's squad leader, and spend more time as the firearms instructor for the sheriff's office." He shrugged.

I knew Pete loved being on the range and I could see the logic in his decision. I also knew that if the doctor told him he had to make changes, then Sarah would see that it happened.

"This way I'm not just losing weight for my health. I get a job that I want."

"And there you are, jumping over sergeant to lieutenant," I said to Phil, who nodded.

"Sad thing is, it won't mean an extra dime in my pocket. As soon as Audrey finds out I'm getting a raise, she'll make me put it into an IRA or something." Phil's wife was a real estate agent and, from what I'd heard him say about her, she was rather frugal.

"Sergeant Macklin. Cara will be proud! And think—for the next four months you'll be my supervisor." Pete gave me another clap on the back that almost sent me to my knees.

As we entered the breakroom, I could smell the Tupperware container full of homemade chocolate chip cookies that someone had left open on the counter.

"I better get back to my desk," Pete said in a voice that sounded a little higher pitched than normal. I looked back and he was already retreating down the hall.

"It's going to be a long couple of months for the poor guy," I said.

"Pete's tough. I was his FTO. As laid back as he seemed, he met every challenge head-on."

Phil went over to the coffee pot and poured himself a cup as I grabbed a cookie. I was about to take the first bite when a sudden horrible thought entered my head. I was now Julio's supervisor. His issues had suddenly become *my* issues. I felt sick to my stomach. I ate the cookie, but all the joy was gone. The adrenaline dump I'd gotten from finding out that I was being promoted disappeared and now I just felt tired.

I wandered back to my desk where I immediately got a call from Sergeant Dill at the front desk.

"Woman here to see you. A Mrs. Nellie Logan."

I had to think for a second before I remembered that Eva Calavera's sister's name was Logan.

"I'll be there in a minute."

The woman pacing in the lobby was younger than Eva.

Her curly brown hair was cut short and her glasses gave her a studious appearance. I introduced myself and gave her my condolences.

"I feel like I'm lost in a nightmare." She wiped at her eyes. "Do you know who did this to Eva?"

"Not yet. We're still gathering information. Talking with family and friends is part of the investigation."

"Do you think someone she knew did this?"

"We won't focus on anyone until there is a significant amount of evidence pointing toward them." Which was my diplomatic way of saying we didn't have a clue who'd killed her sister. I was interested to note that she wasn't immediately blaming Ralph Calavera for her sister's death. The majority of cases I'd worked where a spouse had been killed had seen the families of the victims ready to hang their in-laws.

"Let's go back to the conference room where we can talk."

"I hope it's warm. I'd forgotten how cold Florida can be."

"I can get you some coffee. It's hot. Not good, just hot."

"Thanks, but caffeine is the last thing I need."

Once we were seated in the conference room, I looked across the table and asked her to tell me about her sister.

"That's not as easy as it might be with someone else. Ask me about my husband. He loves to fish. Is devoted to his family. Never happy unless he's working hard and bringing home money, which is just a form of security to him. Eva? She was… complex. Maybe the most complex person I ever knew. I never had any idea what she was going to do next. I can say that almost everything she did was motivated by love. A love of life, of others, of animals and children. That first one, love of life, was what got her into trouble. She wanted to have the most fun, the most excitement that she could find. That took money. Her love for animals and children took money too."

"Is that why she married Ralph Calavera?" I asked.

"Partly. Eva liked the fact that he was a lawyer. She found the courtroom stuff exciting. At least she did before she was living with it day in and day out."

"She got bored?"

"With Ralph? Absolutely. Bored is the perfect explanation for why their marriage had issues. She loved that Ralph worked hard and was dedicated to an important profession that brought home what she needed. Unfortunately, Ralph worked hard and was dedicated to his profession… which meant that he didn't have time to run around and have exciting adventures with Eva. What's a girl to do?"

"Did she love him?"

"Yes. She loved a lot of people."

"Men?"

"I didn't mean it like that. She just had a big heart."

"Were there other men?" Of course I already knew that there was at least one. But the question would tell me how much Nellie knew about Eva's life, or at least how much she was willing to say about her dead sister's secrets.

"I think so. She would tell me about guys that she'd met. From the way she talked about them, I got the impression that a few were… physical relationships."

"Did she ever tell you about fights that she had with Ralph?"

"A few years ago they went through a rough patch. Eva even talked about leaving him. Things never got physical. All the fights were verbal, more arguments than fights. Eva would never stay with anyone that abused her."

I had heard dozens of family members over the years tell me how their child or sibling would never stay in a physically abusive situation, only to learn that that was exactly what they were doing. I'd learned never to underestimate the power of a manipulative personality to control someone who had made the mistake of falling in love with them.

"What do you think about Ralph?"

"Honestly, I've *tried* to dislike him over the years. I guess that sounds funny. But he's a lot of things I don't like. A lawyer. Stubborn. Opinionated. Every time I'd decide that he was a jerk or didn't deserve Eva, he'd do something that made me think he wasn't a bad guy. Also, if I'm being truthful, the arguments between him and Eva were… understandable. Even Eva, as she was bitching about him, would admit that he was probably right. Ralph bent over backward to accommodate Eva. Their separate-bedrooms-shared-house arrangement was his idea and Eva was grateful. She felt like he loved her, but could also give her space to be herself."

"You think he was genuine in his offer to let her live her own life while still being married to him?"

"It wasn't as one-sided as it sounds. Like I said, Eva was a very loving person. She still made it a point to do things for Ralph."

"Like what?"

"Go to dinners or throw parties at the house. She managed the house and grounds. And I really believe that both of them were coming from a good place."

"And he provided the money."

"Yes. I'm sure that was part of the glue that kept them together, but not all of it."

I wasn't ready to let Calavera off the hook yet, even though he seemed to have a fan base.

"Have you ever heard the name Neil Manning?"

Nellie got an inquisitive look on her face. "The name is familiar. I just can't put my finger on why."

"Did Eva ever mention him?"

"Yes. Let me think." She gave me a puzzled frown, then finally opened her eyes wide and said, "A client of Ralph's. I remember now. Eva said that it creeped her out that Ralph was taking him on as a client."

"Creeped her out, why?"

"She said that he'd done something horrible to a young girl. Eva didn't usually talk about Ralph's clients, so something about this guy, or at least what he'd done, must have really squicked her out."

I was dangerously close to crossing a boundary. Or maybe finding out that Ralph had crossed a boundary. If he'd told his wife something that Neil had told him, then he'd be guilty of a serious ethics violation. I didn't want to find out something that could violate Neil's rights and give him a legal out. Still, if he was involved in any way with Eva's death, I wasn't going to back down.

"Can you think of anything specific that she said about Neil Manning?"

"No. Like I told you, I think she just mentioned how much he creeped her out." Nellie pursed her lips and added, "She did say that she'd tried to talk Ralph out of taking this guy on."

I decided to let the subject drop.

"Can you think of anyone who might want to harm Eva?"

Nellie sat there thinking for so long that I decided to prompt her. "Any old boyfriends? Anyone from jobs that she might have held over the years? Or just someone she mentioned who got mad at her?"

"I can't think of anyone that she had a real argument with. I mean, she had breakups and arguments with… businesses or what have you, but nothing serious. No one who kept coming back at her or anything. And she certainly never hurt anyone else. I'll look back through the emails and messages she sent me." Nellie got a pained expression on her face. "Wait. She did mention an email she received a week or so ago. She sent me a copy of it. It was sort of disturbing."

I was on full alert now. Had Eva also received an email about her affair with Julio?

"May I see it?"

"Sure."

Nellie pulled up her email on her phone, scrolled through several messages, then handed the phone to me. The email read: *You have blood on your hands. How can you live with yourself?*

What the hell?, I thought. This definitely didn't seem like it was about the affair. I turned back to Nellie.

"It might be helpful to the investigation if I could get a copy of that email, as well as any text messages she sent you."

"I suppose that would be okay. There's a lot of them. I can't give you my phone."

"We've got a tech guy who can get them off your phone for us."

"Yeah, okay." She didn't look too sure.

I walked her down to the Lionel's office. He was in and, within half an hour, he'd copied all the texts between the sisters, as well as the text of the email.

"I appreciate you coming in and giving us that information," I told Nellie as we walked back to the lobby.

"Don't think badly of anything you read in the messages. We were—" She choked up and I did my best to comfort her in a world where you didn't dare hug a stranger. She continued, "I was going to say that we were just a couple of sisters and sometimes we got a little gossipy."

"I'm just looking for any clues to your sister's murder. No judgments, I promise."

When I opened the front door for her, a strong north wind struck us. She pulled her coat around herself and walked out to her rental car.

I spent the rest of the day trying to prioritize the cases on my desk while avoiding telling Cara about the promotion when I exchanged texts with her. I wanted to talk about it face to face. Besides, I was still trying to come to terms with it.

I left the office right at five and headed straight home. By the time that Cara and Alvin walked through the door, I'd already fed the cats and scrounged up enough pasta and bread to make a semblance of dinner.

"Smells great. A warm dinner is just what I need," she said, giving me a kiss as Alvin ran over to his bowl. I fed him while Cara went in to the bedroom to get cleaned up and changed.

Still exhausted from the loss of sleep the night before and everything that had happened, I was having a tough time thinking through my strategy for telling her about the promotion. When she came out smelling fresh and with a smile on her face, I just blurted it out.

"I got the promotion."

Cara's face lit up and she ran over to hug me.

"What's wrong?" she asked when I didn't seem as enthused as she was.

"I guess I'm just overwhelmed by the idea." I said, handing her a plate from the cupboard.

"You'll do fine." She fixed her plate of spaghetti and went to the table.

"Besides supervising Pete and Julio, there are two other investigators in CID. Both of them are older than me. It's going to be strange," I said as I joined her.

"Remind me who the other two are. You don't talk about them much."

"There's Mick Klein. He's been with the sheriff's office almost as long as Dad and takes almost all the burglary cases. Kind of strange. Doesn't really talk to anyone unless they talk to him first. Has a great clearance rate. Like eighty percent."

"I don't think I've ever met him."

"You've seen him, but I've never had the chance to introduce you. I don't think he's ever come to a department get-together."

"Who else?"

"Lynn Lewis. Sweet, older deputy. She handles sex crimes and takes on some of the other abuse cases where the victim is a child or a woman."

"Oh yeah. Wow. I remember meeting her. She kind of has the ball-busting-grandma thing going on." Cara smiled.

"Exactly. And I'm afraid it's going to be my balls she'll be busting. The worst part is, everyone has been going about their business for months, heck years, without a sergeant. Phil's going to have a hard enough time as the new lieutenant." The more I talked about the situation in CID, the more sure I was that I was getting in way over my head.

"Sleep on it. No one's going to give you a hard time if you're just doing your job."

"What about Julio?" I'd filled her in on that particular situation earlier.

"He's in a bad place, and you're going to have to be both his friend and his boss." She frowned. "Which won't be easy."

"Bingo! How do I walk that razor's edge?"

"Even if you weren't his supervisor, could you let him go on like this?" Cara asked wisely.

"No. I couldn't take the chance that he'd make a mistake that would do real damage to himself or someone else."

"See, now you're in a position to handle it in a way that is best for him and the department."

"You make it sound easy."

"I know it's not. But I also have faith in you." She reached out and took my hand. "Now enough about you. I've got to call Genie. The countdown to the wedding has started." She stood up and took our plates to the sink. "And you can take this as your final warning. The wedding doesn't count as our Valentine's celebration. I expect at least a box of candy hearts."

I knew that last bit was a lie. Cara wasn't materialistic, but she *was* a woman and she was putting me on notice. *Why haven't I already taken care of that?* I cussed myself for being an idiot.

"I'll think of something," I said, confidently hoping I wasn't lying.

Cara spent an hour on the phone with Genie, and with texts back and forth between them and the other folks who were helping to coordinate the affair. I ignored most of it, knowing that Cara would tell me when and where I needed to be at the appropriate time, and tried not to think about my new responsibilities. The only nod I gave to them was a text to Julio, asking him to meet me first thing in the morning. He agreed and apologized for not covering his on-call shift. *We'll talk in the morning*, was my response.

"I'm glad they aren't having a big wedding," I kidded with Cara as we got ready for bed.

"All weddings are big. You know that."

"I'm glad that everyone is excited. After Dad was attacked, I wasn't sure if the wedding would take place. Does Genie ever say how he's doing?"

"She says he still has headaches and sometimes can't think of a word he wants to use."

"The doctors said that was all to be expected." I wasn't surprised that Dad hadn't told me anything about his continuing symptoms. He was the classic guy who could be in excruciating pain and still respond that he was fine if you asked him about it.

"We need to pick Mauser up tomorrow," Cara reminded me.

"I would complain about having to put up with the big nutjob, but I think they're right to stash him with us. He wouldn't do well with all the company coming and going."

"The boy just has a big heart," Cara said. She had a soft spot for the monster and was willing to make excuses for him.

CHAPTER FIFTEEN

Julio's lips were pursed and his eyes distant as I met him in the parking lot on Thursday morning.

"You want to go somewhere for breakfast?"

"I guess." He looked like he hadn't eaten in a couple of days.

"Let's go check-in and then head over to the Palmetto."

"Sure. Congratulations on making sergeant," he said in a quiet voice as we walked toward the building. The morning was warmer than the day before, but still bitterly cold for Florida. At least the wind wasn't blowing so hard.

"Thanks."

"I guess our talk won't be exactly friend to friend." There was a surprising bit of acid in Julio's tone.

I stopped and turned to face him. "Sergeant or not, we need to have a talk. If you don't think I'm looking out for what's best for you, then we can just deal with this in an official capacity." I was starting to get pissed off. I'd wallowed in my own share of self-pity before, so I wasn't unsympathetic to what Julio was going through, but I also wasn't going to let him throw my offer to help back in my face.

"Breakfast will be good," he said begrudgingly.

Inside the office, I was the recipient of the expected ribbing and congratulations about my promotion. I saw Mick Klein, who gave me a noncommittal nod as he headed for his desk in the corner of CID next to Lynn Lewis. She looked up as he approached and they said something to each other. I wasn't sure if I wanted to know what they were talking about.

I glanced quickly through my emails, which included the one from Dad announcing the promotions. Major Parks had had mercy on me and there weren't any new reports in my inbox.

With the morning routine taken care of, Julio and I headed out to breakfast. We drove separate cars to the restaurant because I didn't want to get into a heated discussion while one of us was driving. The Palmetto had a good-size crowd for a frosty Thursday morning. We parked in the back of the lot and as we walked toward the building, I watched Julio. His head was downcast and his usually neat attire looked slept in.

I reached out and put my hand on his shoulder.

"We can work this out," I told him, and for a second I thought he was going to shrug off my hand. Instead, he nodded.

Finally seated and with a plate of macho-man-size pancakes in front of me, I poured an unhealthy amount of maple syrup on them before looking over at Julio. He had just a couple of eggs, toast and coffee.

"Do I have to say anything about the other night?" I asked.

"No. I take full responsibility and apologize." He managed to look me in the eye.

"It never happened if you can tell me that it will never happen again."

He looked me in the eye. "It won't."

"One more thing and then I'll drop it. You can't let the drinking take control. If anyone ever catches you on duty with alcohol on your breath…"

"I know, I know." Julio drank some coffee and looked at the untouched food on his plate like he thought it would bite him. "I don't know what to do about Dani."

"I'm not a marriage counselor, but I think I can assure you that losing your job will not help you get her back."

"Right." He reluctantly forked up some of the eggs. "It's going to be different having you as sergeant."

"Tell me about it."

"And Phil as lieutenant. I'm fine with it. He and I got along well in patrol. Some of the other guys are going to be a little surprised," he said, loosening up and finally making good progress with the eggs.

"Is there anything I can do to help with Dani?"

He shrugged. "I don't know. I just wish…" Another shrug, but he kept eating.

By the time we paid the bill and left the restaurant, the air between us was clearer and I felt better about his mood.

Back at my desk, I did paperwork for half a dozen cases, then went down to the evidence room to box up some items for an upcoming trial.

"What's up with these crazy emails everyone's talking about?" Marcus Brown, Shantel's second in command, asked as he helped me record and box items.

I brought him up to date on the situation. "If you know of anyone who's gotten any of the emails, let me know. We need all we can get for comparison."

He looked right and left like he expected eavesdroppers. "My auntie got one."

"Your aunt? What did it accuse her of?"

"This is crazy, but it's gotten her all upset. The email said she stole another woman's muscadine jelly recipe."

"Seriously?" I smiled and then saw the somber look on his face.

"You don't understand. She takes her cooking seriously. Like drop-dead-in-a-coffin seriously. She's been freaking our ever since she got it."

"And the email claims she stole the recipe?" I wondered

how loony this could all get. "How old is your aunt?"

"Eighty in April," Marcus said.

I was stupidly surprised that she had email, then I remembered that everyone from kindergarten to the grave had email these days.

"She's worried that someone is going to post the lie to Facebook," Marcus said, and one look at his face told me he was serious.

"I'd like to see the email."

"I'll get a copy of it."

"I might want to talk to your aunt too."

"Getting to talk to her is going to be easier than stopping talking to her." He smiled.

Lionel came in as we were finishing boxing up the evidence.

"I've mapped out Eva Calavera's car and phone movements," he told me as he opened the door to his office and flipped on the light. I followed him into the room. "Not sure if it's going to be of much use to you."

"Might not help to find the killer, but it's certainly the type of evidence that can wrap the noose around a defendant's neck."

"Here is the best track I can come up with for the car." He pulled up a map on one of the monitors on his desk. The map showed a dark blue line traveling from Calavera's house to downtown Tallahassee, then returning to Adams County and making a couple of side trips before it ended in the Ditch. There were time stamps next to different points on the route.

"Her husband said he thought she was going to eat in Tallahassee. There are a number of restaurants within a quarter mile of the capitol. I'll have to pull the CCTV and check her credit card records, try to find out where she ate and with whom."

Lionel handed me a sheet of paper. "Here are the phone pings. She'd disabled all the apps that would have given us an exact map of the phone's movements, so going off of the cell tower data isn't anywhere near as precise. What I think it does is confirm the car tracking data."

"You're getting to be quite the detective."

"Thanks, sergeant," Lionel said with an emphasis on the last word.

"The responsibility is already resting heavy on my shoulders," I joked, though it wasn't really funny.

I headed back to my office with a printout of Lionel's map. Before I got to my desk, I was intercepted by Mick and Lynn.

"Could we have a word with you, Sarge?" Mick's use of the word took me by surprise. The sarcasm came through loud and clear.

"Come on, knock it off."

"We're serious about having a talk," Lynn said.

We went into the conference room, but none of us sat down.

"We don't begrudge you the promotion," Mick said, glancing over at Lynn. "Neither of us ever wanted the responsibility. We just want to make sure you understand our positions."

"What Mick's trying to say is that we've got our little cozy spots here and we don't want to feel like we have to defend them."

"We do our jobs. I don't think you could find anyone with better burglary clearance rates than I've got." Mick's tone was defensive.

"And I do pretty well myself. Besides, there isn't anyone else fighting to take over my job." Lynn put her chin out and crossed her arms as she spoke.

What she said was true. I certainly never wanted to spend my days culling through the sexual assault and abuse reports, or rubbing elbows with the creepos that made up the usual suspects in the cases. The few sexual abuse cases I'd had to work had made me angry and left images in my brain that were difficult to put to rest.

"Look, guys, I'm not an idiot. I know how hard you both

work. If something's not broke, I'm not going to try to fix it." I was being completely honest. I was going to have enough work to do without making more for myself. "So are we good?"

They both looked at me with narrowed eyes as though they were suspicious of my motives. Finally Mick nodded and Lynn relaxed.

"Do you think we're going to have any trouble from our new lieutenant?" Mick asked. I was amused at how fast I'd gone from foe to friend.

"Eccles has always seemed like a good guy. Practical. No-nonsense."

"Yeah, that's the impression I've gotten," Mick mused.

"We just don't want to get screwed," Lynn said.

After a little light banter, we went our separate ways. Things seemed fine for now, but I wasn't fooled. The point of that confrontation was clear. It was to let me know that if I asked them to do something they didn't like, I was going to be met by their united resistance. I could already feel an ulcer growing.

After work, Cara drove me over to Dad's so that I could pick up Mauser. I was going to bring him back to our place in Dad's van. Cara went into the house to see Genie, while Dad came outside with Mauser. The dog had already eaten his dinner, which meant that in his mind it was naptime. He didn't even bother giving me his usual over-the-top greeting

"And this is a simple wedding," Dad said as he and I walked out to the barn with Mauser trailing behind us. Dad looked back at the dog as he stopped to sniff some lantana at the base of a pine tree in preparation for lifting his leg. "He's already tired out from all the craziness."

"What about you?" I asked.

"I'll be glad when it's over. Genie is having the time of her life, which makes it worth it."

"What about a honeymoon?"

"I'm working on it. We've agreed to wait until we're recovered from the wedding and can really enjoy it. We might just go down to the coast and chill out for a week."

Dad and I walked in a comfortable silence. At the barn, I helped him feed Finn and Mac, his two twin Quarter Horse geldings. After the horses were done and turned out into their paddock, we headed back to the house. Cara was still working with Genie on the final seating plan for the reception, which would be held at the old Masonic lodge, so I loaded up Mauser in the van and headed for home.

On the way, I had a thought and changed direction. Whether it was a good thought or not, I had no clue, but I'd soon find out.

"Big guy, do you want to make a house call?" I asked Mauser, who was sitting so that he could hang his head between the front seats and drool on my arm. "I'll take that for a yes."

I drove over to Julio's apartment, got Mauser out of the van, then knocked on the door. Mauser shifted from foot to foot and looked anxious. He was probably feeling my own doubts about the wisdom of this errand.

Dani answered the door with an odd expression on her tanned face. Instantly, I knew what she was thinking.

"Don't worry, Julio is fine," I stammered. It hadn't occurred to me that she might take a surprise visit from me as cause for alarm.

"Okay. So why are you here?" Her expression had switched immediately to suspicion.

Before I had a chance to reply, Mauser pushed past me and licked her hand. Dani jumped back, her eyes huge as she looked down and saw what had licked her hand. "Mauser! Wow. Look at you, boy."

Hearing his name and the excitement in her voice was all Mauser needed to start hopping up and down with glee. Dani had forgotten I was even there. I had remembered her reaction to Mauser the few times I'd seen them in the same place, including once at an office barbeque where she'd spent at least half an hour talking to and petting Mauser. The monster had that effect on some people and I confess I'd had this in mind when I made my spontaneous decision to visit.

Dani continued to ruffle Mauser's ears and speak baby talk to him as I stood there, holding the leash and wondering when I should interrupt their reunion.

"I don't mean to butt into your private business," I finally said and she didn't react. "Julio is a good man."

"He's a liar and now he's turning into a drunk." Dani kept her eyes on Mauser and her long, dark hair shielded her face from view.

"I've gotten to know a fair number of liars in my line of work. I also know that everyone who tells a lie isn't a liar. Julio might not have told you the truth about his life before you all got married, but that doesn't make him a bad person. He made a mistake."

"He had an affair with a married woman. That's a sin." Dani shook her head.

"He regrets that. I know how much he loves you."

"Julio hid it from me." She looked up at me with narrowed eyes.

"I'd bet the reason he didn't tell you was because he was afraid that you would reject him if he told you about his past." I was throwing everything at the wall and hoping something would stick.

"So he didn't trust me?" she demanded.

"I think it was more about his own insecurities."

"He shouldn't have sent you."

"Julio doesn't know I'm here."

"Then why did you come?"

"Because Julio is my friend. Because he is an asset to our department. But..." I held a dramatic pause. "...he's not the same without you."

I thought I caught a little weakening of her resolve as her hand paused in scratching Mauser's head. But the beast wasn't having that and barged forward, bumping into Dani and making her pet him again. She smiled at the dog, but I saw tears in her eyes.

"I don't feel I can trust him anymore."

"I wouldn't be his friend, and my father wouldn't let him serve the county as a deputy, if we didn't think he was trustworthy," I stated. When she turned and gave me a hard look, I added, "I'm really not trying to convince you of anything, only that there are more sides to this than one."

"Who killed that woman?" she asked, surprising me.

"We're working hard to find out."

"You… don't think…"

"No, I don't think Julio had anything to do with her death," I said honestly. Of course, the possibility wasn't zero, but there was a big difference between a probability and a possibility.

"Would you let me text my nephew?" she asked, which left me confused until she added, "He lives just on the next block and would love to meet Mauser."

I nodded and she pulled her phone out, taking a picture of the goofball before sending it to her nephew with an invitation to come over and meet him.

Dani invited me inside and I spent another hour as she and her ten-year-old nephew made over Mauser, who mostly just flopped around from couch to floor to the edge of a chair, amusing both of them. When I finally left, Dani refused to give me any encouragement that she'd try and come to terms with Julio, but I tried to be hopeful.

When I got home, the household was sent into chaos as Mauser insisted on greeting Alvin and then jumping around like an idiot as the two cats batted at him from the furniture.

"Always nice to have company," Cara said as she came out of the bedroom.

Her presence sent Mauser into new paroxysms of insanity that threatened to knock the walls down, but with her help and a few treats, we managed to get all the animals settled down.

"Is everyone ready for the wedding?" I asked, giving Cara

a kiss now that I could get close to her without being knocked over by the elephant dog.

"Not even close. I'm taking tomorrow off to help get the hall ready."

"Are you going to be able to take Mauser along?"

"Sure. How'd your first day as a sergeant go?"

I glared at her. "This is going to be fun," I grumbled and told her about being cornered by Lynn and Mick.

It was already late, but I sat down at the table and went through my copies of the emails one more time. This time I was looking for common words or themes. Cara came up behind me on her way to the refrigerator for a drink and looked over my shoulder.

"I probably shouldn't be reading these," she said.

"As long as you understand that some of them are true and some of them aren't. Besides, they don't have the recipients' names on them, so you wouldn't know who they were talking about anyway," I said, letting her scan through a few of them.

"I can make a pretty good guess as to who they were sent to," she said, surprising me.

"Sure, there's the email address, but…" I looked closer at a couple of the addresses and saw that they contained at least the majority of the recipient's name, mostly a first or last name and corresponding initial. Feeling a little stupid, I looked through the rest of the addresses and every one of them contained enough of the name that someone would be able, at least in a small county like ours, to figure out who the addresses belonged to. "Do *most* people's emails contain their name?" I asked myself as much as Cara.

"No. I've seen the email list at the clinic and I'd guess only half use portions of their real names."

"All of these do." My mind was slowly building an idea, using this clue as the foundation stone. "So if I got the clinic's email list and didn't have a way to cross-reference them with the client list…"

"Then the only ones you'd recognize for sure would be

the ones using their name as part of the email address." Cara finished my thought.

"Exactly. Our crazed emailer must have gotten ahold of a list of emails and could only send his ugly little messages to the ones where he could figure out the owner of the address."

"Does that help you?"

"I think it does." I was trying to see all the ins and outs. "Yeah, I think it might." The lightbulb above my head was glowing now. "Maybe he got all of these addresses off of the same email list. If so, then I need to find out what list all of these people are on."

"And you could figure that he or she must be on the same list."

"Right, as part of the same group... or at least with access to the list."

"Access, but not enough to get a list that associated the email addresses with names."

"Good point. A print-out of email addresses?" I speculated.

"No..." Cara snapped her fingers, causing Mauser to lift his head from the floor and moan. "I bet he's on the email list and someone sent an email without making the cc's blind."

"You could be right."

"We had an intern at the clinic do that a while back and we got all sorts of angry calls from dozens of clients who felt that we'd broken their trust and exposed them to spam or stalking from the other people who got the email."

"We'll need to ask all these people what email lists they're on. It would be a local one."

"Maybe you'll get lucky and find someone who doesn't give out his or her email to everyone that asks."

"I don't," I reminded her.

"But most people do. Like when they sign up for the discount card at the Supersave. Or at the vet or any business that wants to communicate with them via email."

"I admit there's going to be some footwork involved, but at least it's a lead to run down. That's more than we've had so far."

"Proud of you." She kissed me on the top of the head, making me feel like a kid. I grabbed her around the waist and pulled her into my lap. She laughed while I gave her a proper kiss before she got up and went to bed.

I texted my revelation to Pete. We swapped messages back and forth exploring the possibilities for a while, then I headed off to bed.

It was with a deep sense of *déjà vu* that I heard my phone ring at five in the morning. I glanced at the phone and saw that it was Julio. I half wondered if I should answer it. I wasn't going to deal well with the situation if he was on a drunken rant. But I didn't have a choice.

"What?" I asked.

"I'm at the Fast Mart on Jefferson. The attendant's been bludgeoned to death and I think it's connected to the emails."

I cursed under my breath. "I'll be there in half an hour," I said, already rolling out of bed.

CHAPTER SIXTEEN

Less than half a mile from the store, I could see the strobing blue and red lights in the moonless winter night. I parked at the curb between an ambulance and a Florida Highway Patrol car.

"Early morning for you," Mike Townsend, the FHP officer, greeted me. "Ortiz is over there." He pointed toward our crime scene van, which was parked farther down the curb.

I looked at the ambulance, wondering why they were there, as I headed for the van. Marcus was digging in the back for his cameras as Julio stood nearby, talking on the phone.

"I left a message with the coroner's service," Julio told me as he put his phone in his pocket.

"Who's our victim?"

"A big guy. I think I've seen him working here. Not one of the family that owns the store. I called their emergency number. The owner is on his way."

"How do you know it has to do with the emails?"

"The witness told me." He pointed toward the ambulance. "The guy's pretty messed up."

"He was attacked?"

"No, just messed up." Julio pointed to his head. "Too much Mad Dog and just crazy, I think. You'll recognize him. He walks around town with a teddy bear and a sign begging for money."

"Terrific." I knew who Julio was talking about. I'd heard the man called by a dozen different nicknames, none of them complimentary. Crazy Bear was the standard and not the worst of the lot. The sign he held always claimed that he needed money to go home and take the teddy bear to his kid. Over the years he'd had a number of different bears. He would use one until it got too grungy to be believable as a prop. I'd told him once that he could beg without the bear, because by now everyone in the county knew it was just a scam.

"When I asked him what happened, he said a guy in a hoodie came in and told the clerk that he hoped he'd gotten the email. The clerk responded that he was wrong, that he'd never hurt anyone. Then the guy in the hoodie said, 'You killed her' before slugging him a dozen times with a piece of pipe."

"Is the pipe still in the store?" I asked.

"No, the perp took it with him."

"Did he drive here?"

"I didn't get very far questioning Bear. He's shook up or drunk or both."

"Let's go see."

We walked to the ambulance where they had Bear in the back, monitoring his vitals while he lay on a stretcher, staring up at the ceiling of the vehicle.

"How is he?" I asked.

One of the EMTs attending him was Alejandro Valdez, affectionately known as Hondo. He was a good friend and one of the best EMTs in North Florida.

"He's shook up, man," Hondo said, patting Bear on the shoulder. "Of course, we have a history with our friend here, so we can look back and see that his vitals aren't too far off from what they were two months ago when he was causing a scene at the post office."

"I don't know anything about the post office," Bear said without looking around.

"Amigo, you were going through the trashcan throwing old mail around and scaring the patrons."

"No, no, not me." There was an odd, childlike quality to his voice. I'd never arrested him or given him an official warning, so I wasn't sure of his real name or actual age. He looked like he was in his fifties, but drugs and living in the rough could add decades.

"Can I talk to him?" I asked. We had a bad guy to find and, if there was a chance Bear could help us get on the killer's trail, the sooner, the better.

"Who wouldn't want to talk to you? Lorenzo, take a break," Hondo said to the other EMT.

"My pleasure. Our friend hasn't had a bath in a while," Lorenzo said to me as he got out of the ambulance so I could climb in.

I sat on the bench across from Hondo with the odorous Bear between us.

"I'm Deputy Larry Macklin," I said, forgetting my new title. "I need to ask you a few questions."

"I don't want to talk about that." He jerked his head and waved his hands.

"First, what's your name?" I asked and waited. I began to wonder if he'd forgotten or didn't want to answer.

"Roy Roper… but Bear's fine," he finally answered.

"How old are you?"

"How the hell would I know?" he shouted.

"Bear, you know you're thirty-eight," Hondo coached him.

"You heard the man," Bear said, pushing out his lower lip.

"Okay, Bear, I want you to tell me what you did today."

"What day is it?"

"Friday. It's early Friday morning. I want you to start with Thursday afternoon. What did you do?"

"Stupid question," he grumbled, but furrowed his brow. "Something. Maybe I asked for money. Yeah. I like to catch the after-work crowd. Not as good as the going-to-work crowd, but who the hell wants to get up at dawn?"

"Where did you do your panhandling?"

"Guess in front of the Supersave."

"Maybe in their parking lot too?" I knew this was one of the infractions he'd been in trouble for. The Supersave had accused him of trespassing years ago, but we usually just gave him a warning and moved him back to the sidewalk. Over the years, the store had gotten used to him. The managers understood that there wasn't much to be done. Arresting Bear wouldn't have any more of a lasting impression on his addled brain than just reminding him that he wasn't allowed on their property.

"Naw, I stay far away from the store 'cause they get mad."

"Did you get much money?"

"Yeah, I guess, some." I hoped we'd never need to put him in front of a jury. He didn't instill confidence.

"So you got some money. What did you do then?" I prompted, hoping against hope that he'd get more coherent.

"What I do. I bought some Mad Dog." He smiled.

"You bought alcohol and then what?" It was like pushing a car with four flat tires.

"Don't know. Drank it. Fell asleep?"

"Let's say you fell asleep. Where did you sleep?"

"Behind the store."

"Which store?"

"The… this one." He waved his hands.

"You drank a bottle of Mad Dog and then passed out at the Fast Mart. Front, side, back of the store?"

"Where they dump the boxes. You lie on a pile of boxes, it's pretty comfy."

"When did you wake up?"

"Wake up? I don't know. It was dark." Bear looked confused.

"Never mind. What did you do when you woke up?"

"Needed some money. My gut was killing me. Thought I might get somethin' to eat. Guess it was late 'cause there weren't no cars coming up to the store. Least aways, not any that had anybody I could ask for money. Some guys, they'll hit you in the face or something. And at night, I don't ask women for money." This last bit was said with an odd tone that made me think he might have run into trouble along those lines before.

"Did you go into the store?"

"Can't till I got money. The Pakis that own the place will throw me out. The old lady hit me with a broom once. You guys didn't do nothin' about that."

"Did you get money?"

"Yeah, I did." He paused and I thought I was going to have to prompt him again, but he went on, "A college-lookin' guy came up and I got the chance to ask him for five dollars. Nice guy. Real nice guy. Gave me ten dollars. Told me to buy a bottle of the good stuff." He smiled at the thought.

"Had you seen him before?"

"Nah, he was just a guy. I knew he was good for money though."

"How'd you know that?"

Bear furrowed his brow. You would have thought I'd asked him to explain how the Large Hadron Collider worked.

"Car. He had some fancy car. Always look at the car. Trucks aren't usually good for much. Maybe if I had a sign sayin' I was a veteran. Another guy I know, he works out by—"

"Stick to tonight. The guy had a fancy car. What did he look like?"

"Never look them in the eyes. That's one of my rules. Good damn way to get punched. Look at the ground or off to the side."

"Come on. You must at least know if he was tall or short,

fat or thin?"

"Good lookin'. Guess you'd say tall. Dressed worse than me. If I had money, I'd dress nice. Torn clothes. Crazy."

"Hair color?"

"Nope. He had a hat on."

"Was he a white guy?"

"No. Black man."

"Was there anyone else in the car?"

"No. I always look. If there's a bunch of guys, I just go and hide and wait for another car. Good way to get beat up is talking to a group of guys late at night."

"What did he do after he gave you the money?"

"Went in the store."

Julio stuck his head into the ambulance. "The coroner is on the way and Marcus is documenting the scene. He wants to know if you want him to do a 3D rendering."

"Tell Marcus to go ahead. I should be done questioning Bear in another five hours." I rolled my eyes. Bear didn't notice.

"Better you than me," Julio said, sounding more like his old self. He jogged back to where Marcus was working.

"Okay, Bear, think. How long was the guy in the store?" I asked.

"Not long. I waited outside."

"You had the money. Why didn't you go in when he did?"

"I don't like to spend the money with people lookin'."

"People?"

"People who give me the money. Makes me feel... guess ashamed or somethin'."

I hadn't imagined that he could have that much dignity left.

"Then after he left, you went in?" I continued.

"I got my stuff and put it on the counter, then I asked that kid for a key to the bathroom. He said I had to show him the money first." Bear sounded offended. I knew that most of the stores in town frowned on the homeless population using their bathroom facilities. The clerks wanted to see proof that they were paying customers.

"So you went to the bathroom."

I saw a shift in Bear's expression. There was pain, or maybe fear in his eyes.

"Yeah, that's what I did. Wanted to make it good, 'cause I don't always get a chance to sit down with running water. Yeah, and it was cold outside, so getting to be inside in the heat was nice. I was in there for a while. Long enough that I was thinkin' the dude behind the counter was gonna start pounding on the door, telling me to get out. They do that all the time."

"But he didn't?"

"No. I got myself together and was comin' out of the back when I heard the front door make a loud noise. Scared me."

"Why'd it scare you?"

He gave me a look like I was stupid. "I been close to a couple shootings and dozens of fights. You don't want to see nothin'. I wasn't goin' to go out the front way if there was trouble. I'd hide or try to get out the back. I ain't stupid."

"So you hid?"

"No. I should have. Stupid, but I heard this guy yelling. Shoutin' about stuff. That's when I heard the guy behind the counter start shouting back about how this guy shouldn't be sending crazy emails to him and stuff. They were just yelling, but then there was only the other guy's voice. He was saying it was payback time or the like. I should have snuck out the back. Stupid."

"Did you see them?"

"Not then. I heard… it. Then again and again." Bear sniffled and wiped his nose with his sleeve. I didn't have to ask what Bear heard. The sound of a blunt object hitting flesh and breaking bones is… memorable.

"That poor guy, he kind of made a noise. Maybe he was beggin' the guy to stop. I don't know. After that, all there was… was that sound."

"When did you see the other guy?"

"After the thumpin' stopped. I looked toward the front of the store and he was walking out, swinging something in his hand. Couldn't see his face. He was wearing a hoodie."

"Where did he go when he left the store?"

"I don't know. I didn't see a car or anything like that. I crawled out and went to check on the poor guy."

"Did you touch the body?"

"Oh no. No. I… He was dead. I…" He looked over at Hondo. "…Y'all aren't gonna believe this, but I was in medical school." He saw the look of disbelief on my face. "Knew you wouldn't believe me. Third year. My head got all screwed up and I kind of lost it. I would have helped him if I could."

"How is he?" I asked Hondo, nodding at Bear.

"The usual. Isn't that right, Bear?" Hondo gave Bear's shoulder a reassuring pat.

"Yeah, that's right."

"I think he could use a night in the hospital. I can take him there, but that doesn't mean they'll keep him," Hondo told me.

I thought for a minute.

"Bear, I'm going to send you to jail for a day or two."

"Hey, what did I do?" he said indignantly.

"Nothing. You're a material witness in a murder, and I want to keep you alive." I looked him in the eye so he'd know I was serious.

"You think that guy might come back for me?"

"I'd prefer that we don't find out the hard way."

"Hard way? You mean me dead?"

"It's a couple nights of protective custody. Hot shower, warm bed, three meals a day. I'll even make sure you get a private room."

"No alcohol?"

"Sorry, but there are limits to the county's hospitality."

"I can't dry out. I haven't been sober in ten years." A

different kind of fear was in his eyes now.

"I'll make sure you have medical treatment. I think they have some stuff they can give you to keep you from having the DTs."

"You *think?*" He was trying to get up off the stretcher. "No way, José."

"You remember Eddie?"

"I don't know no Eddie!" He was struggling to get the blood pressure cuff off his arm.

"Tall Eddie. One of the Thompsons."

"Eddie?" He stopped struggling. "Yeah, doesn't hang out with his ol' friends no more. Got clean. What about him?"

"I could ask him to come over to the jail while you're there."

"I don't want to get clean." He went back to struggling.

"I'll come by tomorrow. If you aren't happy, I'll take you anywhere you want to go in the county." I could see him wavering a little. "And I'll give you two twenty-dollar bills."

"Maybe. Yeah, maybe. I just don't want to get sober."

"Deal."

Hondo and I climbed out of the ambulance.

"Is he really okay?" I asked him.

"I wouldn't trade livers with him, but he's good for another couple of years. I just don't want to get to the jail and have him back out. They're going to want us back in service soon."

"I'll call over there and get someone to handle him. Hopefully Marge is there."

Marge Jones was a large, motherly guard who managed to get most of the inmates to do what she wanted by using her arsenal of dirty looks, jokes and threats. She had a down-home way about her that appealed to the down-and-outers who were locked up in our jail.

"That would be great. Everybody does what Large Marge says," Hondo chuckled.

CHAPTER SEVENTEEN

I called the jail. Sure enough, Marge was working the eleven-to-seven shift. She had a portfolio of grandchildren, so she liked to work at night so she could be with them when they got out of school in the afternoon.

"Sure, I know Bear. Send that reprobate over here. You say he's a material witness. Hope you already got a statement on tape 'cause Bear's memory is good for about an hour." She wasn't making me feel better about my one and only witness.

After seeing the ambulance off, I went over to Julio's car. He was talking to a stout man in a grey overcoat. I recognized the man as Anand Bakshi, the owner of the Fast Marts.

"The clerk's name is Nicolaus Andreas. He's worked here for about three years," Julio told me.

"I will have to look at my records to know who to contact. This is awful. Very, very awful." Bakshi shook his head.

"How old was Nicolaus?" I asked him.

"I don't remember. Thirty or so. He was in and out of grad school at the university. If I am remembering correctly, he had some trouble with his grades. But a nice boy. Quite trustworthy. Never a problem. Other clerks are always calling with problems. Not Nicolaus."

"Did he mention anyone threatening him? Or causing a problem at the store?"

"No, nothing like that. I told you. He never called with problems. Sometimes he'd say, 'Mr. Bakshi, I have to do this or take care of that.' Never bothered me. I wish some of my family were as responsible."

"The store is going to have to be closed for most of today," I informed him.

"Of course. We will need to have it cleaned. This is awful. The last time we had trouble like this was six months ago at our south-side store. Some hooligans got in a fight in the parking lot; shots were fired. A man was badly injured, but no one hurt our employee."

"Do you have any enemies?"

He gave me a philosophical look. "A businessman makes a few enemies."

"Anyone who might get violent?"

"No, not at all. They talk about me and run my business down to others. Yes, that they do. But to kill someone? No one like that."

"Was this Nicolaus's regular shift?"

"He worked the nightshift most of the time because I could trust him. I don't let any of the women work at night. Too dangerous. I only have about a six clerks who I can trust to run the stores late at night."

I remembered a couple of times when Dad had tried to convince Bakshi to close all his stores between one and six in the morning. Those were the bloody hours when alcohol flowed and bad guys thought that it would be easy to rob a minute market. But Bakshi would have none of it. He insisted it was a service to the community to stay open all night. The crime rate at the stores actually wasn't that bad, partly because they would provide free coffee and snacks to any patrol deputies who parked their cars in front of the stores in the early morning hours while they took a meal break or wrote reports.

"You know we're going to need the CCTV footage," I said.

"I called my nephew. He's a good boy. I told him if he got here by dawn, that would be good."

"Fine. We need to process the store before he can get in and pull the data."

"He's been after me to get an off-property server. I... I don't know why I haven't done it. Money, I guess. But what's money to peace of mind?" he said with a shrug.

I left them to go check on Marcus.

"You need any help?"

"Shantel should be here any minute. I've photographed everything and did a run-through with the video. As soon as Shantel gets here, we'll set up the 3D imager. That's going to take a while with all the aisles. Maybe an hour of moving the camera around."

"If you've got the photos, I'm going to put on protective gear and do a walk-through."

"Don't see why not."

I went back to my car and got suited up. I wanted to invite Julio to walk through with me, but there was that million-to-one shot that he could have been involved in Eva Calavera's murder, which in turn meant that he could have been involved in this one. Though I was making a giant assumption about a connection based on Bear's statement that the killer and victim had been yelling about emails.

Wearing my paper overalls and gloves, I made a note of the time that I entered the crime scene. The exterior door was glass and steel, so it would be perfect for picking up fingerprints. Though what were the odds that our killer hadn't worn gloves?

From the doorway, nothing looked disturbed. I could see to the back of the store where a sign pointed toward the restrooms. How lucky had Bear been that the killer hadn't heard him come out of the bathroom? Maybe the hood over his head had muffled the sounds, or he had tunnel vision focusing on the attack.

I looked down at the floor to see if there were any obvious footprints. I saw several scuffs and stains, but nothing identifiable. Then I looked up at the ceiling, scanning for the cameras. We'd pulled footage from Fast Marts in the past and there was always good coverage of the store. I spotted one camera at the back right corner and another one on the left. I crossed my fingers and hoped that they were both working.

The checkout counter was covered with the usual mix of items for sale: energy boosters, lighters, keychains and a large Plexiglas box containing scratch-off lottery tickets. As my eyes focused on the counter, I started to notice the brown-red blood, spots here and splashes there. I walked forward, being careful not to step in any of the spots that dotted the floor.

A couple of feet from the counter, I was able to see the body lying on the floor. The blood trail led from in front of the counter to the opening at the back that allowed access to the area behind it. Apparently the killer had reached across the counter to club the cashier, then walked around to finish his brutal attack.

On the counter by the register were two packs of crackers, a bottle of Pepto Bismol and another of MD 20/20. A ten-dollar bill was tucked under a corner of the crackers. This was obviously Bear's booty from his lucky strike.

I could see several bloody shoeprints near the counter. Solid physical evidence always made me happy. There was a clear imprint of most of the sole of one shoe. With luck, we could match the pattern and name the shoe brand, size and type. If we had even more luck down the road, we'd find the shoes still in the possession of the killer. That was the type of evidence that put killers behind bars.

Or in the electric chair, the voice inside my head reminded me. Funny how the image of Old Sparky had gotten stuck in my brain after talking with Mr. Griffin. No one I'd sent to prison was likely to be executed. Even in Florida, where the state was willing to use its power to punish, the inmates on death row were much more likely to die of old age as their appeals ran through the courts. And the odds that Old Sparky would ever be fired up again were a million to one.

I stepped around the prints. Marcus would have already taken pictures and video, but I wanted to make sure before blundering over them. The energy and violence of the attack on Nicolaus was revealed in the damage to his face and head. I felt a moment of nausea. I turned my head and took a deep breath, grateful that there wasn't any odor beyond the faint, coppery smell of blood.

I looked back at Nicolaus's remains. Was this the same killer? A knife for Eva and a club for Nicolaus? If it *was* the same killer, was there any significance to the use of different weapons? I was anxious to see the email, if there was one. Bear might have misheard them, or been confused, or just made it all up. I gave Bear a pass on this one. Any sane person would have been upset and confused witnessing such an attack and its aftermath.

I left the counter and walked back to the restrooms. Nothing looked out of place. I opened the men's room door and looked around. In the trashcan was a nasty sock and some food wrappers that could have been put there by Bear.

I heard the bell on the door and looked up to see Shantel and Marcus carrying their boxes of supplies for dusting surfaces and taking swabs of blood and DNA.

"We're going to wipe down everything, then do the 3D mapping," Shantel said. "And congrats on that big promotion." She smiled. Shantel was one of the nicest and most sincere people I'd ever met, so I took her comments as they were intended.

"Thanks. We'll see if I can live up to it."

"Our boy is growing up." She nudged Marcus.

When I'd first joined the sheriff's office, because of who my father was I got the cold shoulder from a lot of the deputies. No one liked the boss's son hanging around.

Shantel had been an exception. She showed me all the best practices of evidence collection and time-saving methods to make life easier for me. She also gave me the inside scoop on some of my colleagues. Never to the point of gossip, but just enough to make it simpler for me to navigate the office politics.

Back outside, I called to follow up on Julio's original message to the coroner's office. They answered this time and I explained what was going on, telling them to take their time getting there because it'd be another hour or more before they could get near the body.

"I'm going back to the office unless you need me," Julio said as I disconnected the call. He'd wrapped crime scene tape around the parking lot to keep anyone from driving in.

"I'm good. I'll call dispatch if I need anyone to help out."

"Do you think this is connected to Eva's murder?" he asked.

"I don't know. The MO doesn't look similar, but if it's connected to an email, then all bets are off."

He nodded and headed for his car.

It was quiet before dawn in Calhoun. I shivered and looked at the Fast Mart, where the lights were bright but unable to provide any illumination on the horrific deed that had taken place that night. I was watching Marcus and Shantel move around inside, doing their thing, when a car pulled up to the curb.

My first thought was that it was a customer to be turned away, but as soon as I turned and saw the car, I knew who it was. A man with grey hair and a crooked grin climbed out of the driver's side.

"Macklin!" he called out.

"Lieutenant." I made it sound more upbeat than I felt.

Phill Eccles put his hand out to me.

"We need to sit down and do some strategizing. What a difference a week makes." He shook my hand vigorously. He was a hard man not to like. If he'd been a dog, he would have been a Golden Retriever. Smart, but not too smart, always friendly and loyal to a fault.

"I'm glad you made lieutenant," I said, taking back my well-shaken hand.

"What's this?" He waved toward the store. "Isn't Julio on call tonight?"

"This might be tied to the Calavera murder," I told him. From the puzzled look he gave me, I realized he hadn't been briefed on the case. "There is a personal connection between Julio and Eva Calavera."

"I see. He called you?"

"As soon as he thought there was a chance they were connected." I fretted about whether I should mention any of the other issues surrounding Julio. Most of them were personal, so I decided to keep them to myself as long as they didn't bleed over into the job any worse than they already had.

Phil nodded. "Let's get suited up and you can walk me through it."

I wasn't sure if I was impressed or concerned with how easily he'd stepped into the role of lieutenant.

I went to my car and donned another set of paper overalls. I came back over to Phil's car as he was finishing up with his own suit.

"We have a witness: an alcoholic who goes by the nickname Bear," I told him.

"I know Bear. Not what I'd call reliable."

"No, his testimony isn't going to put anyone in jail. I'm just hoping he can give us a lead on who we're dealing with."

"I'd put more faith in the surveillance cameras."

"The owner's nephew is coming to pull the footage."

"Why aren't you using Lionel?" he asked as we headed toward the store.

"They know each other. The nephew has done this for us in the past. When possible, Lionel says it's best to let the guy who knows the system pull the data. I don't think there's a chance that the nephew is involved. If he was, he would have made sure that the cameras didn't capture anything.

From what we got from Bear, this wasn't a heat-of-the-moment attack. The killer came in with the intention to kill the clerk."

"Anything stolen?"

"Don't know yet. The register was closed. If we give credence to Bear's testimony, then there wasn't time for the safe to have been accessed—not that it can be at this time of night."

I opened the door and got black fingerprint dust on my gloves.

"Marcus, we're doing something wrong. Everybody around here's getting promotions except us," Shantel said as we came in.

"You're one to complain. The sheriff built you your own little kingdom last year," Phil said with a laugh.

"We've swabbed and taken pictures and measurements of the obvious evidence." She pointed to the markers scattered around the store. "Anything else you want us to get, just holler."

We walked back to the victim. I averted my eyes from the worst of his head injuries.

"Whoever it was did a number on the poor guy," Phil said, looking closely at the body. I knew he'd worked more than his share of grisly auto accidents. "I can't recognize him. I'm sure I've talked to him if he's worked here long."

"The owner said he's been here a few years."

"Poor guy gets beat to death." He looked around the small area behind the counter. "These stores need to have silent alarms like the bank. Not that it would have saved his life."

"The first blow must have been near fatal, or at least incapacitated him. From the way the body's lying, he just collapsed. Bear *did* think he heard the clerk mumble something before the killer finished him off."

"The killer didn't hesitate or hold back."

"Looks personal," I agreed.

"Doubt we'll learn much from the autopsy that we can't

deduce with our own eyes. He was killed from multiple blows to the head, and between Bear and the surveillance video, we should be able to nail the time of the attack down to within a couple of minutes."

"We'll round up the local security camera footage from the other businesses and residents. Knowing the time of the attack, we ought to be able to catch the killer's car or him walking away on camera."

"You said that Calavera was stabbed. Are there any similarities between the two murders?"

I thought about it. "No, not really. They were both brutal. She was stabbed nine times and most of the knife thrusts went through the body. Though I have to admit, it wasn't this type of frenzy."

"So the only thing that makes you think there is a connection is the fact that Bear said he heard them talk about an email?"

"Sounds thin when you put it like that."

"I don't want you to get tunnel vision. Still, I don't blame you for going down that path. I'd like you to send me the file on the emails and the Calavera murder."

"Pete's handling the anonymous emailer."

"Fine, tell him to send the file to me." He paused for a second and met my eyes. "I'm going to want to take an active role in high-profile cases like these. I know that's not what y'all are used to, but I will say this. Unless I see you getting way off track, I won't interfere. Is that going to be a problem?"

"No." I thought of Lieutenant Johnson and his hands-off approach. I hoped I wouldn't look back on those as the good ol' days.

"I think this is the beginning of great working partnership," Phil said and clapped me on the shoulder. If I'd hit a prisoner that hard, I'd have been written up.

"Looking forward to it," I said, carefully sliding far enough away that he couldn't hit me again.

CHAPTER EIGHTEEN

Pete and the coroner's van showed up about the same time. The sky in the east was just turning pink as they drove up. Linda and one of her interns headed straight inside the store to take a look at the body.

"How's the diet going?" I asked Pete as he got out of his car.

"Grrrrrr."

"That good?"

"Why do you think I'm up at this hour? My stomach is empty. I can't even sleep." There wasn't an ounce of humor in his voice.

"You'll survive and be the better for it," I said cheerily. He pulled his fist back and I held up my hands. "Sorry."

I had to explain to Pete why I had taken over from Julio.

"Seems unlikely," he said about the possibility of the cases being linked. "Why kill one person and transport the body while, with the other one, you just bludgeon the person to death in front of cameras? Not that other killers haven't changed their MOs, but…"

"I know something seems hinky. If we try to make sense of it, we'll need to explain the change in methods."

"Usually a killer changes MO so that no one will link the

cases. That doesn't make much sense with these if they involve the emails."

"If there *are* emails," I admitted. "If Bear is wrong, then this may not be related to Calavera at all."

"I think that's what you should be hoping for. If this is just your ordinary run-of-the-mill killing, then you can look at the standard motives. Did someone have a grudge against the clerk? Or the store? Was the clerk stepping out with someone else's significant other? Did he date the wrong person's sister?"

"Those are easier leads to follow up on than some mysterious emailer's accusations." I nodded, having thought the same thing after looking at the body.

"Man, that guy is a mess," Linda said, heading back to the van.

"I warned you."

"I need extra bags and swabs for the material not attached to the body. We should charge you all extra," she said good-naturedly. I'd never seen anyone who was as content as she was to pick up body parts.

"You want to go over to the victim's house with me?" I asked Pete, who nodded.

We left Shantel in charge of the crime scene and headed over to the address that the owner had given to Julio.

Nicolaus Andreas was renting a house only two blocks from where Calavera's car had been found. Not surprising as it was an affordable, if not great or even safe, neighborhood. Though the two blocks made an improvement—less drugs and a little less crime.

"Wasn't Calavera's car abandoned near here?" Pete asked as we got out of our cars.

"Yep. Is that another connection or just a coincidence?" I shrugged in response to my own question.

Nicolaus's house was a rundown craftsman-style home that had the look of an off-campus fraternity house. There was an old Toyota and an elderly, beat-up Ford Ranger parked in the driveway. Scattered in groups around the yard were several old lawn chairs. The yard itself didn't look like it had been mowed since last summer.

"Nice place." Pete shook his head and nudged an empty beer can off of the walkway that led up to the porch.

The wooden steps of the porch looked iffy, with rotted wood and peeling paint. I felt better once we'd reached the porch where the wood looked more substantial.

"I hope he wasn't paying much for this," I muttered.

I knocked on the door. Bakshi had told us that Nicolaus had roommates and I presumed the car and the truck belonged to them. After another minute of knocking, I was about ready to give up and get the landlord to come unlock the door.

"Guess no one's home," Pete said, but as soon as the words left his mouth, we heard the sound of heavy footsteps. "Never mind."

"What?" came an irritated voice from the other side of the door.

"Sheriff's office."

"Go ahead and use your new title," Pete whispered to me and nudged my arm. I gave him a dirty look.

"We didn't do anything," the voice behind the door complained.

"Open the door. We need to talk with you. No one's in trouble," I told him.

"Yeah, Sergeant Macklin wants to talk to you." Pete smiled and I gave him a stern look.

I was about to remind Pete that technically this was a death notification when the door opened and a man in his late twenties stood in front of us, shirtless, wearing only a pair of boxer shorts and looking like he was participating in a Chris Farley lookalike contest.

"You got ID or something?" he said, rubbing his hand over his face in an apparent attempt to focus.

Pete and I showed him our stars and IDs in unison. Blurry-eyed, the young man looked at them and nodded.

"If I let you in, can you search the place?" he asked.

"Friend, that's not a very smart question," Pete informed him.

"You can step out on the porch if you want," I said.

"Maybe I should," he said and slid out the door, closing it behind him.

"You can keep us out for now, but we're going to get in," Pete said to himself, but loud enough that we could all hear. A hungry Pete wasn't a very kind Pete, even though he was right. We were going to search Nicolaus's room and the public areas of the house with or without permission. The only question was if we were going to have to wait for a warrant.

"What's your name?" I asked.

"Carl."

"Last name?"

"Loggins."

"Do you live here?"

"I rent one of the rooms."

"How long have you lived here?"

"Eight months."

"Do you know Nicolaus Andreas?"

"Yeah, he's kind of my landlord. I mean, he rents the house and we… What do you call it…?"

"Sublet," Pete said.

"Yeah, right, sublet from him."

"How many people live here?"

"Me, Nicolaus, Twila and Barry. What's this all about?" He was visibly shaking from the cold.

"I'm sorry to inform you that Nicolaus is dead," I said without anywhere near the finesse I would normally use with family members.

"Dead?" he said as though he didn't understand what the word meant.

"We need to ask you a few questions. We're also going to have to search the public areas of the house and his room."

"Oh, shit," he muttered. "Look… crap." I thought he was going to cry—not out of grief, but out of self-pity for his bad luck.

"We aren't trying to nail anyone on drug charges," I told him.

He looked at me like he was shocked that I knew why he didn't want the house searched. "Do I need to call, like, a lawyer or something?"

I was always amazed when suspects asked cops for legal advice. I guess I should have been grateful that they thought we were nice folks who would help them get out of trouble. Usually the very same trouble we were working hard to land them in.

"Not yet. We are just here investigating Nicolaus's death."

"How'd he die?"

"We're still trying to figure it out," I said, sidestepping the question.

"I'm freezing," Carl said. "I guess we can go inside."

Pete and I followed him into the house. There was the smell of stale beer, weed and pizza that reinforced my first impression of a frat house.

From the hall I could see into the living room and the dining room. The living room had trashed, overstuffed furniture and a scarred coffee table

"I'm going to put on some pants," Carl said, turning toward the stairs.

"Pete will walk up with you," I told him and Pete glared at me.

"I don't need help."

"We just want to make sure that you go to your room and don't touch anything that's out in the common area."

"Where else would I go to get my clothes? Duh," he said, which left me with a desire to kick his butt all the way up the stairs.

Pete stomped up after him. I took the opportunity to walk around the living room. I didn't see anything that changed the frat house narrative. There were disc golf bags in a corner by the window. A 72-inch TV with a confusing jumble of game consoles and controls draped around it took up one wall of the living room. The drugs and drug paraphernalia appeared to be limited to bongs and pot. I saw no signs of white powder, syringes, burned spoons or pipes.

The stomping on the stairs signaled the return of Carl Loggins, Pete and, following behind them, a young woman who would have fit in well with my hippie in-laws. She was tall, with long, straight black hair that draped gracefully over a series of rambling tattoos covering everything from pop culture, botany and zoology to myths, legends and gothic literature.

"This is Twila." Carl pointed over his shoulder at the woman. "She lives here too."

"He shouldn't have let you in without a warrant," she said.

"We would have gotten one. Did he tell you that your landlord died?" I tried not to be as confrontational as she apparently wanted to be.

"How did he die?" Twila frowned at me. I couldn't tell if she was holding back her emotions or if she didn't really have any where Nicolaus was concerned.

"It doesn't appear to be an accident." I didn't think I was going to get away with being coy much longer.

"He was killed?"

"I appreciate your passion for information, but I'm here to search the house and ask questions, not answer them," I told her, trying to maintain my open expression and positive body language. Pete was standing behind her, making frowny faces at me.

"I'm a lawyer—well, almost a lawyer. I'm taking the bar exam this spring."

"Congratulations. But we aren't required to give special consideration to almost-lawyers." I took a deep breath and decided to try some honey. "As you know, we can't search your private spaces. But, like a vampire, we've been invited in by one of the people who live here. I can go to the trouble to get a search warrant, but that would waste everyone's time. I'm sorry I can't go into detail about what happened to Nicolaus. Let's just say that we know it involves a person who, for the safety of the community, needs to be apprehended as quickly as possible. Looking through Nicolaus's possessions can aide us in that."

"No one here hurt Nicolaus," Twila said.

"Fine. The sooner we can be satisfied that's the case, then the quicker we can move on. You do understand that we need to look at those closest to him first, and then move outward?"

"Yes," she snapped.

"Besides, there might be clues among Nicolaus's possessions that point toward someone else who would want to hurt him."

"He didn't have any enemies," Carl grumbled.

"That might be true. Let's work together and see if we can prove that." I was about done pussyfooting around these two.

"Whatever, man," Carl said.

Twila looked like I had posed some ancient conundrum. "Okay," was her Final Jeopardy answer.

"We'll talk to you both separately," I told them.

"Where can we talk?" Pete asked Carl, not waiting for me to suggest which of us should talk to whom. They headed for the kitchen.

"We can talk in here," I told Twila, motioning toward the living room.

"The drugs aren't mine," she said.

"I don't know what type of law you've studied, but if they're in the common areas of the house, they may as well be yours where the law is concerned."

She pursed her lips and crossed her arms over her chest. I didn't point out to her that an arrest for drug possession wouldn't help her become a lawyer in the State of Florida. I could see that she was beginning to feel the rock pressing her into the hard place.

"I'll tell you everything I can about Nicolaus," Twila said

begrudgingly. She cleared a spot on the couch and sat down. I reluctantly eased myself onto a ragged chair that looked like it had been picked up from the side of the road.

"How'd you end up here?"

"A referral from a friend of a friend. A guy at law school knew Nicolaus and told me he was a good guy and was looking for roommates."

"This is a long way from campus."

"I was about to graduate and wanted to detox from academia and study for the bar. Seemed like moving out of Tallahassee would help. I wouldn't have rented it if I hadn't found a job over here." She saw my next question in my expression and followed through. "I got a job as a clerk for Mr. Riley."

I'd had a moment when I thought she might say she worked for Calavera. That would have been a nice connection. Will Riley was a local lawyer who specialized in real estate.

"Why aren't you working today?"

"I've taken some time off to study for the bar. My test is two months from now."

"Tell me what you know about Nicolaus."

Twila gave a little shrug. "He's one of the nice guys. Maybe a little too nice. I think the guys in the house take advantage of him. He was working on his MBA but... derailed, I guess."

"What derailed him?"

"Laziness. He didn't seem to have any ambition. Got so he liked working at the store, which gave him enough money to live on. Well, almost. He'd come home and play video games or make videos. He had a little side hustle with YouTube and some social media crap. I think he made enough from that to feed his habit." She saw the look on my face. "His gamer habit. Nicolaus wasn't an addict or anything. He would smoke with the guys, but if they got too wasted he'd just go upstairs and do his thing."

"What about relationships?"

"He was funny about that. I never saw him hang out with anyone. I don't know what he did to get his rocks off, but whatever it was, he didn't advertise it. That's what made it easy for me to stay here. I never got the feeling he was going to start hitting on me. I've had to slap Carl down once or twice, but that's different. He isn't my landlord."

"What about enemies?"

"Nah, nothing like that. He just didn't get emotional, so people didn't get emotional with him, if you know what I mean."

"What about the other roommates? Anyone have any issues with him? Late payments?"

"Oh, a little of that. We had to kick a guy out two months ago 'cause he wasn't paying his share of the electric bill and he was, like, three months behind on the rent. I actually helped Nicolaus with the eviction paperwork."

I wondered how that worked. Was Nicolaus allowed to sublet? I didn't see any point in diving into the legal technicalities.

"What was this guy's name?"

"They called him Putter, 'cause he thought he was going to be a great golfer someday and would spend half the day in the backyard putting a ball around. His real name is Levi Nash. I never liked him."

"Was he angry about being evicted?"

"Pissed, I'd say. Got snarly with me when he found out I'd helped Nicolaus draw up the papers. No love lost there."

"What didn't you like about him?"

She cocked her head to one side and pursed her lips for a minute. "Arrogant. That was part of it. Not that most of these guys don't think they're God's gift. There was just an extra air of privilege about him. Funny, 'cause he was living in this dump with the rest of us and couldn't even pay the rent."

"Did he work?"

"Got a check from his family every month. Said it was some sort of inheritance from his rich uncle, who died when

Nash was a kid. I guess he was more likable then. Like I said, he thought he was going to be a golf pro, but they kicked him off of every course around here 'cause of his big mouth. Nicolaus told me that Nash was always going around telling other golfers what they were doing wrong."

"Where's Nash now?" He seemed like a stretch unless we found out that the weapon used was a golf club.

Twila shrugged. "Haven't seen him since he moved out."

"Did Nicolaus say anything about Nash coming back at him?"

"No. I think Nash was used to wearing out his welcome. Seemed to be a habit of his. Go in, piss everyone off and move on."

"Was there anyone else that Nicolaus ever complained about? Think back to when you first moved in." I was grasping at straws.

To my surprise, she leaned forward. "There was a guy. Crazy Guy, Nicolaus called him. I'd just moved in and Nicolaus came home from work a couple of times complaining that a guy at the store was bothering him."

"Bothering him how?"

Twila leaned back and shook her head. "Don't remember much else. I was just getting settled in and had just met Nicolaus so…" She frowned. "I wasn't paying that much attention. At the time, I didn't know if it was unusual for him to complain about people in the store, so I just nodded and didn't think too much of it. Lucky I remember it at all."

"This would have been?"

"About a year ago. I moved in the first of March. So right around then."

"No description of the man or a name?"

She shook her head.

"There's you and Carl. How many roommates are there?"

"Just one more. An older guy, well, older than me. Barry Greco. He works at the nursery; I don't remember the name. He and Nicolaus got along well. He might have been Nicolaus's best friend." She grimaced. "I hadn't thought about him. He might be pretty cut up over Nicolaus's death."

"Why aren't you?" Her demeanor when talking about Nicolaus grated on me.

"What?"

"More upset."

She shrugged. "I don't know. I've never been upset about people dying. I got it in my head when I was a kid that it's just something that happens. It's like being upset that the sun comes up or goes down. People die. Animals die. I always wondered why people made a big deal about it."

I stared at her, trying to decide if she was kidding or not. I decided she was serious.

"I need to remember you," I told her. "There are a number of murder cases that get off on the wrong foot because a family member doesn't grieve the way the investigator thinks they should. You're a good reminder that people think differently and their emotional responses reflect that."

"I think Barry will be upset. He's an emotional guy. I've seen him upset over a football game."

"When does he get off work?"

"Five-thirty. He usually gets home by six."

"Where were you last night after midnight?"

"The classic murder investigation question. I studied until two o'clock and then went to sleep. I was in bed until I heard you knock on the door."

"What about everyone else?"

"I wouldn't know. I heard noise until one o'clock. There was the sound of a video game, laughter and some music. I don't know if it was from the game or something else. I couldn't tell you who was here or wasn't here."

We talked for a few more minutes and, just as I was standing up, Pete came back with Carl walking a couple of feet behind him. When I caught Pete's eyes, he shook his head and looked up at the ceiling.

"We're going to look around the house. Would either of

you give us permission to look through your rooms?"

Both of them shook their heads no.

"Okay. You can go about your business," I told them. Twila headed for the kitchen.

"I'll be in my room," Carl said and slouched off.

"Where's Nicolaus' room?" I asked him before he got to the stairs.

He pointed to a closed door off of the living room.

CHAPTER NINETEEN

"Interviewing Carl cost me a chunk of brain cells," Pete told me as we started to pick at things around the living room.

Twenty minutes later, I was satisfied we weren't going to learn anything there. What I really wanted was to look through Nicolaus's room, so I went over to the door which I found to be locked. It was an old-fashioned door with the keyhole below the knob.

"Not a problem," Pete said. He walked over to some fast food trash on the coffee table and dug out a sturdy plastic fork. He wiped it off on the couch, then came back over to the door. After breaking off a couple of tines, he took a lighter that he'd picked up from beside a bong and gently heated the fork, bending it into the shape that he wanted.

Pete stuck the fork into the keyhole and started fiddling it around. After a minute or two, I heard a click. He smiled and opened the door.

"Good trick, Houdini," I told him.

"My grandmother would lock us in our rooms when she babysat." Pete smiled. "I learned to let myself out."

Nicolaus's room was cleaner than the rest of the house. Still, there were clothes on the floor, the bed wasn't made and various electronic devices were strewn around the room.

There were a couple of laptops with a layer of dust on them, two phones and an assortment of gameplayer accessories. Nothing looked new. On a bookshelf that took up most of the interior wall were textbooks and fantasy novels. A poster of John and Dean Winchester was tacked up over the bed. With my latex gloves on, I fingered through some change and assorted pocket flotsam and jetsam on the chest of drawers. Next I started opening the drawers while Pete opened the closet.

An hour later, we were no closer to knowing who would want to kill Nicolaus, though I did feel like I had an idea of what kind of person he'd been. There was a childlike quality to his possessions. I wondered why he hadn't grown up, though it seemed a lot more common these days. At least he wasn't living in his parents' basement.

"He'll never grow up now," Pete said, causing me to give him a sideways glance.

"You're reading my mind." I gave him a little smile. "Kind of sad. I've known a few guys who didn't find their way until they were over thirty."

"I think you can include yourself."

"I can't argue with you. Women mature at eighteen, men at thirty."

"I'll go out and get some evidence bags for the phones and laptops." Pete headed for the door.

I took another look around the room. We'd felt under the mattress and looked under the bed. We'd moved pieces of furniture to look behind them. I went into the closet and checked the walls with my flashlight. Looking at the closet floor, I saw a few chips of paint along the side wall. Getting down on my hands and knees, I could see some pry marks in one corner. I took out my keys and was able to get one of them behind the baseboard. With a little leverage on the key, the baseboard came away from the wall.

There were three fist-size bags of what looked like pot hidden in there. They were sitting on a folded newspaper that I figured was there to keep the bags off the floor.

"He had a little side gig," I told Pete when he came back.

"Three bags? With these guys, that might just be him buying in bulk."

"Yeah, you could be right. The space isn't big enough to hide much. Still, another thing we have to consider."

We bagged everything up, including the pot.

"Did you take care of Valentine's Day?" Pete asked as we carried the stuff out of the house under the watchful eye of Twila.

"Made reservations for a weekend getaway to St. Augustine," I said smugly.

"All done through the internet?" Pete asked.

"How else?"

"Sarah rates her presents by how much effort I had to put into acquiring them. Quest for the Holy Grail is the top level. If I don't put in as much effort as the Knights of the Round Table, then I'm not showing her the highest level of love. I usually go for the Lewis and Clark level, which involves several trips to Tallahassee and three or four stores."

"Cara gives less weight to the effort and more to the romantic nature of the gift."

"In that case, you might be okay." He opened the trunk of my car so we could put the bagged items inside it.

"What did you get Sarah?"

"She wanted some earrings that matched a bracelet I got her two years ago for Christmas. Two years ago. I had to get the store to check with their supplier and they had to special order them. Three trips into Tallahassee. She was punishing me for being too cheap to buy the earrings when I bought the bracelet. Not being a total idiot, I had them order the matching necklace so—*voila!*—Sarah's birthday in May is also taken care of. Though I'll have to pretend I had to hunt as hard for the necklace as I did the earrings."

"Isn't that lying?" I asked and got a hard look from Pete.

"This is love, buddy. You've heard of guerrilla warfare. This is guerilla lovefare."

"You're stretching the English language to the breaking point."

We went back into the house and looked through the rest of the public areas. I decided to save any questions about Nicolaus's stash for later. I still wanted to notify the third roommate and interview him.

I sent Pete back to the crime scene as I headed to the nursery to talk to Barry Greco. A body had been found in one of their mulch piles almost a year ago. I wondered if I'd met him while I was working the case. The name didn't ring any bells.

The woman working the front counter directed me to a back corner of the nursery, where two men were offloading camellias from a truck.

"If you're looking for a special type of camellia, we'll have them all unloaded in about half an hour," said a husky man with a beard and wearing overalls as he set down the four plants he was carrying.

"I'm looking for Barry Greco." I moved my coat aside so he could see my star. The look on his face told me he was guilty of a crime or had been in the past. His eyes looked around, searching for an exit, while his brain computed the various risks and benefits of fight, flight or surrender. My muscles tensed in anticipation of his choice. Then his shoulders sagged.

"Look, I didn't do anything," he said in a harsh whisper that belied his words.

"You obviously did, but it probably doesn't have anything to do with why I'm here," I told him. His eyes gave me a half-suspicious, half-pleading look. "You know Nicolaus Andreas?"

"Sure, we're friends." His face was an ever-changing weather gauge of his emotions. Fear was now on display.

"I'm sorry to have to tell you, but he's dead."

After what Twila had told me, I'd expected a reaction. What I didn't expect was to see him faint. I just managed to break his fall and keep his head from hitting an ornamental stone pot.

Barry's co-worker, who'd continued unloading the truck until he saw Barry go down like a felled ox, came rushing over with a bottle of water.

"He's okay," I said after I took Barry's pulse, which was smooth and regular. The co-worker was speaking very fast in a language that wasn't the one I knew.

A little water on Barry's forehead had him moaning and coming out of his faint. No sooner was he aware of his surroundings than he began to cry.

I knew that men do, should and will cry. I've cried. But I always found it awkward to comfort someone who had a beard and outweighed me by fifty pounds.

"I'm sorry I had to bring you this awful news," I said while I patted him on the shoulder.

When he finally managed to sit up, he reached back and got a handkerchief from his back pocket. It was a relief to see him wipe the snot and tears from his beard.

"I… really… Nicolaus was a great guy." He sniffled.

"Can I help you up?"

"Yeah, sorry, man. Just… I don't understand what happened. Did someone rob the store?" he said as I helped him up and over to the truck, where he sat down on the bumper. There were still about fifty plants to be taken off the truck. The other worker was standing to the side, looking confused.

"We're still investigating the death," I said, giving my standard answer. "Any information that you can give me would be helpful."

"I'll tell you anything I know." Then he slammed his fist down on the truck. Hard. My hand hurt just watching him do it. "I just can't believe this."

"Can you tell me about the last time you saw Nicolaus?"

"Last night. Just before he went in to work. I hated him working the eleven-to-seven shift." He continued to cry softly and occasionally pound his first. Most spouses I'd notified hadn't been this emotionally demonstrative over the death of their loved ones.

"Were you and Nicolaus more than friends?" I asked as gently as I could, as much to stem the tide of tears as to spare his feelings.

"No… yes… no. I don't think he felt that way about me," he said with a few more tears.

If I'd thought this great blubbering walrus was capable of it, I'd have added rejected advances to the list of motives for the murder. Looking at his size, I was sure that the surveillance cameras would be able to rule him in or out quickly. A hoodie can only hide so much.

"Exactly what time did you last see him?" I pressed, even though I knew it would bring up more tears.

"Ten-thirty. I drove him to work."

"How was he going to get home?"

"His bike. We put it in the back of my pickup and then in the morning he rode it home. I didn't like him riding his bike in the dark. Especially around there."

I had to agree with Barry. Late-night bike riding wouldn't be advised through some of the neighborhoods between their house and the store. It would barely be safe enough at seven-thirty in the morning when he got off work.

"Was he worried about anything?"

"Like what?"

"Anything." I wasn't sure how to make it any clearer.

"Money. We're always scrambling to pay the bills. He collected the money from everyone and then paid for the electricity, water, cable and rent."

"Any special concerns this month? Anyone not anteing up?"

"He always had to press Carl. But no worse than usual."

"Had he talked about anyone who was mad at him in the last couple of days or weeks?" This question earned me hard look from Barry. "Did someone purposefully kill Nicolaus?"

"I told you, we're still working it out."

I guess I didn't sound very convincing, because he came back at me with: "You're lying! Someone killed him." The tears were gone now, replaced with a fierce grumble.

This guy gives a whole new meaning to volatile, I thought.

"I know you're hurting, but I can't tell you anything at this point. Some of the information I have to hold back, but mostly I just don't have any answers. You have to help me find those answers by telling me everything you know about Nicolaus and anyone that had a grudge against him or who may have been stalking him."

Barry was taking short, quick breaths. I had him take a moment to inhale and exhale slowly. After more water, he looked less like he was going to keel over.

"Everybody liked Nick." Barry stared down at his feet.

"How did you meet him?" I decided to go over their history together in the hopes of jogging his memory. I knew I was risking another breakdown.

"I met him at college. My degree is in agriculture from Florida A&M, but four years ago I wanted to take some business classes. My plan is to save up enough money to open my own nursery. Nick was the assistant teaching the business fundamentals class I took. We got to talking."

"Why did Nick drop out of school?"

"Bored, I think. He told me he was sick of dealing with all the spoiled brats and the self-righteous professors. He came over here and liked the small-town feel. When I told him that the owner of the house I was living in was going to sell it and I had to move, he found the house we're living in now."

"Is there anyone who he rented a room to or met at the store that maybe threatened him or seemed a little off?"

"There were always people at the store who were stealing and causing trouble. Nick just shrugged it off. Maybe the owner of the store would know something. Hey! You could look at the security cameras."

"We're doing that. I'm interested in what you know about Nick."

"I do remember one time, I guess a year ago, maybe longer, that Nick said some guy came into the store and accused him of something. Pissed Nick off 'cause he didn't do anything and the guy came around a couple of times."

"What did he accuse him of?"

"Don't know. Nick didn't say or I don't remember." He looked up and sighed.

"Did Nick have any… significant others?" I asked as delicately as I could.

"No. I think he just didn't care about those kinds of relationships." Barry gave me a sad look. "I'm not just saying that 'cause he didn't think of me that way. I never saw him flirt or act like he was interested in sex. We never talked about it, but I got to thinking he was asexual."

"Last night, was he acting odd in any way?"

Barry looked thoughtful. "I'd had a few beers, so I wasn't paying a lot of attention. Still, I don't think he was any different."

"More talkative? Less talkative? Moody?"

He shrugged.

"You drove him to work." I thought about the beers, but decided to let it go. "What did you all talk about?"

"Not much. Just listened to Corb Lund, my music. That was our deal. We took turns who got to play their music each night. Oh, yeah, and he gave me twenty bucks. Said he was going to get paid, so he gave me the twenty for gas. That was another part of our deal. I took care of the truck and gave him rides, or let him borrow it when he needed to, then when he got paid he gave me a twenty. Sometimes he filled the tank up too." More sniffles, and I knew we were headed toward tears again. "Nick was just a nice guy."

I patted him on the shoulder. "Thank you. I know it's been difficult getting this news and then talking about him. Now what I need you to do is this: think hard. If there is anyone that he ever butted heads with, I want you to call me." I pulled out one of my cards and handed it to him.

He nodded, then tucked the card into his shirt and climbed back on the truck to start unloading plants again.

When I left the nursery I checked my phone, which I'd

switched to silent when we started interviewing witnesses. There was a message from Cara reminding me to pick up our clothes from the drycleaners. She also laid out our itinerary for tonight and tomorrow. We were supposed to have dinner with Dad, Genie and some of the other members of the wedding party tonight at the Palmetto. It wasn't a formal rehearsal dinner, but it wasn't optional either. In fact, it had been my idea way back before I knew I was going to be in the middle of a murder investigation.

I drove back to the store, where they were finishing up. The body was gone and Shantel and Marcus were packing up their equipment.

"Pete went on another call," Shantel told me as I helped her put boxes in the back of their van.

"I'm going to take one more walk through," I told her.

Marcus passed me as I headed to the front door, looking around for any evidence that we might have missed. I didn't want to let the crime scene go so quickly, but there wasn't much choice. The odds were that, if we found a reason to come back, it would be days or weeks down the line. We couldn't ask Mr. Bakshi to keep his store closed for a month. As it was, he'd have to get a professional cleaning crew to come in and remove all the biomass. Most of the items behind the counter would have to be scrapped because of blood or other matter flung up from the blows of the blunt object.

I turned when I heard the front door open. "Forgot to tell you, Bakshi's nephew came by and made a copy of the surveillance footage," Shantel said.

"And you're just now telling me?" I was a little annoyed.

"I looked at it. You can believe me when I say there's no hurry in reviewing it. I wouldn't recognize my own mother with the hoodie, gloves and stocking mask the guy was wearing. I say *guy*, but it could have been a woman from what you can see."

"Figures." I should have known that if it'd been a hot lead, Shantel would have called me.

When I pulled away from the store, I headed for the drycleaners, then went two blocks down to the library to talk to Eddie Thompson. All the while I was looking at my watch, trying to balance the time. I needed to either not have a professional life or not have a personal life, because I didn't have time for both.

There were about two dozen cars in the library parking lot, and a young man was holding the front door for an elderly man whose arms were full of books. *Maybe I could get a job at the library*, I thought. *It's one of the last bastions of civilized behavior.* Maybe that's why my ex-confidential informant was doing so well after getting sober. What better place to stay clean than the library?

"I don't like the looks of this," Eddie said as I walked up to the front desk.

"What? I can't come see an old friend?"

"Now you sound like a 1930s gangster." He was sorting books as we talked.

"Can we go somewhere to talk?"

"See, I knew I wasn't going to like this. If you just wanted to be chatty, there's tomorrow."

"You got an invitation to the wedding?" I said in mock surprise. Cara had told me they planned to invite him.

"Yep, and my plus one is Jessie." He gave me a big smile.

"Glad to hear it. I need a favor," I told him.

He stood up. "I knew it."

After Eddie asked a woman who was restocking books to take his place at the front desk, he led me to a small meeting room.

"Go ahead, hit me." He dropped down in a chair and looked prepared for an actual punch.

"You know Bear?"

"Smelly Bear? 'Cause that's what we call him."

"I think we can assume we're talking about the same man. He was a witness to a murder. I need you to... be his friend."

"What the hell does that mean?"

"I can't keep him in jail, which is where I put him this morning, but I want to keep him reasonably sober and safe."

"So…" Eddie said.

"I want you to put him up at your apartment."

"No way! That drunk? You remember that I have a little problem with substance abuse, right?" He was sitting bolt upright in the chair, looking at me with a no-way-that's-going-to-happen expression.

"You could be his…What do you call it? Sponsor. Take him to an AA meeting," I suggested, even though I knew it was a ridiculous idea.

"No, no, no. And I've got lots of reasons. One of them is that I've got a quasi-date with Jessie tomorrow."

"I'll make it worth your while."

"I'm not going to let you buy me."

"Come on," I cajoled. "For an old friend."

"Old exploiter," he shot back.

"Civic duty, then."

Eddie gave me a petulant look. "I've got my own life to think about. Bear is… disgusting."

I sat down in a chair so we were eye to eye.

"I need your help. Bear saw a murder over at the Fast Mart this morning and, as bad of a witness as he is, he's my only one."

"I heard something went down at the Fast Mart. One guy said it was just a robbery."

"On the QT?" I asked him.

"You know I can keep my mouth shut." And Eddie was right. For all his faults, being a blabbermouth was not one of them.

"Someone entered the store and bludgeoned the clerk, Nicolaus Andreas, to death."

Eddie reacted before I'd even finished speaking. He looked stunned and leaned back in his chair, mouth hanging open.

"Nicky? Are you sure?"

"You knew him?" Which was a stupid question. Eddie had hung out around the store quite a bit when he was using.

"Damn. Nicky was one of the few guys who would help me out when I was messed up. I talked to him a couple of weeks ago. Wow."

"Bear was in the store when it happened."

"Damn." Eddie cupped his face in his hands. "Like, three years ago, I passed out behind the store in January. Nicky got me up and carried me inside so I didn't freeze to death. No joke. I thought about that when I got sober. I could have died that night. Just gone to sleep and never come back. Before I met you, I think that was one of the nicest things anyone had ever done for me."

"So will you take Bear back to your place and look after him?"

"One condition."

"What's that?"

"He gets a shower at the jail and some clean clothes," Eddie said reasonably.

"We can work with that," I said and smiled.

CHAPTER TWENTY

Back at the office, I headed down to see Lionel with the hope that I'd be able to get a look at the security camera footage. I trusted Shantel's judgment, but I still wanted to see it for myself. The more eyes on it, the better.

"You just missed him," Marcus told me, pointing back down the hall. "He said he was heading to our new lieutenant's office."

I went back that direction and found Lionel talking to Phil, who was moving furniture around.

"I'm going to keep the desk there," Phil told Lionel, who was holding a box with a desktop and monitor. "Are you sure you can't just figure a way for me to dock my laptop instead of having a whole new setup?"

"Major Parks said you'd need at least two monitors."

"Great," Phil said with a scowl. He smiled when he saw me. "What can I do for you?"

"I wanted to talk to Lionel about the security footage from the murder this morning."

"Just put the box down on my desk. You can hook it up later," he told Lionel. "Before you go, Larry, brief me on where we are with the murder. I got a call from two of the TV stations in Tallahassee and they were asking questions about the emails. They've gotten wind of them somehow."

"What did you tell them?"

"That we're looking into them. When one of them pushed, I told him I'd get back with him on Monday. So we need to come up with a plan to deal with the media on it. It's not like we haven't been soliciting people to come forward with information anyway."

"We can give them some tidbits. I don't want to let them know there could be a link to the murders."

"Agreed. *Is* there a link?"

"That's one of the things I'm hoping to find out from Lionel."

Lionel set the box down. "I did find an email on Nicolaus's phone. We're lucky that his phone didn't have a passcode and he'd left his email open."

"What about the security footage?"

"It's good for what it is. The problem is that the killer was prepared for the cameras. You can't make out much. Average height, most likely male. I'd say Caucasian, but he could be light-skinned or Hispanic."

"I'll let you know what's going on as soon as we learn anything new," I told Phil. It was going to be different having a supervisor who took an active interest in my cases. Of course, on the other side of the coin, there were going to be cases where I was the supervisor and not the primary. How was I going to handle that? *Not a clue*, I answered myself.

Back at Lionel's office, he pulled everything up on his monitors.

"Here's the email I think you're looking for." Lionel had it on the monitor at the center of his array. "I transferred everything from his phone."

I leaned forward and read the email aloud. "You deserve what you get. Killing a woman is evil."

"Who'd he kill?" Lionel asked.

"I don't know." This seemed out of left field. Was it a mistake? Almost twenty percent of the emails' accusations seemed to go wide of their mark. Just from the little bit I'd learned about him, Nicolaus seemed an unlikely killer.

"Sorry I couldn't give you a smoking gun," Lionel said. "Here's the security footage." He made a few rapid clicks and an image of the interior of the Fast Mart appeared. "There were two cameras, but this is the best angle. I'll show you both."

I could see Nicolaus working at the counter. A minute into the footage, Bear stumbled through the front door. Nicolaus looked up and Bear gave him a big wave. They talked for a bit, then Bear picked out his items and set them on the counter. More talk, then Bear headed for the bathroom and Nicolaus pushed the items to the side.

"Your killer is coming up," Lionel said. "Let me know if you want to see it at half speed."

"Let it play through the first time, then half speed."

The door opened and a person in a hoodie came in, holding their head down. They had gloves on and opened the door in one smooth move with their right hand. Down at their side, they were holding what looked like a pipe in their left hand. Their approach to the counter was an easy swagger, with maybe a little stiffness as though their muscles were tense.

"The clerk doesn't seem to notice the weapon." Lionel was leaning back, watching the footage with a look of concentration on his face.

"It was chilly last night, so the hoodie and heavy clothes wouldn't raise any red flags."

"Hell, in that neighborhood people dress like that in the middle of summer. Got to hide what you're selling."

"You have a point."

"There, that's the first reaction." Lionel had stopped the video. He pointed to Nicolaus, who had tensed up as he looked at the approaching figure.

"He's wearing pantyhose over his face." I'd seen enough CCTV with a bad guy wearing pantyhose to recognize the look.

"These days, I swear I see more bad guys wearing pantyhose than women," Lionel agreed.

"Question is, is he wearing the pantyhose to disguise himself from Nicolaus or the cameras?"

Lionel clicked the *play* icon. The killer increased speed as Nicolaus reacted. Within a second or two, the attacker had landed the first blow that sent Nicolaus to the ground.

"He came in there to kill Nicolaus," I stated. "Which means the disguise is for our benefit."

We continued to watch as the killer made his way around the counter and bludgeoned Nicolaus to death.

"Man or woman?" I asked Lionel.

He hemmed and hawed while staring at the monitor. "Can't tell. First time I saw it, I was sure it was a man. After watching it a couple more times, I'm not so sure. If it's a man, he's not very large. Certainly could be an athletic female. A woman with some muscle."

"I'm leaning toward male, but I can't be sure with all those clothes," I said, watching as the killer made their way back to the front door. There was one slight hesitation at the very moment when we could see movement at the bottom edge of the image. The killer might have heard Bear come out of the bathroom. If they did, they ignored the sound and exited out the front door. Once the attacker was outside the store, I could just tell that they went to the left. That might at least tell me where they parked their car or in which direction their home was.

I watched the footage two more times.

"Make me a copy and put it in the shared folder," I told Lionel. I wanted to be able to review it some more. "I had a revelation about the emails. All of them were sent to email addresses where the person's name was part of the email. As though they got a list and didn't know the recipient if the person's name wasn't imbedded in the address."

"Not the clerk's email," Lionel said, shooting down my balloon.

"What?"

"See." He showed me Nicolaus's email address. I hadn't thought to check it.

Sure enough, his address was a character I vaguely recognized from a game and the number 4769. No hint of his name. Had I checked Eva's? I wasn't sure. The list I'd been looking at was from Pete and I'm not sure he'd added Eva's email.

"Do you have Eva Calavera's email?"

Lionel pulled it up. Her email address started with equineprincess.

"But you're right about the rest," Lionel said, scanning the list.

"If Eva's and Nicolaus's don't fit the pattern, then maybe the emailer and the killer aren't the same person. Or the killer wanted to target Eva and Nicolaus, but needed to muddy the waters with a bunch of bogus emails."

"Why send the emails in the first place?" Lionel asked.

"Good question. There are a lot easier ways to mislead an investigation."

"By sending all these emails, the killer is giving us more chances to catch him." Lionel frowned. "If I can get on his electronic trail."

"I like the idea that they aren't the same person. The email threats are circulating out there and the killer decides to take advantage of them."

"Makes more sense if they aren't the same person. The emails just seem to be a kind of internet troll spreading venom around town. The murderer is focused. You saw the video."

"If they can be two people, then why not three? An emailer, Eva's killer and Nicolaus's murderer. The MO of the two murders is very different," I said, hating myself for suggesting that there might be a *third* person we were looking for.

"Above my pay grade," Lionel said. "The emails are too short to get an idea of the syntax. Get me some long samples and I could run them through a program that can compare them."

I stood up. "I've got a feeling that footwork is how these murders are going to be solved."

I glanced at my watch and walked a little faster than normal to my desk. I had a dozen things I needed to take care of before I left.

When I opened my emails, there was one from our human resources department asking me to call and schedule a tutorial on the software that the department used to keep records on employees. I'd have to use it to enter evaluations, reprimands and referrals for the deputies under me. The thought of spending half a day learning about a stupid software system made me want to pull my hair out. *I'll call them on Monday*, I told myself and closed the email. I scrambled to transfer my notes from that morning to a crime scene report, ending up with more of an outline than a full report. Then I returned a few calls and emails on other cases that couldn't wait until Monday.

On my way out the door, I ran into Deputy Sanderson.

"I've got hours of footage from the cameras around the Fast Mart." She was walking toward the back of the office where patrol had their lockers.

"Remember you volunteered this time." I smiled.

"*You* need to remember it the next time a position opens up in CID," she said, her tone joking, but not really.

"If I have any say, you'll get a shot at it."

"Hold you to that."

By the time I left the office, I knew I was pushing my time limits. Halfway home, I got a text from Cara. I didn't have to read it to know what she wanted: me, home, now. I let my foot ease down on the accelerator as I left the town behind me. Five minutes later, I was driving up to our doublewide in the woods. The door opened before I got to the steps.

"Did you pick up the laundry?"

"It's in the car." I hurried back to the car and took it out of the back seat.

"We don't have a lot of time."

"I'm going as fast as I can," I said, letting a little irritation slip into my tone.

"I need to get there a little early and help with the decorations," Cara said as she took her dress. We were standing on the porch with the sun slipping down behind the trees as the temperature dropped.

"Then maybe you should take your own car," I snapped, even though I knew she wouldn't want to do that. The waters were just getting very deep and I felt like I was already standing on tiptoes to breathe. When I saw the hurt expression on her face, I sighed. "I'm a little overwhelmed right now."

"You don't need to take it out on me," she said, again telling me something I already knew. A loud woof came from inside the house as Mauser heard our raised voices.

"I shouldn't have applied for the sergeant's job." I stared down at my hands, not wanting to meet her eyes. "I'm in over my head. I've already bungled the problem with Julio, and I've got to take a class in the stupid software that HR uses. On top of that, the brand new Lieutenant Eccles wants briefings on the murders and strategy meetings on how to run CID. I need to just admit I'm not going to be able to do the job." I was angry at myself for being inadequate and failing before I even got out of the gate.

"Larry, you'll do fine. You've just got a lot going on right now. Your dad's marriage, the fact he's still recovering from his injuries, the murders, the emails… which, I might add, are not your responsibility."

"They are now that I'm Pete's boss." As soon as I said it, I knew I was being silly. "Okay, you're right, the emails aren't in my basket. Especially if the writer isn't even my killer." I sighed again. "I just want to get this wedding done. And you don't know I can do the sergeant's job."

"I remember when you didn't think you were a good deputy or an investigator."

"I'm not very good. I screwed up my own revelation about the email addresses."

"It made sense to me."

"I forgot to look at Eva Calavera's email. It doesn't fit the pattern. Lionel pointed out that the email address of today's victim doesn't fit either. So that puts us on a different trail. I don't know how much longer it would have taken me to notice."

"Quit beating yourself up. Now let's go inside before Mauser knocks the door off its hinges." As if on cue, the buffalo threw himself against the inside of the door hard enough that I could feel the house shake as I stood on the deck.

"Hurry." I opened the door to the slavering monster.

After thirty minutes of flurried activity, we were in my car and driving toward town.

Cara waved to the hostess as we entered the Palmetto and headed straight to the private room in back, with me in tow carrying a couple of boxes with centerpieces and assorted decorations.

"This is just family," I complained.

"It needs to be special for Genie and your dad."

"You're sure that your parents aren't going to make a surprise visit?"

"They'll be here," she said, causing my stomach to drop. Her parents were good people, but their hippie lifestyle and her mother's odd ways always brought chaos in their wake.

"You promised they were up in Tennessee," I stammered.

"Don't worry. That's why I brought my laptop. They wanted to have a five-minute Zoom visit during dinner."

"I guess they can't cause too much trouble if they're only here via Zoom." If I sounded unsure of that, I was. "I'm surprised your parents would do Zoom. They're more of the smoke-signal type."

This last comment got me *the look* from Cara. Not that she didn't feel the same way, but she just didn't think it should be said out loud.

"The commune they're staying at is an odd mix of high tech and low tech. Hydroponics controlled by computers to grow cloth-grade hemp for them to weave on looms."

"Is it legal to grow hemp in Tennessee?"

"I doubt it," Cara said nonchalantly. She was already taking the centerpieces out of the boxes.

I helped as best I could. Mostly I stood around holding things until Cara either took them from me or told me where to put them. Just as she spread the last pieces of wedding glitter, Dad, Genie and her son, Jimmy, walked in.

"Wow!" Jimmy said.

"You didn't have to go to all this trouble." Genie hugged Cara and, from the light in her eyes, it was clear how much it meant to her. My mood when I arrived home felt stupid and petty. After Genie released Cara from the hug, I took Cara's hand and gave it a gentle squeeze.

"This looks official." Dad moved over to Genie and gave her a side hug. She buried her face in his chest to stop her happy tears.

It wasn't just family. The minister and other people who'd helped Cara and Genie plan the wedding, including Pete, Sarah and their two daughters, had also been invited. By the time everyone had arrived, the twenty-five chairs and two long tables were filled with people chatting and laughing.

Dad and Genie were seated in the middle of one of the tables. I was seated on Dad's left and Cara was next to me. Across from us were Pete and Sarah. I wanted to talk to Pete about the emails and what I'd figured out about the email addresses. However, I realized that the sharp elbow to my ribs from Cara when I started to discuss it over the table was a warning with claws behind it.

"We'll talk after dinner," I told Pete.

Jimmy looked at me several times and covered his mouth to hold in his laughter. He was seated on Genie's right and kept trying to get my attention.

"What's gotten into Jimmy?" I asked Cara.

"What?" she said, eating her salad and avoiding eye contact.

"He's looking over at me and laughing."

"Your dad might know." She had just the hint of a smile on her face.

I didn't have to be psychic to know there was a secret going around that I wasn't privy to.

"What's up with Jimmy?" I nudged Dad, who'd been in an animated conversation with a friend of Genie's.

"We'll talk about it after dinner," Dad told me, waving the issue away with his hand.

"I'd like to know," I said, feeling a little of the irritation from earlier in the evening creeping back into my head.

"It's nothing really. Just a slight change in the wedding ceremony." Dad smiled with a gleam in his eyes that I didn't like.

"Tell me."

"Fine." He turned in his seat to face me. "We thought that Mauser should have a larger role in the wedding."

I frowned. "And…"

"In your role as best man, we thought it would be nice if you lead Mauser up to the front so he can stand with us during the ceremony."

"You're kidding, right?"

"Mauser is a big part of our lives."

"He's going to be your best man. You're replacing me with Mauser," I said through clenched teeth.

"No. You're still the best man. He's just going to be up there with us."

"I'm just the handler. He's going to be the best man." I felt the idea crawling under my skin.

"Larry, you're taking this too much to heart," Dad said in the same tone he used when I got cut from Little League.

"Fine, I'll be the moose handler. I guess I'll give him my suit and I can wear overalls."

"You're being silly."

I turned to Cara. "You knew about this?"

"We discussed it the other night."

"You discussed it without me? I guess Mauser was included in the discussion, but not me." I knew my voice was getting too loud. As irritated as I was, I managed to bring my voice down a couple of notches. "Great. Second fiddle to thunder paws." I shoved my plate away and tried to get control of my emotions.

Dad had turned away and was talking to Sarah. Pete was concentrating on his salad and I could tell that he was trying not to laugh. Cara took my hand under the table and leaned in close to my ear.

"You love your dad and Genie. If this makes them happy, is that a bad thing?"

I gritted my teeth. I wanted to point out that I was the one who was going to have to walk up the aisle with the big buffoon while everyone laughed.

"I'll do it," I managed to say.

By the time dessert arrived, I'd almost gotten my good humor back. Once we were up and mingling, Jimmy's excitement at having Mauser as part of the wedding party made the upcoming ordeal seem more palatable. Jimmy's joy at anything unusual was contagious.

"Mauser is grrrrreat!" Jimmy said, imitating a commercial tiger I'm not sure he'd ever seen. "It's going to be neat having him at the wedding. Do you think he'll pee on anything?"

"No telling." Which was true. "I'll do my best to make sure he doesn't. Good thing the wedding isn't in a church."

The thought of Mauser peeing in a church caused Jimmy to go into spasms of laughter.

"It's not nice to make fun of me," I said with a grin.

"I not making fun of you, brother," Jimmy told me and raised his hand for a high five. He'd taken to calling me brother, and I had to admit that it didn't bother me at all. Jimmy had been born with Down Syndrome. Despite the challenges he faced, he easily found joy in so many things. There was a lot I could learn from Jimmy.

"So you're the wedding's dog handler," Pete said, walking over to us. This sent Jimmy into another round of laughter. "You learned more about the emails?" he asked me in a serious tone.

Once we'd high-fived Jimmy again, Pete and I meandered over to a semi-secluded corner of the room where I explained about the email addresses.

"I think you're on to something. The fact that the murder victims' emails don't fit the pattern reinforces the theory in my mind." Pete nodded to himself.

"What it means for the murders remains to be seen," I said.

"There are two paths to follow. One: the emails and murders were done by the same person. Two: they weren't."

"Thank you, Captain Logic. I could figure that out."

"With this revelation, I'd say that it's more important than ever that we each pursue our own lines of inquiry. In the end, we'll either meet in the middle or we won't."

"When one of us solves their own case, we'll be able to decide whether they are connected or not."

"I'll take the low road and you take the high road," Pete said. "If the emails were taken from a business or someone's private email list, then maybe we can backtrack to which list they came from. If we do that and figure out how they got the list, that might lead us to the sender."

"My thinking exactly."

"This is at least a new avenue to go down. Talking with Lionel, I'd about decided that without a suspect, analyzing the small amount of writing in each email wasn't going to get us anywhere."

I was about to tell him that Lionel and I had talked about it when Sarah came over to us.

"No business talk," she scolded us. "You two can take a day and a half off from murder and mayhem to give the happy couple their due."

"They are happy," Pete said, raising the glass in his hand toward them. Dad and Genie were laughing along with Cara and Jimmy.

Cara looked at her watch and then at me. She said something to Dad and Genie before clapping her hands.

"Everyone, there are two other people who want to send Genie and Ted their best wishes tonight. Give me just a moment to get them connected."

Cara went over to her laptop that she'd set up earlier on a table against the wall. After a little bit of button-pushing and soft cursing, she managed to connect the Zoom meeting with her parents.

"Ted!" Anna, Cara's mom, shouted while Cara herded everyone in the room over to the laptop.

I was elbow to elbow with Dad as we watched the image of Henry and Anna sitting in what looked like a rustic cabin. Behind them were an assortment of plants.

"Are those pot plants behind them?" Dad whispered to me.

"Only some of them," I told him.

"We want to wish you and Genie the very best! We wish we could be there. Don't we, Henry?" Anna turned to her husband, who was looking particularly Nordic with his silver hair and beard and wearing a wool tunic.

"Indeed we do!" Henry said. "Hello, Cara, Larry!" He waved to us. "It looks like a great party. Ted?"

It took a second for Dad to realize that Henry was waiting for him to acknowledge the greeting.

"Yes, Henry?"

"Remember what Odin said: 'Only the mind knows what lives near the heart; a man is alone with his own spirit. There is no sickness worse for any wise man than to have nothing to love.' Cherish Genie."

"Genie?" Anna called.

"Yes, Anna?" Genie stepped toward the laptop.

"Hold him tight yet set him free, be always with him that he may see, stand behind him so he stands strong and guide him swiftly through all life's flights." With that, Anna and Henry clinked their goblets, which contained heaven only knew what.

Folks began to drift off after the cyber-visit from Anna and Henry. I told Cara I'd take the laptop out to the car. A little fresh air would be nice. There was a light breeze and a clear, starry sky with a brisk promise of frost.

I didn't notice that Dad had followed me outside until I stopped and opened the car door.

I tensed and Dad said, "I thought we taught our deputies about situational awareness?"

"I guess I missed the class that warned officers about sneaky old men," I bantered back.

"Thank you." Dad's tone held a softness that had always made me feel uncomfortable.

"For what?"

"Accepting Genie and Jimmy into our family."

"They're good people. I'm really happy for you." I paused. "I'm happy too. I like that my family has grown."

"Grown a lot in the last couple of years. Cara, her crazy parents, now Genie and Jimmy."

We leaned back against the car, both looking up at the cold black night.

"I've been thinking about your mom lately. I remember our wedding day so clearly. She wouldn't let us or my parents pay for anything. Her dad was a very proud man. She told me he'd be devastated if he thought anyone else was picking up the tab 'cause we thought he couldn't afford it. Once I got to know him, I knew she was right."

"I only met him a few times," I said, barely remembering my grandfather.

"He'd had a bad heart since he was a kid. Worked like a horse on his farm, even though the doctor told him his heart could go at any time. Proud and stubborn."

"I've seen pictures of the wedding. It was out at his place, right?"

"In the old tobacco barn. They'd quit growing shade tobacco five years earlier. It took us a week to clean it up. Your grandmother made your mom's dress."

"I've seen it in the old steamer trunk. Grans really did all that lace work?"

"Her and her sewing circle. Our wedding was as much 1900 as it was 1984. I don't have words to tell you how much… love, caring, family… I don't know how to explain it, but I felt raised up by being there and allowed to become a part of her life."

"Mom was special." I felt tears forming.

"I don't think Genie has ever been a part of a real family. Her mother put her up for adoption when she was less than a year old and she has no idea who her father is. I want her to feel like I did when I married your mother."

"In my heart, I know that she and Jimmy belong with us," I told him, and he raised his hand and put it on my shoulder.

We stood up and walked back toward the restaurant where Cara, Genie and Jimmy were coming out, carrying the boxes of decorations we'd carried in three hours earlier.

"See you in the morning!" Genie called.

"Ten?" Cara said.

The times were agreed on and more orders given.

"We don't do this much planning for a major drug raid," Dad commented to me *sotto voce* and got a playful thump on the back from Genie.

Cara and I got home and dealt with the pillow that Mauser had decided to eviscerate while we were gone.

"I hope the minster doesn't accidently splash holy water on you. You'll burst into flames and take all of us with you," I told Mauser as he methodically sniffed every tree and plant within a hundred feet of the house before picking the spot to do his business. "I can't believe I've got to escort you up the aisle. I should have left you where I found you, or turned you in to the pound."

Finished with his business, Mauser came over and leaned against me as I looked up at the Milky Way girdling the night sky. "Do you think there's another guy and a hundred-and-ninety-pound alien looking back at us?"

Mauser's heavy breathing pumped out clouds of smoke in the frosty air, his only answer to my question.

"We better go in and get some sleep. We've got a big day tomorrow." We started toward the house. "If you want to make Jimmy's year, pee on something in the lodge," I advised him.

CHAPTER TWENTY-ONE

Morning came too soon. I could have slept in another hour, but Cara was a nervous ball of energy, worried that she had forgotten something.

"You weren't this nervous before our wedding," I said, eating my cereal standing up so that Mauser wouldn't try to take it from me.

"I don't mind disappointing myself, but I couldn't stand it if Genie and your dad don't have a wonderful day."

"I'll help with anything you need as soon as I finish my breakfast."

"At least the weather is going to be perfect." Cara looked out at the sunshine sparkling on the frosty ground.

With her car packed, Cara headed to the hall to meet the others. My marching orders were to stay with Mauser, get myself ready and get both of us to the hall an hour before the wedding.

With a couple of hours to kill, I sat down at the kitchen table with my laptop to work on my cases. Before long, I was drawn to Pete's reports on the most recent poison-pen emails. Even though we'd agreed to treat the murders and emails as separate cases, I couldn't get the messages out of my head. *Technically, it's my day off*, I thought as justification for opening the file.

As I read the latest emails, I tried to understand the person behind the words. Why had they been sent? Was the creator of the emails the murderer of Eva and Nicolaus? I saw a couple of names of people I knew on the new list of victims, including a friend who worked at the bank and an older woman who had been one of my history teachers in high school. It was as though someone was doing a story about the secret lives of the people of Adams County.

Mrs. Hicks was accused of vindictively giving out bad grades to students she didn't like. There were a couple of problems with that accusation. First, she hadn't been that type of teacher. Second, she'd retired three years ago. Why would someone bother with ancient history, pun intended? I remembered that some of the other kids in her class hadn't liked her and accused her of not being fair. But I'd heard the same thing about every teacher I'd ever had. Sometimes it had even been me who'd thought they weren't being fair. Maybe the writer of the emails had taken a class from her. Or maybe they had just heard it from someone else.

Jack Morten, who was a loan officer at the bank, was accused of visiting prostitutes in Jacksonville. Morten wasn't married, so I wasn't sure what the hook was. Maybe the bank wouldn't look favorably on one of their employees paying for sex. Prostitution was illegal and came with a lot of unsavory baggage. Still, it was a fact of life. According to Pete's report, with a promise of immunity, Morten had admitted that he used a sex worker who presented herself as self-employed and clean of drugs and diseases. He'd seen the same woman for two years now. Pete went on to say that Morten appeared mortified that he had to talk about the "affair." The reason he stated that he'd come forward was because he wanted the "creep" who'd sent the emails to get caught before he bothered his "friend" in Jacksonville.

The fifth addition to the list of recipients was the most interesting. My new boss had received one. Phil Eccles's accuser said that he had bungled an investigation and allowed a killer to get away with their crime. Phil's email threatened him with "severe repercussions." Our new lieutenant had told Pete that he couldn't imagine what case the emailer was talking about. He'd only been involved in a handful of murders as an investigator, and only two as the primary on the case. In both of those cases, he'd caught the criminals involved in both of the murders.

Looking over all of the different people who had received emails, I wondered when I'd get mine. What would it accuse me of?

"Probably having a four-legged brother," I told Mauser, who was flopped on the floor next to my chair.

Next I dug into all the phone interviews that Pete had done with the email recipients, trying to identify a common email list that all the addresses had come from. The list of people he'd talked to could be divided into three groups. The first were people who didn't understand what an email list was. They were generally the over-seventies. There were four of them. The second group was made up of young people who, for all practical purposes, had all said that they signed up for dozens of different email alerts a week. One guy said he got over two hundred emails a day with various offers and announcements. The third group, and maybe the most interesting, was made up of people whose online security radar was set to max. They had been able to give Pete specific lists of the different groups they belonged to and the companies they allowed to email them information. Of course, one of the geeks in the second group had pointed out that, even if you didn't give the company permission to send you offers and updates, they still had your email on a list.

The emailer had to get the list from somewhere and I didn't think it was from hacking a big company. I was also sure that it was a local company or organization. My guess was that it had come directly from the business's office or from someone forgetting to hide the cc's on an email.

Several companies in town kept regular email lists,

including the nursery, which ran some pretty good specials to get folks to sign-up for emails; the Supersave, which provided a discount card if you signed up—Cara and I had one of those; the local music theatre was another; and so was the library. Most folks in town used the same internet provider, so they would also have everyone's email. Those seemed like the best bets. I planned to get together with Pete on Monday and double down on this theory by talking to those businesses and trying to find out if they'd leaked their emails or if they could have been stolen.

I was about to get up when I got a text from Julio asking if he could come by and talk. I hated the fact that I had to think about it. Not because I needed to get ready for the wedding, but because I was now his supervisor and probably shouldn't be discussing business in my home on the weekend. I sighed.

Sure – though I'll need to leave for the wedding soon.

Be there in 5 was his reply.

The knock on the door awakened the sleeping giant, who let out two woofs that shook the house. Mauser bounced over to the door in a race with Alvin, who was almost run over in the process. I opened the door and let Julio in so he could be beat about the thighs by Mauser's tail.

"I still can't get used to his size," Julio said while petting and scratching the menace. "Then there's you," he said, managing to bend down and pet Alvin. We finally convinced Mauser and Alvin to give Julio enough room to come all the way into the house.

"What's up?" I asked.

"I just wanted to clear the air."

"We're fine," I said, trying to mean it.

"Dani is talking to me again. I think I might get her back."

"She's a nice woman."

"I know. I just don't want to screw this up."

"I hope she wasn't too irritated that I talked to her."

"I guess it would have been easier if you'd stayed out of

it. You getting involved… I know you were trying to help. Maybe it did, maybe it didn't."

"In our game, too many marriages fail," I said, thinking of all the deputies I knew who had gone through several marriages already.

"I also appreciate you not reporting me for… not being on call when I was scheduled to be."

I didn't point out that being drunk was a little more serious. There were times when you had to just let things go and hope they didn't come back and bite you in the ass.

"I just lost some sleep," I told him.

"All I want is to be a good investigator."

"You *are* a good investigator. Learn from this. That's what I'm trying to do."

"I had another reason for coming by. I thought of something that happened with Eva. This was a long time after we'd ended our affair. I had stopped at the Supersave and saw her coming out. She… looked upset. Maybe crying. I was already married to Dani by that point and I didn't want to stir anything up with Eva, so I almost let her go, but she looked shaken. I looked back and saw her just sitting in her car with her head down. After thinking about how it might look if someone saw us talking, I decided to take a chance and went over to the car." His eyes were focused on the past as he remembered the encounter.

"What had upset her?"

"Eva said a man had accused her of something horrible. When I asked her what, she just shook her head. When I pressed her, she said the guy wasn't being rational. Bad things just happened. She was pretty rattled and not too coherent. After talking for a few minutes, things got a little awkward between us when she asked how I was doing and I mentioned Dani. At that point, she said she was feeling better and needed to get home."

"It didn't have anything to do with her husband?"

"No. I'm sure of that. I got the feeling she'd run into someone in the store that bothered her. She said the guy was crazy."

"Can you remember exactly when this was?"

"Maybe about two years ago. Fall, I think. I don't really know."

"Anything else you can remember?"

"No." He shook his head.

I glanced at my watch, "I've got to get ready for the wedding," I told him.

"Wish your dad my best."

By the time I got to the Masonic Hall, I already had drool on the shoulder of my coat from Mauser hanging over the seat as I drove.

While the hall was still used by the Masons, it was governed by a board of directors who oversaw its management. Albert Griffin had given me a rundown of its history when I'd told him that Dad was getting married there. According to Mr. Griffin, in the early 1990s the Masons had been having a hard time financially and couldn't afford the upkeep that the building required. A foundation had been established which received endowments from several members of the community, allowing the hall to remain as a significant county landmark. Built of stone in a classic Federal style, it lent an air of prestige to the town square.

I found a parking space as close to the back door as I could and got Mauser harnessed up with the usual amount of pig-wrestling. Cara came out to make sure that Mauser and I were presentable.

"You're here," she greeted us. "I'm going to need some help with the ladder. We're trying to string up some of the garlands." She went on with more wedding talk that I let flow over me, knowing I'd be told what I needed to do when I needed to do it.

I walked Mauser around the flowerbeds before going inside, hoping to avoid Jimmy's best-case scenario.

Guests started arriving just as the women finished decorating the hall.

"I thought this was going to be a small wedding?" I said to Cara as we watched folks come in.

"The guest list might have gotten a little out of hand. It's your father's fault. He didn't want anyone to feel left out."

"The sheriff *is* an elected position," I mused, wondering what the final tab would be for this shindig.

"The reception is just cake and finger food," Cara said, reading my mind. There was a dining room connected to the main hall by a set of double doors. The reception would be held there immediately following the wedding.

"What was the final decision on booze?" I asked. A week ago, they'd still been trying to decide what the best course would be.

"There is beer on tap and champagne, but no bar. And there's just enough beer that I doubt anyone can get more than two glasses."

"We don't need anyone getting drunk at the sheriff's wedding and causing trouble."

"There's Eddie and Jessie," Cara said.

When I looked up, I had to do a double take. "Wow!" I said in admiration.

Eddie was wearing a black suit and Jessie had on a knee-length green dress that gave her a surprisingly sophisticated look. Her dark hair was elegantly styled and free of colored dyes. They headed straight for us. Luckily, Jimmy had taken on Mauser duties, so I didn't have to wrestle with the moose while trying to talk to people.

"You look amazing!" Cara told Jessie.

"Thanks. The training doesn't hurt." She made a muscle with her arm.

"Who'd you steal the suit from?" I asked Eddie, putting on a smile to let him know I was kidding.

"I'm lucky Bear didn't puke on it or try to sell it for a bottle of Boones Farm." He stepped in close to me and whispered, "You got to get that guy out of my apartment."

"In a few days," I assured him. I did feel a little bad. "Who's watching him now?"

"Albert is letting him help clean up the garage."

"How's the academy going?" Cara asked Jessie.

"I'm fifth academically, top woman in the physical training and tenth overall," she said with pride.

"I'm impressed," I said. And I was.

"What was your final academy standing?" Cara asked me.

"I don't remember," I lied.

She elbowed me. "Come on."

"There were a hundred-and-thirty-some-odd cadets. I was twentieth academically and forty-second for the physical portion," I muttered.

To change the subject, I asked Jessie, "Have you heard from Major Parks?" I knew that she'd been told her application would be considered when she had successfully completed the first third of her training. Before our recent budget crunch, we'd sponsored cadets. Now we would give them letters of support to get them into the academy, and then finalize their employment once they were most of the way through with their training so they could seamlessly go from the academy to our probation program.

"He said that they're going to have a committee meeting at the end of the month to decide what positions will be open and which applications to consider."

"I don't think you have anything to worry about."

"Still be a few years before I work my way up to CID."

"Who says CID is up?"

"I can't believe they made you a sergeant," Eddie said, causing the rest of us to look at him. "I mean, good guys never get promoted."

"Nice save." Cara smiled.

"No, I'm serious."

Jessie pulled him away as more folks came up.

"You should probably go and do your usher duties," Cara told me before turning to greet Dr. Horvath.

I headed for the entrance where Jimmy and Mauser were

handing out programs and telling people where to sit. Unfortunately, the big dog was such an attraction that they were creating a bottleneck instead of helping the flow.

"Jimmy, why don't you take Mauser out for one more pee break before we get started?" I told him. "We don't want too much laughter during your mom's wedding, do we?"

"I guess not," he said with a sigh.

"Out back would be the best place to take him for a walk." I pointed toward the back door, where they wouldn't run into all the folks coming to the wedding.

Five minutes later, I was handing out programs and pointing people to the left or right when Phil Eccles and his wife came in. There was just enough of a pause in arrivals for us to get in a few words.

"It's great to see you, Audrey," I said, nodding to his wife. She was a nice-looking woman, almost as tall as me, with blonde hair and clear blue eyes that smiled when she looked at you. Anyone in the county would recognize her, since her face was on two billboards in town. She was the top agent for Adams Realty and they took advantage of her photogenic qualities to promote the agency.

"Larry, always a pleasure. I'm so glad that you and Phil are going to be working together."

"I think I've got a good suspect in those murders, or at least the Fast Mart murder. We'll talk later," Phil said with a pat on my arm.

Soon everyone was seated and waiting expectantly for the ceremony to get started. I was standing in the hallway with Mauser, who was pumped up from the collective excitement.

"Are you sure you want him up front during the ceremony?" I asked Dad, who looked unusually nervous.

"I'm not sure about anything right now." He brushed at non-existent lint on his dress uniform. There'd been some back and forth about his clothing options, but we'd all agreed that he should wear his sheriff's uniform after seeing him try on a tuxedo. He kneeled down and ruffled Mauser's ears. "You're going to be a good boy, right?"

Mauser made a gurgling sound in agreement while swinging his head back and forth.

"He'll be fine!" Jimmy said, and I was one hundred percent sure that Jimmy was hoping Mauser would perform some of his usual antics and have the whole hall laughing hysterically.

The music began and Dad started down the aisle with Mauser and me falling in behind. I'll admit that, this one time, Mauser rose to the occasion. He almost looked regal as he strutted beside me to everyone's smiles and finger-pointing from the younger members of the audience. Meanwhile I tried to maintain my own dignity as the dog's handler.

The minister was Reverend Pritchard, who had conducted my marriage to Cara just ten months earlier. He had a grin on his face as he watched Mauser and me take our places. As soon as we were in our spots, the music changed to "Ode to Joy" and Genie walked with Jimmy down the aisle.

By the time Dad and Genie were pronounced man and wife, the crowd was lost in the romantic milieu of the moment. Applause and cheers rang out as they kissed.

After spending time with the happy couple as they thanked everyone, I helped Cara make sure that the reception was ready before opening the doors. The cake was cut and the pictures were taken.

As I was eating my piece of cake, Phil Eccles came over to me. Taking our plates, we drifted over to the side of the room where we could talk without being overheard.

"You have a suspect?" I asked.

"A guy that I helped arrest two years ago. He attacked a clerk at the feed store in town. Beat him pretty bad. Matt Green was the investigator who did the follow-through with the State Attorney."

"He's out of prison?"

"Yep, released a month ago. At the time, he worked a plea deal that got him some mental health treatment and jail time. The guy's name is Walter Fowler."

"How crazy is he?" I was thinking of the two murders. While anyone that stabbed or bludgeoned someone to death had to be a little insane, the murders were committed in such a way that I knew the person we were looking for was able to organize a plan and carry it out. So crazy, but not too crazy.

"He's a psychopath. Organized and capable when he's doing what he wants. His craziness doesn't shine through until he's confronted by a roadblock to his plans."

"Where is he now?"

"Here in town. I checked with his probation officer. Guess where he lives?"

"Don't tell me. Down in the Ditch?"

"Bingo. I looked over your report and he lives less than three blocks from where Eva Calavera's car was found and only a block from Nicolaus's house."

"What's the rest of his record look like?"

"Minor stuff, for the most part. Stalking, exposure and lots of public disturbance stuff."

"Sounds like a charmer."

"He's thirty-three years old and of average height and weight, so he's not ruled out by the video from the security camera."

"Since he's on probation, we can search his place."

"I'm game. Tomorrow or Monday?"

"You're the boss."

"You're the lead investigator."

"Tomorrow morning would be a good time. We'll find out if he's breaking any other conditions of his probation. Can you get ahold of his probation officer?"

"Sure, she's an old friend. You know her, Rosalie Valdez."

"Rosalie's great to work with. Tomorrow at ten?"

"I'll give her a call. See if she wants to be there."

"Stop hugging the wall." Cara had walked over to us.

"Yes, dear," I said and got a punch in the arm for being a

smartass. "Ouch. She's mean," I said to Phil, who got his own punch in the arm from Audrey.

"You heard the woman: quit hugging the wall," Audrey said, taking his hand. "You all did a beautiful job with the decorations," she told Cara, who almost blushed from the compliment.

"We did what we could. The place is cavernous."

"I bet Genie and the sheriff are thrilled," Audrey said.

"It meant a lot to Genie. By the way, has Sarah invited you to the get-to-know-you dinner we're having for Genie on Wednesday?"

"We talked about it yesterday. I had to cut it a little short because a client walked in just as she was getting into the details."

Cara and Audrey meandered off toward the spread of appetizers and left us guys still hugging the wall.

"Audrey is very nice," I said.

"She's my all. You'd think that, with her looks and the job she has, she'd be stuck-up or demanding, but nothing could be further from the truth. I have a son from my first marriage, which was an unmitigated disaster. I'm glad to say that Audrey has made him her son too. After my first wife, I was almost too scared to take a chance on Audrey. I kept thinking that she was too good to be true. Ten years later and I know you get what you see with her." He paused and I think he actually choked up a little. "Looks like you did great marrying Cara."

"I'm glad I didn't have to go through a bad marriage to get here." I thought about my conversation with Julio earlier. I prayed things would work out for him and Dani.

"How about Bill Louis? He's on his fourth wife and she'll rattle the windows when she gets up a head of steam."

"I was at a scene last year with him when she called him on his phone. From ten feet away, I could hear her screaming at him." I winced at the memory.

"Of course, he's no great shakes himself."

Phil was right. Louis was a competent deputy, but after

twenty years, that was the best that could be said of him. He would argue with you for an hour about what charges a suspect should get, or which patrol car he should have.

Cara and I helped get Dad and Genie out the door and I promised to take Jimmy home. He had been staying overnight at Dad's during the last couple of days building up to the wedding, but he needed to get back to the group home where he lived in Tallahassee so he could go to work at Publix in the morning.

I traded cars with Cara so that she could take an exhausted Mauser home while I drove Jimmy back to Tallahassee. Jimmy was almost as tired as Mauser and spent most of the trip leaning back with his eyes closed. When we got to his place, we both got out and I handed him his duffle bag.

"I'm glad you're my brother now," he said and gave me a hug. "Come meet my friends."

"Some other time, buddy," I said. It was getting late and I still had to drive back to Adams County. "High five." I held up my hand. He ran back and we slapped hands.

Back home, all was quiet. We ate a few leftovers before I fell asleep on the couch, only to be woken up at eight by a text from Phil Eccles that read: *All set. Rosalie will meet us at ten tomorrow at Fowler's house.*

CHAPTER TWENTY-TWO

Early Sunday morning, I left the house while Cara was still lounging in bed. I figured she'd earned it. Before I left, I made sure that everyone had their breakfast. I took a moment while Mauser was bouncing around waiting for me to put down his food bowl to tell him that he was headed home on Monday afternoon.

"And I'm not sure you'll be missed," I joked, giving him his food. As though Alvin had understood what I'd said, he left his own food for a moment to come over and rub his head against Mauser's leg. "Okay, I guess Alvin is going to miss you."

Before meeting with Phil, I stopped by the office. As I checked my emails, I was dismayed to see even more messages from Major Parks and the other brass. I found it tough to resist the temptation to mark all of the office and personnel management emails as spam. Instead, I skimmed through them to see which were things that I needed to think about and which were just cc's gone mad.

Finished with my inbox, I had just enough time to read the file that Phil had shared with me on our suspect. Walter Fowler was a piece of work. Looking through his record, I found a couple of mental health evaluations. Like most of the evaluations I'd read, the two in Walter's file avoided the real question, which was: How dangerous was he? All the reports said was that he showed signs of this issue or that, and with proper medication blah, blah, blah.

I went through the reports and looked at the jobs he'd been working each time he'd been arrested. They varied from short-order cook to roofing laborer. Cook showed up most often. *Makes me not want to eat out*, I thought.

His most recent trip to jail had resulted from a confrontation with a clerk at the feed store. Witnesses said that he had argued with the clerk near a store display, then started beating the clerk with a fencing tool that he'd picked up from a shelf. Both Walter and the clerk were lucky that the clerk had been agile and avoided most of the blows. When Walter was arrested, he'd claimed the clerk had insulted him and abused him on numerous occasions. But it turned out that that particular clerk had worked at the store less than a week.

Walter got the plea deal and was a model prisoner. Being good when he was being watched was a recurring theme in Walter's life. Was he Nicolaus's killer? Could he have been Eva's? I found one mention of a knife being used in his file. He'd pulled a butcher's knife on a fellow cook at a restaurant.

Thinking about what I'd learned, I headed out to meet Phil. The morning was cloudy and warmer than it had been over the last few days. I drove to within a couple of blocks of Walter's duplex and parked. There wasn't anyone moving around at ten on a Sunday morning. I wasn't surprised. This neighborhood wasn't full of the church-going type. Most of the residents would still be in some form of a stupor from the night before.

Phil pulled up beside me and rolled his window down.

"Rosalie is right behind me," he said. "She'll join us after we get in."

I could see her car behind his.

"You got your vest on?" he asked.

"You know, it's not my first rodeo."

"Always double check. I won't be insulted if you check-list me."

"Front door or back door?"

"I'll take the front."

"Or we could do it like in the movies and leave the back of the house open so we can have an exciting chase scene," I suggested and received the one-finger salute in return.

We talked logistics for another couple of minutes before Phil let the watch commander and dispatch know that we were going in to question someone on a possible murder charge.

With my star in plain view on my belt, I made my way through the neighbor's backyard. The fences dividing the properties weren't even a challenge. They consisted mostly of rotted wood and broken wire.

The back of Walter's duplex was a jumble of debris left by dozens of former tenants. I wanted to make sure that I didn't have to try and run through this obstacle course of rusty metal and broken plastic. Being a duplex, I only had to worry about one side of the house and half the back. Luckily, the windows had bars so the back door was the only way out on this side of the house.

The plan was simple. Phil would knock and I'd see who ran out the back. I heard his voice loud and clear as he thumped on the front door. A ten count and the back door opened. As soon as I saw the half-dressed form of Walter Fowler emerging from the house, I stuck my foot out and pushed him over. He crashed to the ground with an *oof* and a curse or two.

"Don't even think about running. Roll on your belly and stretch your hands out." I used my radio to tell Phil that I had him.

Now that he was caught, Walter did as he was ordered.

"I didn't do nothin'!" It was the cry of every person ever arrested.

"We have a right to come inspect your home."

"My probation officer does," he sputtered as I cuffed him.

"Mr. Fowler, what are you doing making these fine officers get down on the ground and cuff you?" Rosalie said as she and Phil came around the side of the house.

"Ms. Valdez, I wouldn't have never run if I knew you were here. I didn't know who these guys were."

"The fact I was yelling 'sheriff's office' at the top of my lungs wasn't a clue?" Phil said.

"Let's take you to the car. You can wait there while we search your house." I pulled Walter up off the ground. I watched him as he walked through the house ahead of me. *Was this the man in the Fast Mart footage?* I asked myself. Nothing about his appearance ruled him out.

The duplex was just over seven hundred square feet. It took us almost as long to put on our personal protective gear as it did to search the place.

Phil was the first to strike gold—a metal pipe that could have been used to beat Nicolaus to death. The pipe raised fewer red flags than the fact that it was clean. Cleaner than almost anything else in the house. In the back of his closet, I found a used but well-cared-for set of cooking knifes. Like the pipe, they were also very clean.

There was a fresh stain on the nasty couch in the living room that looked to be blood.

"I'm going to call in Shantel's crew," I told Phil as my mind mulled over the possibilities.

"Absolutely. He's looking dirty to me."

"Does he have a job?" I asked Rosalie.

"Had one as a cook for about a week at the truck stop."

Phil and I looked at each other. The truck stop was only a few hundred yards from where Eva's body had been found.

"We need to go slow and be careful," Phil said. "We don't want to make a mistake that his lawyer can use to get him off."

"Hello!" we heard Rosalie sing out. "Walter's been a

naughty boy. This will let you lock him up while you check him out." She was holding up a lamp and inside the base was a bag of weed and a small bong.

"Nice!" I was feeling good. We could lock him up for a violation of probation and take our time digging into his alibis, background and any evidence we found among his property.

When Marcus showed up, I took Walter and headed for the jail with Rosalie following behind. Once we had booked him, I thanked Rosalie, who went on to enjoy the rest of her Sunday while I headed back to Walter's house to help Marcus. Darlene's black-and-white Escape was parked outside.

"Working on a Sunday. I hope they're paying the new sergeant time-and-a-half," Darlene said as I walked up to where she and Phil were talking. "Is he good for the murders?" She nodded toward Walter's place.

"Who knows until we've shaken all the trees," I told her, but I held up crossed fingers. "I'm cautiously optimistic."

"If you've got this, I'm heading home," Phil told me.

Darlene and I watched him drive off with a wave in our direction.

"I leave and your dad's handing out promotions like Easter candy," Darlene said lightly.

"Go on, make fun of me being sergeant," I urged her, knowing she couldn't resist.

"Make fun of you?" She looked shocked. "You're my protégé. I'm proud that you're rising up through the ranks. I always knew you had greatness in you. Shame you had to wait until I left to let it out."

"There it is," I said.

"I'm going to get serious. Supervising people is a complicated business, especially in this day and age. You've got to watch your back more in the office than out on the street, otherwise you'll find yourself at the center of a lawsuit."

"You're doing okay."

"You think so? As chief of police, I've had to dodge a dozen lawsuits already. A couple have been from the community, but there have been a few internal squabbles that have almost turned into lawsuits."

"You're kidding?"

"Remember the first thing I had to do was get rid of some of the sycophants that Chief Maxwell had surrounded himself with. I got one to resign and the other shaped up enough that I can live with his job performance. Both of them dropped the name of their lawyer into the tougher conversations we had."

"You're the chief of police. I'm lucky to just be a sergeant."

"Keep telling yourself that when you're doing evaluations. They're sitting in that office with you, not your dad."

"See, and that's why I didn't really want the promotion."

"Nonsense. What did JFK say? We do it not because it's easy, but because it's hard."

"I saw you and Hondo at the wedding together yesterday," I said, changing the subject. Darlene and Hondo had been an item for a few months.

"You came with Mauser. Are you all dating?"

"Fair point."

"I don't know what Hondo and I are except good friends," Darlene said. My impression from talking with Hondo was that he liked Darlene, but didn't like commitments.

Darlene also did a search of the house just so we had as many eyes as possible giving it the once over. She discovered a hiding place in the bathroom tucked in behind the water heater, where we found drug paraphernalia wrapped in a newspaper with headlines touting the second invasion of Iraq.

"Just a guess, but I'd say it's not related," I told her as we bagged the yellowed syringes and crusty-looking heroin.

"I'd bet you a dollar you could get some poor sap out on

the street to melt it down and inject it into their veins," Darlene said with a sad shake of her head. "I miss being able to get out in the country. Same drug-fueled issues, but at least there's some fresh air."

The knives and the pipe were the big takeaways. The million-dollar question was: Could our crime scene techs find any blood or DNA evidence to tie Walter back to either of the murders? We also had another ace in the hole—Eva's car. Would we be able to find some evidence that Walter had been in that car? Finding evidence inside the Fast Mart would be more problematic. Everyone from the wrong side of the tracks ended up there at some point, so finding his DNA there wouldn't be as significant as finding it in Eva's car. As far as I knew, Walter had no reason to have ever been near her.

I wanted to start digging into his alibis for both murders, but that would have to wait. Questioning him too soon could just muck things up. Everything would have to wait until Monday.

By the time I got home, Cara had set out my Valentine presents on the table.

"Tomorrow is Valentine's Day," I pointed out to Cara, who seemed very proud of the wrapped gifts on the table.

"I know, and we don't have to give each other our gifts today. I just thought it might be nice to do it when we have a lazy Sunday afternoon rather than after work tomorrow."

I didn't have to be a mind-reader to know that she'd already decided we were celebrating Valentine's Day today.

Ivy was walking around the gifts, sniffing them while Ghost was playing with the ribbons.

"I got everybody gifts," Cara said, explaining the cats' interest. Mauser even came over and put his head on the table, as interested in the cats as the presents. "Even you." She ruffled Mauser's ears, and I assumed this remark was aimed at him and not me.

"Give me a few minutes to get your gift ready."

"You got me something?" She pretended to be shocked.

"I had a choice?" I laughed.

Luckily, I'd already printed out the reservation confirmation for the trip to St. Augustine. I'd booked a "romantic weekend package" at a bed-and-breakfast on the edge of the old town. I'd also devised a clever plan for presenting the gift to her. I'd bought a cheap box of chocolates from the Dollar General and hid the confirmation underneath the candy. In case anyone thinks I'm suicidal, I also included some candy hearts and a mushy card.

As I opened my own gifts, Cara was looking at her meager pile with suspicion. She'd gotten me a fancy desk plaque with my new title on it and a new leather folder for my badge.

"What?" I asked innocently.

"Thanks," she deadpanned, "for the gifts." She had opened the box of cheap chocolates without discovering the confirmation underneath.

"My pleasure. I sure like mine. I *did* get you a nice card."

Cara looked ready to go from *Very funny, wise guy* to *This isn't funny at all.*

"Look under the chocolate." I tapped the box.

Next thing I knew, she was double-checking her calendar to make sure that the dates for the trip would work and talking excitedly about what the weather would be like and what clothes we should pack. My little ruse had been a success.

We distributed gifts to Alvin, Mauser, Ivy and Ghost. With Cara doing all the buying for two vets, she received a bunch of free samples of animal treats and toys. Everyone came away from the table happy with their Valentine haul.

CHAPTER TWENTY-THREE

Monday dawned wet and blustery as warm air blew in off of the Gulf. I got to the office to find Pete working on his emailer case.

"I don't think it's fair that you solve your case and leave me hanging in the air," he said, looking up from his monitor.

"I'm not sure that the murders *are* solved. I'm almost positive that Fowler didn't send any emails. I don't see him as the type to bother and, on top of that, his laptop looked… ancient. I'm going to get Lionel on it as soon as possible, and with some luck we'll have the answers sooner rather than later."

"It seems like an odd coincidence that two people are murdered and the threatening emails they received don't fit the pattern of the other emails."

"I agree. I would have bet that the killer either sent all the emails, or was taking advantage of the fact that someone else was."

After dealing with other cases for most of the morning, I sent out a group text to Shantel, Marcus and Lionel asking for a time when we could all get together and discuss how we were going to move forward on the Fowler evidence. We had him locked up for as long as we needed, but I wanted to know as soon as possible if he was our killer. If he wasn't, I still had two murders to solve.

Lunch on you was Shantel's response, which received a rousing second from the other two. We agreed to takeout from a new barbeque joint, Mama's Boy BBQ, which had recently opened up in an old fast food restaurant. The young man who ran it had had a few problems as a teenager, but his mother, who ran a soul food catering business out of her house just south of town, had pulled him back on the straight and narrow.

At eleven-thirty, I was halfway to my car to go pick up lunch when I caught sight of a silver Porsche pulling into the lot. It squealed into the spot next to me and Ralph Calavera jumped out.

"You've arrested someone for Eva's murder."

"I don't know where you get your information from, but you've got the wrong end of the stick."

"Walter Fowler." Calavera was visibly shaking.

"We arrested him for probation violations."

"I was his attorney two years ago," he stated through clenched teeth.

I took a minute to consider this. The information was the proverbial bombshell. Our suspect now had a potential connection with one of the victims. As close as one degree of separation.

"I need to get a formal witness statement from you. Are you willing to do that?"

"Absolutely. So you're admitting that he's a suspect?"

"He's a person of interest." I looked at my watch. If Calavera was our usual type of witness, I'd want to get it all down as soon as possible before he changed his mind or forgot something. In Calavera's case, I didn't need to worry about that. "You look like you could use something to eat. I'm on my way to pick up lunch for our crime scene techs. We're going to go over a few notes, or I'd ask you to join us. But you can eat in the conference room, and we can record the interview after lunch."

Calavera shifted from foot to foot, clearly anxious to blurt out everything he knew. Taking a couple of deep breaths, he nodded, "Yeah, I could use something to eat."

Thirty minutes later, I had him set up in the conference room while I went down to the evidence room with the rest of the food.

"We have Fowler's DNA, so that's a positive," I said.

"You know we won't have results from the DNA collected from the two bodies for months," Shantel said. We'd finished our pulled pork sandwiches and were getting down to business.

"Evidence from Eva's car and Eva's person is the top priority. That's evidence that he can't easily explain away." As I said it, I hoped that Ralph Calavera wouldn't tell me that Walter Fowler had ridden in Eva's car at any point during his legal representation.

"I've already gotten into the laptop," Lionel said. "Accessing his email accounts might prove harder. If he sent the emails, he didn't use a traditional email service."

"I'll make a note and see if he'll voluntarily give us his email password. Have you found anything suspicious?"

"Nothing that sends up big red flags. From what I've seen, he doesn't look very sophisticated. His browser history hasn't been cleared in weeks. Lots of porn. He likes fancy cars. Has a Facebook account that has less than a dozen friends, who all look like relatives."

"What about the knives?" I asked Marcus.

"I'm going to get them over to FDLE. I don't want to try looking under the handles for trace evidence and screw it up. They have the microscopes and talent to do it right. You know what the tradeoff is," Marcus said.

"Time."

"Weeks, at least."

"At least he's in jail," I said, glad that this wasn't one of those make-a-decision-now-or-lose-him deals.

We talked a little more before I cleaned up my trash and headed to the conference room to interview Calavera.

"I'm glad you came in," I told him as I turned on all the recording equipment in the room. "I'll be recording our interview."

"I'd like a copy."

"That can be arranged." I felt awkward sitting down across from Calavera and trying to look on him as an ally.

We went through the formalities of the time and place of recording, who was present and the circumstances that had brought it about.

"Tell me about your relationship with Walter Fowler."

"I do my public service by serving as a public defender on occasion. Two years ago I was given the case of a man charged with aggravated assault at the Sunny Side Feed Store here in Adams County. The man in question was Walter Fowler. I counseled him to plead not guilty to the charges."

"Tell me about the charges and your first meeting with him."

"He was charged with assault, but it was also clear that he had been trying to steal several items from the store. Items that he thought he could sell to addicts. Bute, to be specific."

"Is he an addict?"

"Not to my knowledge. When I represented him, he told me that he drinks to excess, but surprisingly draws a sharp line between that and hard drugs. At least he did at that time. Anyway, he attacked a clerk when the man discovered him stealing."

"Tell me about your interactions with him."

Calavera looked thoughtful.

"Standard first meeting. It was in one of the interview rooms at the jail. He came in and dropped down in the chair across from me." Calavera signaled for me to turn off the recording equipment. I didn't want to, but I was curious to know what he wanted to say.

"You're off the record," I told him.

"When I agreed to be recorded, I wasn't thinking about what it might sound like if I speak my mind about Fowler. The truth is, I didn't like his attitude when I met him. He came across as an asshole. Having that in an official record doesn't look good. He could sue me for defending him when I admit that I didn't like him. See my point?" Calavera looked conflicted.

"I want to hear your real impressions about Fowler, but honestly, it's the timeline and his motivation that's important to get on tape. So we'll do this: if you have an opinion, signal me and I'll turn off the recording."

"One more thing off the record. He told me it was a good thing that someone stopped him, or he might have killed that guy. That statement is covered by attorney-client privilege, but if he killed Eva and that clerk, I'll be glad to get disbarred and tell it on the record."

"We'll see where we are after our people go over the evidence we've collected and I've had a chance to interview Fowler."

Back on the record, Calavera continued, "We met two more times. The second time, I brought him an offer from the State Attorney for a plea bargain, which was fair if not generous. He agreed to it, so the third time I saw him he signed the papers and we were done."

"Did your wife ever come up in conversation?"

"No."

"That was the sum total of your interactions with Fowler?"

"No." Calavera pulled out his phone and showed me an email that Fowler had sent him.

In it he claimed that Calavera had talked him into the plea agreement and that Calavera was lazy and just didn't want to take the time to go to court. Fowler claimed he could have beaten the charge and that Calavera would pay for landing Fowler in jail. The email was long-winded and meandering.

"Fowler had it sent to me while he was in jail. You'll see that it came from his sister."

I looked at the beginning of the sender's email: BFowler.

"I could have forwarded the email to the State Attorney.

Making threats from prison is frowned upon. But this isn't the first angry email I've gotten from a client suffering from plea-bargain regret. Funny thing is that it's always the ones I help get a light sentence. No good deed…"

It would have been handy if the email had mentioned Calavera's wife. However, a threat was a threat. This wasn't a smoking gun, but it was a gun in Fowler's hand.

Later that afternoon, I got a decent mugshot of Fowler and six other characters that looked sort of like him. On the off chance that we were headed in the wrong direction, I included Neil Manning's mugshot. Maybe Calavera's response to Fowler had all been an act. With my mugshot lineup, I headed over to Eddie's place to show them to Bear. It was a long shot, but occasionally the long shots paid off.

I pulled into Mr. Griffin's driveway and went up the stairs to the apartment above the garage. My couple of raps on the door apparently weren't heard over the TV blasting inside. I pounded a few more times and finally heard the volume go down.

"Who is it?" Bear shouted from the other side of the door.

"Larry Macklin, from the sheriff's office. Remember me?" I smiled toward the door's window when he peeked out.

"Oh, sure." The door swung open and a blast of heat hit me. Bear stood there in boxers and a T-shirt. I'll say that the few clothes he had on looked clean and there wasn't an odor coming off of him.

"I just want to show you some pictures and see if you recognize anyone."

"The guy was wearing a hoodie, so it probably won't help." Bear shook his head. "Hey, do I got to stay sober? It's killing me." I looked at the coffee table where there was an open beer. "That's only beer. Eddie is letting me have a couple a day so I don't get the DTs too bad. But I got a real hankerin' for the hard stuff."

"Just do what Eddie tells you for now. Have you remembered anything new from the night of the murder?"

"Yeah, I pissed myself. That's how scared I was," Bear said with raised eyebrows.

"I don't blame you. I saw the security camera footage. Sit down."

I waved him toward the couch and laid out the eight mugshots on the coffee table. "I want you to take your time and look over these. Don't rush it. I want to know if any of them look familiar." I purposefully stood up and walked behind him so I couldn't inadvertently clue him in on any one picture.

I will say this: he looked them over slowly and carefully.

"I know him." He pointed to the picture of Walter Fowler. "I know him too." He pointed to another mugshot, one of the random ones I'd picked out.

"Was either one of them at the Fast Mart the night of the murder?"

He paused. "I don't think so. I ain't seen Turk for a while. I heard he was in jail for selling." He was tapping the second picture. "This one." He pointed at Fowler's picture. "He's mean as a snake."

"When was the last time you saw him?"

"A week ago. He was at the Petro station across from the Supersave. I saw him pull up and so I went back across the street to the store to get some more money and wait for him to leave."

"Why are you so scared of him?"

"'Cause he's mean. He's kicked me before." I saw Bear hunch over, remembering the blows.

"He did that for no reason?"

Bear was quiet for a minute. "I never really did nothin' to him. He's just mean. Some people are like that."

"You know Turk and you know the mean guy. Could either of them be the person that hit Nicolaus?"

Bear didn't think about it long before he gave a big shrug.

"I don't know. He had a hoodie on and I only saw him from the back."

We talked a little bit longer before I got a text from Cara telling me that she was over at Dad's waiting for me to pick her up. I thanked Bear and told him to listen to Eddie.

Cara had taken Dad's van and the mastodon back home. I picked her up and took a minute to say hi to the newlyweds before we headed home to dinner.

"Happy Valentine's Day," I said, and she leaned over to give me a kiss as we drove home. "It will be nice to have our house back."

"It's going to seem empty without Mauser," she said half-jokingly.

"Now you can give Alvin his fair share of attention without that ox getting in your face."

"I'd feel bad for Alvin except that he worships Mauser."

The next day was filled with all the tasks that had to be done to investigate and push forward the stack of cases in my inbox. Returning phone calls and emails, chasing down witnesses, pushing the labs to move our evidence up on their lists. Wednesday morning, I got with Pete and Phil Eccles to come up with a strategy for interviewing Walter Fowler.

"This isn't his first time around the playground," Phil reminded us.

"I say we two-time him," Pete suggested.

"Our advantage is that he doesn't know for sure that we're coming at him for the murders," I said. "I'm with Pete. Having two of us in the interview room might help throw him off his stride."

"Normally I'd say that just one of us goes in there. But he's not the kind of bad guy that's going to be softened up with the buddy-cop routine," Phil said.

"One thing in our favor is he can't afford a lawyer. Of course, he gets one for free as soon as he asks, but that's a lottery. One thing's for sure: he's not going to get Ralph

Calavera, pro bono or otherwise," I said darkly.

"Even a bad lawyer is going to tell him to keep his mouth shut, so we need to move now," Pete said.

"I want both of you to go into the room. Larry, you be the primary and get in close. Pete, hang back and when Fowler gets too comfortable, ask a question out of left field and knock him off his stride. Let's see if we can rattle his cage."

Walter Fowler looked smug as he walked into the interview room. He was wearing the usual orange overalls provided by the county. I told the guard to unlock his handcuffs. Pete wasn't there yet. We'd agreed he'd come in after Fowler got it in his head that there would only be one interviewer.

"Have a seat," I told him, pointing to the chair at the corner of the small metal table. The table and chairs were arranged so that he couldn't have the table between us. He was working hard to look comfortable as he leaned back in the hard metal chair.

"Who are you? And what hell do we have to talk about?"

Pete opened the door and came in. Fowler looked up, surprised.

"Have you ever met a woman by the name of Eva Calavera?" I asked, and watched as his eyes grew into saucers.

"I never did anything to no woman!" he yelled loud enough to hurt my ears.

"Do you know who she is?"

"No, no, no. I don't know any women!" He was shaking his head adamantly. I was thinking we didn't need Pete to rattle him. He was doing a good job getting himself worked up.

"Just answer the questions. Are you saying you've never met Eva Calavera?"

"Yes, no. No, I've never met her." His head whipped back and forth. This was not the hardass nut to crack that he'd been portrayed as being. He acted more like a fourteen-year-old kid in the principal's office.

"But you know Ralph Calavera," Pete said.

"No."

Pete and I just looked at Fowler. I gave the name time to sink in.

"Wait, Calavera was that idiot lawyer I had. He talked me into taking a plea bargain. I wish I could sue him." He stopped talking and his eyes got squinty. "Is Eva some relative of his?"

"Yes. Did you ever meet Ralph Calavera's wife?" I held up my hand. "Think about it before you answer."

"No. Maybe. I… Maybe at the courthouse. There were women around him at the courthouse. One of them could have been his wife. Listen to me, I didn't do anything to any woman. I don't touch women. Ever." He leaned forward and was looking at me with sharp, clear eyes that seemed a little haunted. His manner caused me to think about my next question.

"What is it about women?" I left the question very open-ended because I didn't really know what I was asking.

He leaned back. Not arrogantly this time, and there was a pained expression on his face.

"I got accused of… bothering a girl when I was in high school. I. Never. Touched. Her. Got it? Not only did I go to a detention center, but I was beat bad by my father. He broke two of my teeth. See." He showed off two gold teeth on the left side of his jaw. "I never touched no girl then and I haven't since."

"You never went for a ride with Eva Calavera?"

"No. Ask her. I'll do a lineup, whatever you want. I'll take one of those lie detector tests." If he was faking this, he was a great actor.

"Have you ever been in the Fast Mart on Jefferson?"

"I didn't kill that guy!" Now he was on his feet.

"Sit down," I told him.

"I want my lawyer!" he yelled.

"Do you have a lawyer?"

"You bet I do." He reached into his pocket and brought out a folded and spindled business card. "I talked to him the other day about my probation violation."

"You can ask for permission to call your lawyer. We're done here," I said, getting up. I saw the look on Pete's face. "For now," I added.

Phil Eccles met Pete and me when we came out of the interview room. "Why'd you stop the interview? Just because he asked for a lawyer?" There was irritation in his voice.

"That and the fact I don't think he did it." I continued before he could object: "The evidence might prove me wrong, but I think we need to have something solid before we interview him again."

"He put up a good front," Pete admitted.

"The list of circumstantial evidence against him is solid," Phil said with a frown. It was clear he didn't like letting up on Fowler.

"I'll be the first one to go after him if we have some physical evidence," I assured him.

"You have a point. As long as he isn't out on the street. We need to keep an eye on his court appearances and make sure that the State Attorney knows that we're interested in him staying behind bars for now."

"Absolutely," I promised.

We picked up our firearms as we left the jail. Pete headed for his car while Phil and I walked toward the crosswalk.

"You get the email?" Phil asked me.

"Which one?"

"Lunch tomorrow."

"Yeah, should be properly embarrassing," I grumbled. There was a lunch and pinning exercise scheduled for noon on Thursday.

"You need to embrace it." He smiled. "I remember when you became a deputy. You spent half your time acting like you were being punished. Now you're doing the same thing with your new position. Don't. The people who want to be promoted will resent your attitude, and the rest of the deputies won't respect your authority if you act like you don't have any. You've been doubly blessed."

"How's that?" The light changed and we crossed the street.

"First with the promotion and, second, most investigators who get a promotion while in CID have to go out on patrol. You get to be sergeant and you get to stay in CID."

I saw the truth in what he was saying. No one likes a bad winner. "You might have a point," I admitted.

CHAPTER TWENTY-FOUR

For the rest of the morning, I turned my attention to other cases. There was an ugly one where a man tried to take revenge for a drive-by shooting where his father had been wounded. Two days later, the son had rammed the car of the shooter. Sadly, the shooter's young daughter had been inside the car and was injured in the accident. The revenge-seeker was now facing multiple attempted murder charges, with additional penalties because of the age of the girl. The only good news was that the original shooter had also been arrested. It was one of those cases with just one depressing interview and report after another.

About two o'clock, my mind started going back to the murders of Eva Calavera and Nicolaus Andreas. I fought off the urge to look through the files awhile, but finally I gave in. I sat back and started opening the folders on my computer. Something about Eva's case was bothering me. I read back through the interviews of Ralph, her sister, Margret Whittle and others. I identified two main things that had disturbed what was otherwise an idyllic life.

The biggest was the trouble with her marriage. Calavera said that they had reached an understanding. Was this true?

Then there was the statement from Julio that a "crazy

man" had been bothering her in the store. Could that man have been Walter Fowler? He'd been described by more than one person as a "crazy man." If so, why had he been bothering her? He'd given a convincing performance in the interview when he'd claimed not to know her. Still, anyone who believed that they couldn't be fooled was a fool. True psychopaths could tell a lie with enough conviction to convince anyone.

Then I opened the files on the emails. We knew that there was a pattern to them and the email addresses were a clue. Our murder victims were exceptions to that rule, which meant that they had been specifically targeted by the emailer.

I saw where Pete had made a spreadsheet of all the email addresses and various facts about the recipients and the emails. I scanned the columns. The first two were the names of the people who had received emails. The third was the date they'd been received. The fourth column noted the number of emails received, while the fifth listed the email addresses of the recipients. It went on with columns for number of words used, physical addresses, and so on. I was impressed. Pete had put in a lot of time compiling the spreadsheet. I methodically scanned all the columns, looking for connections or something that had been missed.

I didn't see it the first time I looked. But maybe it registered in a small part of my brain, because I went back and looked at each individual email address again. Then I sat bolt upright.

Phil Eccles's email address hadn't been his sheriff's office email like I'd assumed. It was a personal email. The address began with: Forevergreen. Which, if you didn't know that he was a sheriff's deputy, might also make you think it was the email address of a funeral home. I called Phil.

"The threatening email you got came to your private email," I told him.

"Yeah, I guess that's right."

"I think you might be the murderer's next target." I reminded him about the pattern in the email addresses.

"Maybe." There was silence for a moment. "Still, killing a middle-aged woman and a store clerk is a bit different than killing a deputy." I heard a firmness in his words. Maybe even a challenge.

"Where are you?" I heard his sirens in the background.

"I'm on my way to a traffic accident. I'm still filling in the gaps in patrol's schedule. They had me scheduled through this week. I didn't want to leave the watch commanders in the lurch," he said.

"If you get the chance, I'd like to meet and talk about this. If I'm right then you, Eva Calavera and Nicolaus Andreas all have a link to the murderer."

"I'm coming up on the scene. I'll call you when I can."

I looked at my phone for a minute, thinking about what I should or could do. All I could think of was to put together as much information on the backgrounds of Eva and Nicolaus as I could. When I caught up with Phil, I wanted to let him look it over and see if he could figure out where he fit into the narrative.

I pulled up the email that Phil had received: *You are incompetent and allowed a killer to escape justice. There will be serious repercussions!*

Similar to the other emails, I had one question for Phil. What killer had he let escape?

It was almost five by the time Phil called me to meet him at the Fast Mart. Not the one where Nicolaus had worked, but one that was on the north edge of town. Here the clientele was more commuter and less druggie.

Phil was sitting in a marked unit, writing up the accident report.

"Three cars totaled. Luckily, airbags and seatbelts kept the injuries to a minimum and everyone was reasonable, so there weren't any shouting matches. Just took forever to get the road cleared," he said as he typed.

"I reread the email you received. What killer did you let escape?"

He pushed his laptop away and looked at me. "I don't

know. I've worked at the department for fifteen years. I've been involved in dozens of murder investigations, but mainly as an officer on the scene. Like I told Pete, in the two cases I worked as the primary investigator, we caught the murderer both times. And there's no possible link with Eva or Nicolaus."

"Can you remember anything happening at the Fast Mart where Nicolaus worked?" I wondered if Nicolaus could have been a witness to something Phil had been involved with.

"You know what that place is like. I'm surprised the dealers don't have a sign out front advertising the current price of meth and heroin."

"Any murders?"

"I went to a shooting and a stabbing there. A couple of overdoses. A poisoning."

"What's the story with the poisoning?"

"The drugs were laced with a toxic substance that was never identified. We caught the person who sold it to the victim, but the rest of his stash was clean. We couldn't ever charge him with anything except possession and dealing."

"Was Nicolaus a witness?"

"I wasn't the investigating officer, just the first on the scene. Pete was the investigator. Let's see." He searched his files. "Wow, he was. Nicolaus was the clerk on duty that day. I guess I met him then. So that's a connection between me and Nicolaus and a death. I wonder if Eva had any connection to the victim?"

"I'll ask Ralph Calavera." I made a note. "You should inform the watch commander about the possible threat to your life," I told him.

"I'm not worried, but I will. I'd want any deputy under my command to let me know if they're at added risk," he said. "I think I'll put up a little extra protection."

"What's that?" I asked as he got out and went to his trunk.

"I hate the thought of being shot in the back of the head." He showed me where he'd taken an old Kevlar vest and made a screen that hooked into the roof of his car, running from just behind his ear to the car frame's support beam. "At least they'll have to step up beside me. I rigged this up when I found myself sitting in parking lots doing reports late at night."

"I've heard the stories," I said. More than one officer had been shot in the back of the head when some asshole came up on their blind spot while the officer was parked. I made a mental note to look at a shield like that for myself. A couple of hooks, an old vest and you'd gain a couple more seconds of reaction time. "Makes you wonder why our cars don't come with a piece of bullet proof Lexan," I mused.

Phil made the call to the watch commander and told him that there had been a credible threat made against him. The watch commander asked what Phil wanted to do about it.

"Just make sure you don't forget I'm out here. And don't give me too much grief if I'm a little quicker to request backup."

"10-4," was the response.

"I'll review the cases we talked about. Still, I think Fowler's the best suspect."

"You might be right."

I closed down things at the office and was home by six, just as Cara finished feeding Alvin and the cats and was heading for the shower.

"Remember, we're taking Genie out for a girls' night in Tallahassee," she said as she stepped into the spray.

"I'd forgotten," I mumbled. At least that would give me time to read back through the cases. I'd call Ralph Calavera too and ask him some questions about the death at the Fast Mart.

"Wow!" I said when Cara came out wearing a sparkly blouse, well-fitted jeans and ankle boots, with her red hair brushing her shoulders in soft waves. "You sure it's just you girls?"

She laughed. "You never know who we might pick up."

"I'll be here when you get back." I took her in my arms

and kissed her.

With the winter night closing in, I settled down on the sofa with my laptop to go through the files and make a few calls. My first was to Ralph Calavera. There was no answer, so I left a message for him to call me back. Meanwhile, I reread the reports. At some point, I fell asleep. The ringing phone brought me back to consciousness. It was Calavera.

"I want to ask you a few questions about a poisoning that took place in the Fast Mart parking lot a while back."

I reviewed the details with him, but he couldn't think of any possible connection to Eva. We briefly discussed Walter Fowler and the possibility that he'd sent the email to Phil Eccles. We hung up without coming up with any new ideas.

I called Pete and asked him about the poisoning case.

"Sad. The woman was in her mid-twenties. Not deeply involved in drugs. Came and bought some ecstasy that had been laced with something. Never found out what. Darzi thought it might be something imported from China. I was afraid we were going to have people dropping all over town. Luckily that didn't happen. And when we found the dude that sold it to her, his stash was clean. We sent him up for five solid years."

He couldn't recall Eva being involved in any way.

"What time is the hen party supposed to break up?" I asked.

"Sarah said she'd be home by eleven."

I looked at my watch. Still a couple of hours.

After I hung up with Pete, I used my laptop to search the department's records for all cases that Phil had worked on that had involved a death, whether intentional or accidental. After reading several reports, I found myself staring again at the one regarding Kristy Holloway's death at the Fall Family Festival. Since Doug Holloway had also received one of our mysterious emails, I read through the report more thoroughly until a fresh detail stood out. Doug Holloway had gotten a text from his wife half an hour before the accident. The text read: *Hon, my coffee addiction is making me late. Clerk is filling the coffee maker now!*

Where had she been?

I called Doug Holloway. Maybe he would know what store it was. The call went straight to voicemail. I left a message and explained what I was after.

Something bugged me. I looked at the phone. Doug Holloway's wife had been a writer. Books. I wondered if the email addresses could have come from the library's email list.

I called Eddie.

"What?" He sounded less than pleased to hear from me.

"How secure is the library's email list?"

"Good," he said suspiciously.

"When y'all are sending out emails, do you ever fail to use the blind cc feature?"

There was silence, then: "Maybe."

"I'm going to read you off a list of names. Tell me if they sound familiar."

I read the list of email recipients.

"I guess most of them come into the library. Some, I'm sure. Others not so much. Look, you have to get Bear out of here."

"Forget Bear for a minute. Who would be a good person to ask about people who might have spent time at the library a couple of years ago?"

"Tenesha has been there for, like, five years. Worked the desk before I got there. Now she's the program director."

"I want to ask her a few questions."

"She'll be there tomorrow."

"Now." My gut was rolling over. I had a sick feeling something bad was going to happen soon. The threat to Phil was making me nervous. And while I didn't know much about Doug Holloway's personal life, I didn't like his phone not being answered at almost ten on a Wednesday night.

"It's late."

"This might be important."

He hesitated. "Let me call her first."

"Sure."

Five minutes later, Tenesha called.

"Crazy Eddie said you wanted to ask me some questions?" she said cheerfully.

"Did you know a woman named Kristy Holloway?"

"She was so sweet. Hit by a car. Just awful. I was going to be at the festival that day too. The library always has a booth. I'm glad that my mother-in-law needed to go to the hospital that day. Oh, I know that sounds awful, but I just don't think I could have handled seeing Kristy killed like that."

"She came into the library a lot?"

"Oh, yes. She did volunteer work and lots of research for a book she was writing."

"Did her husband ever come into the library?"

"Not much before she died. Right afterward, the poor man seemed to live there. I think he wanted to be close to her. Now he just comes in occasionally. Sweet man."

I didn't bother asking about the email list. Seemed obvious that someone could have gotten ahold of it pretty easily. I was about to thank her and hang up when I had another thought.

"You said the library always has a booth at the festival. Do you remember if Eva Calavera was involved with it?"

Tenesha didn't hesitate. "Absolutely. She used to coordinate all the booths. It won't be the same without her."

Feeling very edgy, I hung up with Tenesha and called Phil Eccles, who had just gotten off duty.

"I think I know who might be behind some of this. Maybe all of this."

I explained my theory.

"You think Doug Holloway blames *me* for his wife's killer escaping justice? How do you figure that?"

"The man was broken by his wife's death. I think he blames a bunch of people. I'm wondering about the death of the man who killed Holloway's wife. It was suicide, but I think we need to look into his death closer. Eva served on the festival committee and was probably the person who asked Kristy to participate. Finally, there's the clerk at a store who made her wait while he fixed her coffee. It may have been Nicolaus."

"Sounds a little weak to me, but at this point it's worth checking out. You said you called Holloway and there wasn't an answer?"

"That's right."

"I just got off work. My ass and my feet are killing me." He paused. "Where do you want to meet? I think we should go in one car. No sense spooking him if he's there."

"I'll meet you at the Supersave parking lot. We can leave one of the cars there."

I texted Cara: *Got to go out. Meeting Lt. Will keep you updated.*

If you have to. Almost done here. Be safe. She added a heart emoji at the end.

I headed out into the cool, damp night.

CHAPTER TWENTY-FIVE

Phil Eccles got out of his patrol car when I pulled up next to him.

"We'll take your unmarked," he said.

He popped the trunk of his car and pulled out a duffle bag, which he then tossed into my back seat. Folding himself into the front seat beside me, he said, "Let's go. It's your circus."

We drove to Doug Holloway's house in silence. I don't know what Phil was thinking. For my part, I was expecting to roll up on a suicide or something worse. And I hadn't forgotten about the threat he may have sent to Phil.

The house was dark. The streetlights lit up the yard, but I doubled down on my bad feelings.

"You take the front door," Phil said, pulling a vest from his duffle bag. I'd put mine on before I left the house.

With handgun drawn, Phil headed around the side of the house with the weapon's light illuminating his way.

I walked cautiously toward the front door with my head on a swivel. Were we over-playing this? As cliché as it sounds, it was better to be safe than sorry. Once at the door, I stood to the side and knocked, then rang the doorbell. I heard its chime inside, but no one came to the door. I pounded harder. Nothing.

"I'm not getting any answer. Any action on your side?" I asked Phil over the radio.

"No joy."

I heard knocking from the back of the house, a pause, and more knocking.

"Circle east around the house. I'll circle west and check the windows," Phil said.

"Roger that." I started around the east side of the house. All the windows were secure and the blinds were down.

We gave up and met in front of the house near the garage.

"We have nothing that would justify a warrant," he said.

"No. We may have to wait until morning. He's an electrician, and when I was here his van was in the driveway. Let's ask a neighbor if he ever parks it in the garage."

"Good idea."

We went to the house on the east side of Holloway's property. The lights were on, and as we got close, we could hear a TV inside. With our guns holstered, I rang the doorbell.

"Who's there?" asked a man's voice from the other side of the door.

Phil held his star up to the peephole. "Sheriff's office. We'd like to have a word with you."

"Yeah, okay." We heard the lock turning. The door opened partway to reveal a forty-something-year-old man in sweatpants and T-shirt. He looked a bit annoyed.

"Have you seen your neighbor, Doug Holloway, today?" I asked.

"Something wrong with Doug?" There was more curiosity than concern in his voice.

"We don't know. We're just doing a welfare check."

"Noooo, I don't think so. Tough, 'cause I see him all the time. I don't think anything about it. You know?"

"What about his work van? Have you seen it?"

"It wasn't in the driveway when I got home. I did notice

that."

"Does he ever park it in the garage?" I asked.

"Never. Kind of annoys me. The HOA got pissed at me when I had a cousin staying with me and his RV was in the driveway for a week. That RV wasn't much bigger than Doug's van and it's always sitting in his driveway."

We thanked him and turned to walk away. My phone vibrated as we headed back toward my car.

"What's up?" I asked Cara.

"I don't know." Her voice sounded hesitant and concerned. "Maybe nothing."

"Tell me."

"Audrey left the restaurant about ten minutes before Sarah, Genie and I did, but when we got to the parking garage, her car was still here."

I looked over at Phil, who hadn't heard the conversation. He was standing at the passenger-side door waiting for me to unlock the car.

"Are you looking at the car?"

"Yes. What's scary is this is downtown Tallahassee on a weekday night. Nothing else is open."

"Do you see anything odd about the car?"

"No."

"Can you get down and look under the car?"

I heard her getting on her knees, then a short gasp. "Oh, shit!"

"What?" I was waving Phil over to my side of the car. He saw the look on my face and moved fast.

"Keys. There's a set of keys, not under her car but the one next to hers. Should I get them?"

"No. Don't touch them. Take a picture with your phone and send it to me. Phil is with me."

He was getting agitated. "What's going on?"

In seconds, I heard my text message alert go off.

"You get it?" Cara asked.

"Yes, hold on."

I pulled the photo up and showed it to Phil with a quick

explanation of what Cara had told me.

"Tell her to call 911."

I did that, then Phil and Cara put together a description of Audrey and what she was wearing.

"I take it you're headed that way?" I asked him after I hung up with Cara.

"No. Got something to do first."

He took out his phone and called a friend who was a major with the Tallahassee Police Department. Phil told him what had happened and asked him to make sure everything was done by the book at the crime scene. When he hung up, he turned to me. "How sure are you that this guy," he pointed at Holloway's house, "is involved?"

"I'm *not* sure. But I've got a gut feeling, and I think the circumstantial evidence supports my gut."

"Then I want you to sit in your car. That's a direct order," he said, then turned and started marching toward Holloway's house.

"Wait!" I called, trotting to catch up. "You don't want to break in without a search warrant."

"No time. This isn't about charging someone; this is about finding my wife. Consequences be damned!"

"Seriously, we need to call the watch commander and get a BOLO out on Holloway's van. We can get a search warrant within the hour," I said reasonably, taking hold of his arm to stop him.

He turned and planted his palm on my Kevlar vest, sending me backward onto the lawn.

"Don't mess with me, Larry. Write me up, if you need to. Tell the watch commander I've gone rogue. Whatever you feel you need to do. But stay out of my way."

I was shaken, more from my own confusion than from the physical altercation. Trying to stop someone from doing what I knew *I* would do was an odd position in which to find myself.

Phil turned and headed for the back of Holloway's house. I got up and jogged after him.

"Think about what you're doing," I argued when I got within earshot. "Calling in reinforcements will get more eyes looking for Audrey."

"The person who sent that email plans on killing her. It's a matter of time. It's also a matter of me getting to him quickly and without sirens. Assuming it's Holloway, you said he sent an email blaming himself for his wife's death. That's messed up. It also means he's probably on his own list. Some cop or deputy pulls him over or approaches the van, he's going to kill Audrey and himself without a second thought."

Phil was at the back door now, where he was feeling around the frame in order to figure out where to put his boot.

"That makes sense," I allowed, but was about to give my counter-argument when I realized I didn't have one.

Before I could say another word, Phil stepped back and landed an impressive kick to the spot just below the doorknob. The door gave way with a crack. He reached inside and flipped on a light. Reluctantly, I crossed the Rubicon and followed him into Holloway's house.

The house was neat as a pin. It almost looked like he had professional cleaners come in.

"Watch for booby traps," Phil advised me. "If the guy is an electrician, he could rig up some nasty stuff. Let's clear it. You take the right; I'll take the left."

We checked the whole house. There weren't any dead bodies and no one was hiding under a bed.

One of the bedrooms was fixed up as an office, with one wall covered with shelves of Kristy Holloway's books. She had written dozens of contemporary romance novels. The covers showed various muscled, half-dressed men with sophisticated women looking them over or being held in their arms.

On the desk there were several binders, each with the words *Ideas and Notes* printed on the spine. I picked one up and flipped through it.

"I think this might explain the emails," I said to Phil.

I was looking at snippets of gossip from all over the county. There'd be a name and date, with a tidbit like: *Wife is taking a cut of the sales. He thinks she might get fired.* There were hundreds of them and I recognized many of the names.

"I think Kristy must have mined local gossip for plot ideas. Doug must have used these to send out the poison emails."

"Pretty smart way to lay down a smoke screen for the murders," Phil agreed.

"If we could call in Lionel, there are probably clues to what his plans are on the computer."

I was looking at the desk, where a couple of monitors and a nice gaming keyboard were set up. Underneath the desk was a computer tower that looked like it could do a lot more than surf the internet.

"There's no time. No hard feelings, but if you want to bail, go ahead. Just don't try and stop me."

"I'm with you. I'm just used to being the one going on a rampage."

My phone rang and both of us jumped. Before I could even answer mine, Phil's phone also buzzed. We both answered.

My call was from Cara.

"They're asking some questions that I'm not sure how you'd want me to answer." Her voice was nervous and tense.

"I know. Just tell them what you know while leaving out anything you might suspect Phil and I are up to."

"What *are* you doing?" she asked in a harsh whisper as if she was trying not to be overheard.

"Looking for Audrey. We have a lead." A thought occurred to me. "Did you see a van parked in the garage, either when you arrived or when you got back to your car?"

"Maybe. What type of van?"

"An electrician's van." I sighed and decided to let her in on it. "Specifically Doug Holloway's van."

"I don't think so. He was doing work for us on Monday," Cara said, confusing me for a moment.

"For us?"

"The clinic. He was rewiring one of the examination rooms because Dr. Barnhill wants to put in some new equipment that requires more power... Anyway, he was there. I talked to him. Oh, no!" She choked up.

"What?" I asked, worried.

"I was talking to Holloway and we were discussing the wedding and everything." She paused, then said softy, "I told him about us getting together tonight." I could hear the tears in her voice.

"You couldn't know. We'll find him. Though I guess I should let you know that I might be out of a job soon. We didn't have a warrant to search his house, but Phil was determined."

"I'm just scared. Do you think Audrey's in real danger?" She asked the question by reflex, but I was sure she didn't need me to tell her how bad this could be.

"We just have to find Holloway."

"Wait! When we were talking at the clinic, he mentioned a cabin he goes to. It's on the west side of the county."

"Does he own it?"

"Yes. He and his wife owned it and used to go there all the time. I think me talking about the wedding made him think of his wife."

"Did he say anything about where it is?"

"He said that it has access to the Magnolia Ridge hunting plantation."

"Great. Thanks."

"Be careful."

"Love you."

"Love you too."

Phil hung up about the same time as I did.

"They haven't found anything else at the scene," he said, anxiety and anger etched clearly on his face.

"I think I know where he might be."

In the living room we found pictures of Holloway and his wife at a cabin. From the trees and vegetation, I was sure it was local.

I pulled up the property appraiser's website on my phone. "I should have thought of this earlier." Within a minute, I knew where the cabin was.

"Let's go," Phil said, heading for the back door.

I put out my hand and stopped him. "Holloway told Cara about the cabin. He *wanted* us to know about it."

"That's fine," Phil said with a fatal resolve, then he ran out the door.

CHAPTER TWENTY-SIX

"I'll drive," Phil said when I joined him at the car, holding out his hand for my keys.

"I don't think so. You're too worked up. Better I drive and you navigate."

He didn't look happy, but he didn't argue.

"We should call for backup," I said as I pulled out of the driveway, even though I knew he wouldn't go for the idea.

"No. I told you, if we go in there with a bunch of deputies he's going to execute Plan Omega." He turned in his seat to face me. "You know why I can't call in anyone else?"

"You just told me," I said, confused.

"That's part of it. But the other reason is that if someone else bungles the rescue and Audrey gets hurt or killed, I would hate that person. I know that's irrational, but it wouldn't matter. It would be a white-hot hate that would end in something bad happening."

I didn't doubt he meant it. I slowed down a little and turned to him.

"I'll only let this go so far. You have to promise me that if we can arrest him, we will."

"I've got one mission and that's to save Audrey. As soon

as she's safe, I'm done playing *Die Hard.* You have my word on that."

I was sure he meant that too. I sped up.

"Tell me when the turns are coming up." We were already out of town and the roads were narrow and dark as the speedometer edged up past eighty.

"About three miles," Phil said, looking at the map on his phone.

My phone rang with a distinct gunshot tone that told me it was Dad. I hadn't put the phone in its the holder on the dash like I usually did, so I pulled it out of my pocket with one hand and handed it to Phil.

"Put it on speaker."

"Where are you?" Dad's voice was on the edge between being worried and being very pissed off.

"Looking for Audrey." I knew he would have already heard about her abduction.

"What do you know? Is Phil Eccles with you?"

"I'm here, Sheriff," Phil said, then pointed a finger at the windshield. "Half a mile on the left."

"I want you both to come in and coordinate the search," Dad ordered.

"We've got something to check out first," I told him.

"What?"

"A cabin."

"Not without backup."

"Give us half an hour to check it out. We'll let you know what we find," I said, stalling.

"You know I can track the GPS on your car," Dad reminded me.

"Sheriff, your wife was nearby when Audrey was kidnapped," Phil said. "This man could have hurt her. All I'm asking is a chance to get it right before a bunch of good-natured flatfoots come on the scene and get my wife killed."

"Damn it, Phil! You know you can trust me. I won't send anyone who's going to screw the situation up worse than it already is."

"I'm asking you to trust *me*. If I need help, I'll call for help."

"Larry, am I an idiot for asking you to talk some sense into Phil?" Dad asked.

"I think Phil's right. Let us go check on the cabin. Holloway might not even be there."

"You're both going to be writing traffic tickets for the next ten years," he growled. "I'm sending assistance, but I'll hold them back two miles. If I don't hear from you in forty-five minutes, they're coming in." Then he hung up on me.

I'd made the turn and we were now on a narrow dirt road with ditches three-feet deep on either side. The land out here varied from swamp to upland pine woods. Tonight, with no moon, I could only see a few feet in front of my headlights.

"We're going to stop half a mile from the cabin and walk the rest of the way," Phil said. "Stop a quarter mile after the next turn."

We were lucky and found a wide enough spot to pull off the side of the road to park, though the road was little more than a Jeep trail at this point. On either side of the trail was nothing but palmettos and pine trees.

"We'll walk in the ditch," Eccles said as he stood at the back of the car. "What have you got in the trunk?"

"A Remington 870 and extra mags for my Glock."

"A rifle would be handy, but we've got what we've got. Grab the shotgun."

I popped the trunk, pulled out the gun and loaded it with several buckshot shells and a slug—the slug first in case we need to open any doors. I stuffed another handful of slugs and buckshot into my pocket. I filled my remaining pockets with the extra Glock mags.

"Here's a flashlight," I said, pulling two out of the trunk and handing one to Phil.

"I don't like it, but without the moon we'll have to use them." He dug in my trunk and found an old T-shirt, which he tore and tied over his flashlight so that most of the light was suppressed, leaving just enough glow to see the ground.

"That'll have to do. Let's go."

We climbed down into the ditch and started moving as fast as we could in the cold mud. I didn't feel the cold as my mind imagined what we would find at the cabin.

I kept close and watched Phil's feet as best I could so I wouldn't stumble. I was still trying to decide if I was insane for going along with him or not. The truth was that, without knowing the future, there was no way of being sure what the right answer was. Coming down on the side of action was natural for me. *Hopefully it won't bite me in the ass this time*, I thought.

"It's going to be a long walk back if she isn't there," I whispered. I'd barely gotten the words out when we saw the glow of lights ahead and heard the rumble of a generator.

We reached the path leading up to the cabin. We could see Holloway's van clearly as we climbed out of the ditch and moved into the palmettos. The closest we could get to the cabin without being out in the open was about fifty feet.

The cabin was small with a narrow porch across the front. It was a simple hunting layout with a door and one large window in the front. The shutters were closed, but light shone through the cracks.

"I know you're out there!" Doug Holloway shouted from the cabin. "Someone tripped a sensor."

Phil and I cursed in unison.

"I'm coming out onto the porch. Don't shoot me or rush up on me. I have a deadman's switch rigged up that will kill Audrey if anything happens to me. Do you understand?" His voice sounded calm and even slightly amused.

I could feel Phil vibrating with anger next to me. "We hear you!" he shouted.

"I'm opening the door."

Light streamed out around him as he stood in the doorway. We could see he had something in his hand and wires running out behind him. He moved to the window. "Before I open the window, I'll warn you that you might see something that will upset you. Remember the deadman's switch."

He unlatched the shutters and swung them back to reveal Audrey tied into a straight-back wooden chair with wires wrapped around her and a gag in her mouth. Her eyes were frantic. I had to grab onto Phil to keep him from running out into the clearing.

"Come out into the light!" Holloway shouted at us, almost as if he'd seen me restrain Phil. "I want us to talk."

I took out my phone and called Dad.

"We're at the cabin. Holloway's here with Audrey. I'm going to leave the line open," I whispered when he answered. Dad was cursing as I put the phone back into my pocket.

Phil had already walked out into the open. I thought about remaining hidden. Maybe I could slip around the back. Then I thought of the motion sensor we'd tripped. Holloway seemed to have his bases covered and I didn't want to cause him to do anything stupid, so I stood up and walked into the clearing behind Phil.

"That's better. Don't come any closer than thirty feet. I wouldn't want you to be tempted to do something stupid." Holloway waggled the switch in his right hand. The piece of plastic was the size of a small remote control and had a button on it that he was keeping depressed. Several wires ran out the end. One went up his sleeve while the other snaked back into the cabin.

"Lieutenant Phil Eccles and Sergeant Larry Macklin. Y'all did good. How'd you find the cabin? Was it the clues I left in my house or did Cara tell you about it?"

I felt my own blood beginning to boil.

"This was all part of your plan," I said, suppressing my anger as best I could.

"Unlike the chaos that brought about my wife's death." He paused in dramatic fashion. "My wife was killed by the bungling, oblivious actions of a group of idiots. Eva Calavera invited her to be a part of that stupid fall festival. If it hadn't been for Nicolaus Andreas, Kristy would have been there on time and not rushing around to get set up. And we can't forget Daniel Zywicki, the driver of the car that killed her."

"Did you kill him?" Phil asked before I could.

"No. He escaped my justice. Of course that was after you let him get away with the murder of my wife."

"He was going the speed limit and your wife stepped out in front of his car," Phil said calmly. "It wasn't murder."

"Didn't he see that there were people walking around their cars and crossing the street? Don't you think he should have slowed down and been paying closer attention? Yes, he damn well should have! His negligence killed Kristy and you let him walk free." Even in the cool night air, I could see the sweat clinging to Holloway's forehead as he ranted.

"So kill me. Audrey didn't do anything to you or your wife," Phil argued.

"No. You're going to know what it feels like to have the love of your life killed and not be able to punish the man who did it." He nodded toward the wire running up his sleeve.

"You're wearing a bomb," I said, making sure it was loud enough for my phone to pick it up.

"No. Not a bomb. Your wife and I are both going to be electrocuted. I think I've rigged up a pretty serviceable electric chair for her." Through the window, I could see Audrey squirming against the straps and wires holding her to the chair.

"You bastard," Phil hissed.

"You know Old Sparky over in Raiford? My interest in electricity came first, but when I learned about electric chairs as a kid, I was fascinated with them. I wrote an essay on their history and how they work for a seventh grade history class. Got an A-plus too. Fourteen states have an electric chair named Old Sparky; three states have one named Old Smokey. I think Sparky is better."

I felt sick to my stomach thinking about poor Audrey strapped to this madman's homemade electric chair. Phil was swaying slightly. I could only imagine the thoughts going through his head.

"Tell me what I have to do for you to let Audrey go. I'll do anything," Phil told Holloway, who had a sneer on his face.

"All I want is for you to suffer like I did."

"Look, let's talk about this," I said. "Turn yourself in and we can work a deal. People will understand why you had to kill Eva and Nicolaus." I figured the longer I could keep him talking, the better. I could tell that Phil was frozen, unable to do anything while wanting nothing more than to save his wife.

Holloway wasn't listening to anything at this point. He was just ranting.

"I talked to them. I talked to everyone. Talked and talked. They were all so sorry. Very sorry for your loss. I wish things had been different. Even that stupid clerk was sorry. At first they were sorry, and then they wanted me to go away. I was bothering them. They didn't want to dwell on her death, and I shouldn't either. That's what they told me. I should get over it. A year was long enough." I caught the glimmer of tears running down his cheeks.

"Don't cause any more pain," I told him. "How will it help to create more suffering?"

He turned and glared at me.

"Shut up! This is my purpose. I didn't know it at first. I thought maybe they were right. Maybe I should try and get over my grief. But all I wanted was for the people who caused my wife's death to die. I got my wish when I found out about Zywicki's suicide. And do you know what?" He paused as though he expected us to answer. "I felt better. I was pissed that Zywicki wasn't officially punished, but at least he was dead. Death was the answer. Kill the people who caused her to die."

"Why the emails?" I asked, trying to get him off the subject of death.

"I hate this town. My wife was the one who wanted to move here. She said she could write better in a small town, but I despise all the small town clichés. *Quaint* is just another word for *shabby*. Honestly, this whole town is responsible for what happened to Kristy. I wanted to stir things up. Plus, it made you all look like idiots and gave me good cover for the murders."

"Do you really think that killing my innocent wife will bring you any peace?" Phil was visibly shaking with rage.

"I don't know and won't ever know the answer, because I'm going to die when she does. You see, the person most responsible for Kristy's death is me. It's only fitting that I execute myself too. Speaking of which, I think it's about time to get on with—"

Holloway never got the last word out. There was a *hiss-pop* sound that I could barely hear over the roar of the generator. I recognized it as the sound of a suppressed rifle. At almost the same instant, wood splinters flew into the air where the wires trailed back into the cabin.

Holloway went rigid, with his teeth chattering and body arched and twisting in the air for what seemed like minutes, but had to have been only seconds before he slumped, smoking, to the porch floor.

Phil ran toward the cabin door as I followed, trying to see Audrey through the window. As I jumped on the deck behind Phil, I was aware of someone else running toward the cabin.

Inside the cabin was a very-much-alive Audrey Eccles, straining at her bonds. The wire was now draped loosely around the base of her chair. Phil rushed to her side and hurriedly unstrapped her from the makeshift electric chair. I helped him pull her to her feet, then turned when I saw movement on the porch.

"Damn," Pete said. In his hand was a Remington 700, made eight inches longer by the suppressor fitted to the barrel. "I'm glad you're all alive." He stuck his head in through the cabin door.

I went over to him.

"I got most of it," he said, pointing at the two wires

twisted together. The bullet he'd fired had split both of them without severing either.

Audrey was still being supported by Eccles.

"I'm glad I didn't wait for the cavalry to save me." Still shaking from adrenaline, she explained, "When he went out on the front porch to talk to you, he pulled the wire close enough to the chair that I was able to snag it with my foot. It took me almost the whole time you were talking to him to get the wire loose enough that it fell from the chair."

Phil gave Pete a look that would have caused me to melt right down into the ground. "Good thing Audrey saved herself, 'cause she saved your ass too," he snarled.

"I…" Pete started, but I put my hand on his arm to stop him.

"I think I almost dislocated my ankle in the process," Audrey said, limping a little as she walked away from the chair.

Outside, there were blue and red lights flashing through the pine trees as a bevy of patrol cars and an ambulance rolled into the clearing. Dad came marching toward the cabin, his green eyes flashing. I knew that look. *I should hide,* my inner voice advised me.

After making sure everyone except Holloway was alive, he unleashed his ire.

"Do I need to remind you that this is a crime scene? Pete, take control of this. Keep everyone back. Call in Darzi's office and Shantel. I want her and Marcus here."

As Pete got up and moved toward the deputies outside, Dad put his hand on Audrey's elbow. "I'm glad you're okay," he said with kindness, before he turned back to Phil and me. His face turned to stone.

"You two are both on unpaid leave. The promotion committee will decide whether you get to keep your new positions or not. And believe me, I'm being generous. If I were to make the decision right now, you'd both be washing patrol cars at half salary for the next year."

Phil started to defend himself, but shut his mouth before

anything came out. Wise man. I knew that any attempt to defend the indefensible right now would result in a worse punishment down the road. Been there and done that.

"You will both distance yourself from this investigation, except to answer questions from Pete or internal affairs. Is that understood?"

"Yes, sir," Phil and I said in unison.

"And I have some special punishment for you," he said, pointing his finger in my face. "I'll text you later."

I thought he was going to leave it at that, but he took a deep breath and held his hand out to Audrey. "I'll take you over to the ambulance so they can get a look at you."

"I'll be all right," she assured him.

"I'd feel better if you were checked out, and Pete will want to get a statement from you. I'm also sure that he'd prefer to talk to you before there's any opportunity of you being influenced by others..." He gave Phil and me his death stare. "...involved in this incident. We'll bring you home afterward."

Audrey glanced at Phil, who gave a stiff nod.

"You two get the hell away from this crime scene. Pete will contact you when he's ready to interview you. Also, don't talk to each other or anyone else about the events that transpired. Is. That. Understood?"

We nodded and walked away from the cabin with our proverbial tails between our legs.

Once we were out of earshot, I turned to Phil. "Welcome to my life."

"Audrey's okay. For right now, that's all that matters." He clearly wanted me to believe him, but there was tension in his voice.

"Pete had to take the shot. You heard Holloway. He was ready to die and take Audrey with him."

"Maybe." His teeth were clenched. "I'm glad I have a week off to cool down. Pete should be glad too."

I thought about arguing Pete's case more, but I knew it would be best to drop the subject for now.

As we drove back to town, I called Cara to let her know that we were all fine. I could hear that she was fighting back tears.

I dropped Phil off at his car and headed home. Cara was waiting for me at the door. For a long time, we just held each other tightly. My text alert went off as we parted. It was Dad.

Since you have the week off, you'll be watching Mauser. Jamie has some work he needs to do and you can save me some money. Be at my house to pick him up at seven.

I looked at my watch. With luck, I could get five hours of sleep.

"The good news is, I don't think I'll be fired," I said to Cara.

"Better get to bed," she told me. "I have a feeling that your Dad has a long day planned for you."

Larry Macklin returns in:

St. Patrick's Cross
A Larry Macklin Mystery—Book 18

ACKNOWLEDGMENTS

As always, thanks to my wife, Melanie, for her editing skills and support; to H. Y. Hanna for her inspiration, assistance and encouragement; and to all the fans of the series. Larry never would have come this far without all of you!

Original Cover Concept by H. Y. Hanna
Cover Design by Florida Girl Design, Inc.
www.gobookcoverdesign.com

ABOUT THE AUTHOR

A. E. Howe lives and writes on a farm in the wilds of North Florida with his wife, horses and more cats than he can count. He received a degree in English Education from the University of Georgia and is a produced screenwriter and playwright. His first published book was *Broken State*. The Larry Macklin Mysteries is his first series and he released a new series, the Baron Blasko Mysteries, in summer 2018. The first book in the Macklin series, *November's Past*, was awarded two silver medals in the 2017 President's Book Awards, presented by the Florida Authors & Publishers Association; the ninth book, *July's Trials*, was awarded two silver medals in 2018. Howe is a member of the Mystery Writers of America, and was co-host of the "Guns of Hollywood" podcast for four years on the Firearms Radio Network. When not writing, Howe enjoys riding, competitive shooting and working on the farm.

www.ingramcontent.com/pod-product-compliance
Lightning Source LLC
Chambersburg PA
CBHW061534210726

48287CB00006B/1947